Weddings Can Be Murder

The Painted Lady Inn Mysteries

By

MK Scott

Chapter One

THE TALL PALM trees strategically placed along the Miami shoreline reminded Donna of a former crime show set in a similar locale. Even though it was early morning, many cruisers crowded the deck as the huge ship was guided into its berth. Steel band music played in the background.

Mark nodded at the people below them on the next deck. "No one is going anywhere fast."

Heloise spotted them from below and waved with both hands, trying to get their attention. Even though her mother had taken Legacy's best-known gossip under her wing, Donna had had more than her share of the opinionated female. She pretended to gaze in a different direction as if missing the woman's flamboyant gesture.

Not easily dissuaded, Heloise cupped her hands around her mouth and yelled, "Donna Tollhouse, I know you can see me! Your mother wants to know if you and loverboy…"

Fortunately, the appearance of her mother stopped the ship-wide announcement.

Mark wrapped an arm around her and dropped a kiss on her hair. "How about we just stay on the ship instead of going back to Legacy?"

"It's do-able, but what about the wedding? I'm sure Heloise has already called in the news." Even though any of her family members who were onboard could have made an early morning phone call once they came into cell range, her money was on Heloise beating them all to the punch.

"The captain could marry us."

"True." They'd played with the idea while sunning on sugar white sand beach. Bypassing the pageantry and trouble associated with weddings appealed to her. However, her hidden soft side relished the possibility of using the silver candelabras and cut-glass punch bowl she'd bought at an estate auction. "It might be hard to run a bed and breakfast from the sea."

Mark lifted one eyebrow and asked in a mock serious tone, "Have you considered a floating bed and breakfast? It's bound to be unique."

"Do you think I could jack up the mansion and load it onto a pontoon platform?"

Laughter greeted her suggestion, but before her fiancé could offer any alternatives, Security Director Ramirez hurried their way. Even with his olive complexion, he still appeared flushed.

"Mark. Donna. Glad I got you before you disembarked. Your neighbor," he pointed back to Heloise who trailed him, "spotted you from below and showed me where you were. The authorities would appreciate it if you'd do a rundown of everything that happened. Just for the record, of course."

Donna made a dissenting sound that caused Ramirez to explain more. "It won't take long. They only want facts. That's all."

Heloise had crept close enough to join the conversation. "I'll be glad to help."

An urge to be mischievous tempted Donna. "That would be wonderful! After all, you were there for so many of the pivotal events."

The woman practically glowed as she moved closer to Ramirez, talking as she did so. "Well, I knew there would be trouble as soon as I saw…"

Mark and Donna hurried away. They avoided glancing back, afraid an anguished look from the security director might have stopped their escape. Giggling, they jogged down the corridors holding hands, darting around passengers until they reached Mark's cabin. Once inside, Donna slammed the door and leaned against it. "Woo-wee, that was fun! I feel like a kid again."

"Yeah, I know what you mean." Mark wiped his sweaty brow with his forearm. "You bring out the secret rebel in me."

"Ha!" She moved away from the door to deliver a playful push. "It was always there."

"Hey, I didn't say it wasn't there. I said you brought it out." He blew out a long breath and announced what they both knew was inevitable. "We will have to go and talk to the police about the case. Without our help, murderers and would-be murderers could walk. We will give our depositions, but there's a possibility we will need to fly back as witnesses for the trial."

That would certainly throw a monkey wrench into their wedding plans. Should they even plan anything knowing they might get called in as eyewitnesses? She groaned heavily before speaking. "Why is it always so much trouble being on the right side of the law?"

"Don't dwell on it too much. Unless you're planning on a long engagement, we'll be married before it even comes to court. We might end up missing our flights though. I've already been through the rescheduling thing. Maybe they'll give us a break on fees if we explained we're helping keep the cruise lines safer."

Even though it sounded good when Mark said it, she knew the airlines wouldn't see it that way. "I wish. They might view the cruise lines as the competition."

"True enough. Did you put your bag out last night for disembarking?"

The dear, sweet man thought she had only one bag. "Yep, but I still have my carry-on and my tote bag. If we get stuck in Miami…" She splayed her hand against her chest as if the idea horrified her. "…I can get by."

Personally, she wouldn't mind another day, just her and Mark. Half of the cruise Mark had missed, while she was busy being Janice's wing woman, and the other half was spent on fingering the killer. Not exactly what she'd call a restful vacation. It would be less stressful to get back to the inn.

"Everything I have, except for my sports coat, wallet, passport, and airline tickets, should already be on their way to the airport."

While this was her first cruise, she seriously doubted the luggage went to the airport. "I don't think so. I met a lady at midnight bingo who always uses a bright yellow suitcase since they line up the suitcases on the dock where you came on." Remembering Mark's entry through the Puerto Rican Port Authority, she corrected, "I meant where I came on. Anyhow, the woman joked about people with black suitcases often snag the wrong one."

A pained expression knitted Mark's eyebrows together briefly as he lamented. "I have a black suitcase."

"Oh!" She hadn't thought of that, but men tended to go for the nondescript bags. "Well, surely you tied a colorful scarf on it?"

His disbelieving stare meant no color ribbon or material of any kind was attached to his black conformist suitcase.

"A whimsical luggage tag such as a shark or Mickey Mouse?" she asked.

"I used the tag that came with the bag. It matched the bag."

She shrugged her shoulders. "Maybe when we're done talking to the police, everyone will have picked up their bags and ours will be the only ones left."

"Let's hope not. I heard a couple up on deck talking about staying onboard as long as they could, which appears to be hours."

A knock on the door stopped their obsession on bags and disembarking.

A voice announced from the other side of the door, "It's Ramirez."

When Mark swung the door opened, the man shook his index finger at Donna. "You did a very naughty thing up on the deck. I will overlook it since you helped me track down a killer."

Helped him? That's not at all how she remembered it. Ramirez accepted that an elderly man, who had access to all kinds of drugs, decided to commit suicide by taking a swan dive from the uppermost deck that had a chest high railing. If that didn't have suspicious death written all over it, she didn't know what did. A shudder passed through her body when she realized it could have ended there. All the cruisers may have been a bit put out that a fellow cruiser had the bad taste to die on their cruise, while their memory of the incident would last about ten minutes to be brought up again only when they arrived back home.

Before she could correct his reference to himself helping, Mark spoke. "What can we do for you?"

"It's me helping you." Ramirez used his thumb to point back at himself. "You won't have to go through the protracted process of leaving the ship. I've had your bags pulled out of the baggage area, and they're waiting in a courtesy limousine. All we have to do is take the freight elevator, and you'll avoid the hassle, give your statement, and make it to the airport before your chatty friend." A flash of white teeth signaled a grin, although his heavy mustache overshadowed it.

Limousine could sometimes be code for *aging white passenger van*, but a ride was a ride. She'd beat everyone to the airport, whiz through security, and be one step closer to home. "Sounds good to me. We'll need to stop by my room and get my carry-ons."

Ramirez held up one hand. "Done. Your kind roommate passed them out to me, and they should be on their way to the limo."

Because the man was being super accommodating, Donna's antennae went up. People weren't that nice without reason. What was Ramirez's angle? Mark would probably advise her to wait and see and to stop being so cynical. It's hard to make plans for attack or defense if you didn't know what type of ground you're standing on. The best way to deal with the unknown was full speed. Her lips tipped up into a forced, sweet smile that made Mark wince the tiniest bit.

"You're being awfully nice to us. Fast checkout, limousine, which is appreciated, which brings me to, what do you want?" she asked.

Mark coughed, patting his chest as if all the air in his lungs had just been sucked out. Her eyes stayed on her fiancé, and judging by the lack of sweating and redness, she deduced it was nothing more than a distraction.

"A woman who speaks her mind." Ramirez slapped Mark on the back. "You've found yourself a treasure."

After clearing his throat noisily, possibly to make a coughing fit appear more legit, Mark responded. "I often tell myself that."

She doubted it. There was a good chance the men would waste time exchanging pleasantries, and she'd never get an answer. Donna resorted to waving, which was such a Heloise move she resented having to use it, but it stopped the men from their pointless exchange.

Ramirez nodded to her as if he'd somehow forgotten she was there. "Did you have something to add?"

One hand fisted and ended up on her hip. Some people might call it her *I mean business* stance, but anyone who knew Donna knew it was both hands on the hips that really meant business and not the other way around. "As you know, we're interested in catching our plane. To facilitate everything in a prompt fashion, I need to know what you want." She held up her index finger. "If I don't know, I can't give it."

"Ah, yes." Ramirez's hand stroked his mustache slightly, muffling his reply. "It would be helpful if you allowed me to take the lead. I suspected something wasn't quite right while you and your associates unwittingly contributed details."

Before she could even formulate an answer, Mark shook his head. Did he think she'd allow the security director to take credit for all their hard work? What she really objected to was the word *unwittingly*. It made it sound like she was a ditzy old lady, which she certainly was not.

The hand not balled on her hip went up. She pointed her index finger again as she spoke. "First, you should know I am a seasoned sleuth. Mark," she cut her chin in his direction, "is a thirty-plus year police officer, now detective. He has solved numerous cases, many being murders. Truthfully, I think it is unlikely that you would have solved this case on your own. This is what the police will think as well. Maybe you should say Detective Mark Taber consulted on the case." The point made, she returned her hand to her side.

He continued stroking his mustache, but then allowed his hand to drop. "This sounds workable, but..." He held up a finger mirroring Donna's earlier actions, "...what's in it for you?"

Since it seemed as if she gave up all claim to solving the case, she'd wait the tiniest bit, letting him think he had received everything he asked for. When Ramirez dropped eye contact and turned to Mark for an answer, she knew she had waited a tad too long.

"I'd like another cruise, free, of course," she stated, to get his attention again.

"A free cruise!" His hands fluttered in the air as if he were ready for take-off. "That's impossible!"

"No, it isn't." It probably wouldn't be an appropriate time to mention she'd researched possible compensation before stepping onto the ship. Anything from fires to piracy could result in a free or discounted trip, not that she'd had any plans before hand to ask for reimbursement. Her plan had been to sun by the pool while various crew members waited on her. What she'd wanted to be sure of before booking her cruise was that she had chosen the line with the least number of lawsuits filed against it. "I've read about cruise lines offering credit for a new cruise when something horribly goes wrong."

"That applies to a fire or the entire ship getting sick, not playing at being a lady sleuth."

"*Play!* I wasn't playing when I hunted down clues. Nor was I playing when I spoke to the suspects. Should I ask what you were doing when I was supposedly..." She put her fingers up to make air quotes, "...playing."

"You shouldn't have said that," Mark murmured under his breath, then shot the confused security director a pitying look.

Ramirez pushed his shoulders back and thrust his chin out. "I was conducting the ship's business."

Donna considered mentioning the casual chit chat the director made with the various passengers when he wasn't hanging out at the pool ogling bikini-clad women. She didn't. Instead, she changed tactics. "You did help when Maria went into labor. Anyone dealing with Heloise when she was in full rage deserves some sympathy, too."

"Yes, yes. This is true. I'm sorry for saying *playing*. I misspoke. My English isn't so good."

She had her doubts about the last part since any ship that carried mostly Americans would hire a security director who could speak English fluently, but she'd give him that one. "The cruise?" She raised her eyebrows.

"I'll see what I can do. Perhaps a discount, maybe half off?"

"Let me think about it."

Mark made a face at her reply then mouthed the words, *"Take it. Honeymoon."*

It would be nice to get away, especially in the winter. "Don't we have some people to see?"

"Of course, right this way." He opened the door as Mark gathered his sports coat and Donna picked up her purse.

They both followed the man keeping back far enough in the hall for Mark to whisper. "You should take the half-price cruise. It would make a good honeymoon. This time we can get on the ship together."

"I plan on it, but no reason to let him know just yet, especially since I have to hold a straight face while he makes himself out to be the hero."

His fingers entangled with hers. "Don't worry. We both know the truth. That's what matters."

"I agree."

She gave his hand a squeeze while Ramirez stood by the elevator clapping his hands. "Hurry! We don't have all day."

Maybe she should hold out for seventy-five percent off. The way he immediately offered the half-off discount meant that was the standard compensation package. You'd think for the services of two skilled professionals, they could be a touch more grateful.

The freight elevator shot downward without the three of them saying anything. Perhaps the men were thinking about their statements, but Donna had already moved on to wedding plans. Since neither one of them was getting any younger, there was no reason to plan a blowout wedding. Once home, she'd contact Herman, who was a justice of the peace. She suspected he'd be itching for a return visit to his former home in Legacy. He might even bring some of his friends along. She'd need to have rooms open for them, which meant the wedding couldn't be during the busy season.

Summer could be busy. As well as fall when Columbus Days occurred. The entire town re-enacted one of Columbus's ships shipwrecking off the coast of North Carolina. Even though originally Columbus was supposed to have landed on Christmas day, everyone agreed that sailing was not a winter sport in North Carolina. Last year, they couldn't even round up three tall sailing ships and had to settle for one cabin sailboat, a smaller Hobie Cat, and Jamison's Motors pontoon boat, which had a picture of a tall ship painted on one side along with the name of the company stenciled across it.

The elevator shuddered to a stop, and Mark reached for her hand. Ramirez led them past the waiting people who jostled each other with their carry-on bags as they waited to disembark. As they passed the group, a few grumbled about Mark and Donna getting preferential treatment.

By the time they reached a Staff Only door, comments concerning them being arrested for smuggling now floated through the corridor. One lady piped up loud enough for Donna to hear.

"She even tried to buy an ivory bracelet. You know those things are taboo."

The words stopped her. *Smugglers?* Did they look like smugglers? Wait a minute, that voice sounded familiar. Heloise. She should have known. Even though she wanted to correct Heloise and explain ivory was banned outright as opposed to only being tabooed, a slight jerk on her hand had her looking up at her fiancé.

"Ignore her. Gossipers gossip. End of story."

Maybe. In the end, it made her sound rather mysterious, not that smuggling was ever on her bucket list as something she wanted to do. Right now, getting home, seeing her dog, and everything getting back to normal sounded just about perfect, although, normal tended to be a relative word at the Painted Lady Inn. If all went well, no one would die in her vicinity in the next six months. With her free hand, she crossed her fingers just to be sure.

Chapter Two

THE FIRST HURDLE to navigate on the journey home was the busy Miami airport. At least they were able to get out at the curb and right beside the courtesy baggage check for their airline. They checked the large bags, but Donna was determined to hold onto her tote bag and carry-on.

The palm trees outside the airport building gave it a tropical flair and gladdened the hearts of all those who traveled from snowy climes in the dead of winter, hoping for some sunshine and warmth. There was plenty of both in Miami.

Music blasted from a nearby car with a Latin flavor. Donna tried to pick out the words. Not only were they too fast, she suspected they weren't English, either.

Mark brandished their tickets tucked into an envelope with their gate number on it. "Let's go, honey. We can bypass the counter and head directly to security."

He held out his hand to her. Donna gave him the handle of her carry-on, which she surmised wasn't what he was expecting to hold on to. "I'm only allowed one carry-on. I didn't want to check my souvenirs since some of them are delicate."

Mark switched the carry-on to his right hand and reached for Donna's hand with his left. "I understand. With any luck, we should get through security fast." They walked in the same direction a huge herd of people were heading. The human blob broke apart and headed to various concourses, reassuring Donna they might not have to wait forever as passengers unpacked the innards of their carry-ons and placed them in plastic bins for the x-ray.

Their concourse security line snaked around the various roped dividers rather like a Black Mambo or something equally lethal. Mark sighed heavily while Donna entertained herself by sniffing the air.

"I smell cinnamon rolls," she announced.

"Not surprising."

Being able to distinguish scents, even ingredients that went into something, she considered her unique skill. "There's the smell of bacon and..." her nose wrinkled as she identified the aroma, "...hotdogs. It's not even lunchtime."

Mark waggled his eyebrows playfully. "Not everyone is on the same time, and some folks wouldn't mind hot dogs for breakfast."

"Philistines." She joked, using her great grandmother's label for anyone who didn't do things her way. Donna rocked up on her toes trying to figure out why their line wasn't moving.

A shrill, angry voice carried through the airport security area.

"You will not rifle through my personal things, young man!"

Donna slid Mark a knowing look. "Good gravy. I had high hopes of getting through security and on the plane before Heloise arrived. Our stop put us behind schedule."

"Well, it is what it is." He gestured to the area where Heloise was shouting down a TSA employee while Cecilia stood slightly away from the commotion, looking in the opposite direction. The TSA man pulled a wine bottle out of the suitcase and held it up high, causing the angry woman to reach for it.

"Give it to me. It's mine. Do you have any clue how much they charge for wine on the ship? An arm and a leg. I intend to keep it."

The uniformed man handed it to another employee who threw it away. Heloise deflated a little, especially when the sound of breaking glass carried in the suddenly quiet area.

"Ma'am, do I need to call security?"

The question forced Cecilia into action. She swung around and grabbed Heloise's arm in a firm grip. "I'll take care of her. Mother's mind tends to drift at times."

"Mother!"

Anything else Heloise might have to say was lost as Cecilia hustled the woman toward the gates.

Donna sighed and leaned against Mark, who asked, "We aren't on the same plane, are we?"

"Be real. The closest airport to Legacy is Charleston International, and there aren't all that many airlines that stop there. The chance is very real we'll be on the same plane."

"Maybe we'll get bumped. We could volunteer." His eyebrows arched as he grinned. "What do you think?"

"Don't even think of it. I have a lot to do and need to get started. Besides, it's a short flight. With any luck, Heloise will be thrown off before the flight takes off."

"We can hope. If nothing else, we can plug into the entertainment unit and watch a movie on the way back. That way we won't hear the complaining and demands."

It made sense, but it wouldn't do much for her mother.

Once the commotion ended, they moved a few feet. All the TSA employees who had hovered nearby thinking they'd be asked to assist went back to screening people.

An older man in a parallel line waved and called out. "Ahoy there!"

The gentleman with the wide smile and the silver hair did look familiar.

Mark put up his hand to acknowledge him, telling Donna, "Look, it's Simon, your mother's on-ship beau."

Oh, yeah, that's who it was. She gave a finger wave. "He seemed nice."

"He's saying something. Can you make it out?"

"I'm not sure. Something about my mother."

"It figures. We might see him after we get through security." The agent gestured for them to approach the stand. Mark went first and flashed his identification. He took Donna's carry-on, leaving her with the tote bag. Remembering the scene with Heloise, she mentally reviewed all of her items she'd added, hoping they would pass security.

Were her toiletries small enough? Mark would easily give up her expensive night cream she'd shoved in her carry-on with intentions of moving it to her checked luggage. She rattled the tote bag, urging Mark to take it. He refused, due to it having high heels and lips stick tubes all over it.

The t-shirts, hats, and jewelry she'd brought back as souvenirs would have made it through security easy enough, especially since they'd already been processed by customs at the port terminal. Everything had been loaded into the limo, which did turn out to be a van as she previously thought. It would be difficult to say what went on during the inspection. She hadn't had a chance to check her luggage and assumed everything was still there.

Her time came. She hurried to the conveyor belt and placed her tote bag and purse into one bin as she toed off her shoes. Donna walked slowly to the metal detector, wondering if her underwire bra would be her undoing. The metal detector remained silent as she walked through. With the hard part of the trip over, she pulled her shoes back on and gathered her supplies which, to her delight, passed inspection.

The flight home was uneventful except for Simon Lightwater being on the plane. Somehow, he had brokered a deal with Heloise to take his seat in first class while he joined Cecilia in coach. Daniel bumped up his and Maria's tickets to first class to celebrate his status as a family man and keep a safety zone between coughing passengers and Baby Cici.

She fastened her seatbelt as Mark nodded to her mother and beau a few seats ahead of them. "Love is in the air."

Donna held out her own hand and admired the way the light bounced off the diamond. "I agree."

"I'll not be fool enough to disagree with you, but I wasn't refer-ring to us. I was referring to your mother and Simon."

"Oh." She shrugged her shoulders. "I believe his interest is sin-cere. It's my mother who I have doubts about. She told me she had no interest in love or marriage. She is quite content to be wined and dined, but that's it."

Who could blame her? Her parents married young and may not have even dated anyone else. Suddenly, her mother was the most popular girl at the party. Who would want to give that up?

The flight went fast. There were no outraged screams from first class nor were there any harried looking attendants, which must mean Heloise had fallen asleep or was living life to the fullest.

BECAUSE HER FIANCÉ had driven himself to the airport, Donna managed to bypass riding home with the family. As the newly engaged couple, they'd think all they'd do is whisper sweet nothings to each other.

"You have no clue how much I appreciate you driving."

Mark laughed as he placed the luggage in the trunk. "Yeah, I kinda got that impression. Why would you not want to ride home with the family?"

"And Heloise." She added the one name because it made a major difference. "Still, it's not just her. When you get my mother and Maria together, they want to talk wedding. They start asking me about dates, food, music, who to invite and who not to invite. The two of them are worse than editors at a bridal magazine."

"Maybe they're frustrated wedding planners."

"Could be." A sudden epiphany occurred to her as she maneuvered into Mark's car. "You know, I mentioned having the wedding at the inn. We will take pictures, right?"

"People usually do." He closed his door and started the car.

"Exactly."

He worked his way through the parking garage and fiddled with the navigation system. "Not getting anything. It should clear once we get outside."

They paid the parking fee and exited. Donna figured that somehow her sweetie missed out on her having an amazing insight. She cleared her throat.

Knowing the routine, Mark didn't look away from the road. "What is it?"

"I said *exactly*. You never bothered to ask why I said that." She crossed her arms, attempting to make her point.

"No need to ask since I knew you'd tell me."

She made a slight snort, not sure if she should be offended or not. "Well, I guess you got me there."

"So, exactly what?" He eased onto the road.

"As you probably know, I just about gave up on my wedding chapel. Originally, I thought some photos of a cute, young couple tying the knot on the website might do the trick, but now I'm not so sure."

"Why is that? I know you've never tried it."

"I meant to, but with working at the hospital, there never seemed to be time. Still…" She held up one finger. "I may have been aiming at the wrong demographic."

"How so?"

He really didn't understand. As a man, he probably hadn't been planning a storybook wedding since he was twelve. Most of her friends had cut pictures out of magazines and pasted them into notebooks as they planned their extravaganza ceremony. By the time they did marry, the notebooks had been tossed. The obsession with weddings she blamed on the movies and pretty much every tale that featured a prince and a wedding.

"When you're young and Daddy is footing the bill, you spend outrageous sums on catering, horse-drawn carriages, and designer gowns because the couple has no concept of money. They even have to hire a wedding planner. Up to this point, they've had everything provided for them. Our wedding chapel would not attract the pull-all-the-stops group. Instead, people marrying a second or third time would be more likely to want a quiet wedding. We could also offer a vows renewal."

"Sounds good. Would you be the designated wedding planner?"

"Good Heavens, no!" She threw her hands up in the air to emphasize her point. "Those women are impossible. They're controlling, always interfering where they aren't needed. I'm not a bit like that."

Mark cut his eyes in her direction but said nothing.

"What was that supposed to mean?" She knew the man's moods and often he managed to say a great deal by saying nothing.

"Hmm. Nothing."

"I don't accept that. Come' on. Tell me. You know I won't leave you alone until you tell me more."

He gave a heavy sigh. "Call me stupid because I know anything, I say will get me into trouble."

"Quit stalling. Spit it out."

He held up one hand as if gesturing for a halt. "I never said you were anything like a wedding planner. Never even met one as far as I know."

She realized a buildup when she heard one. "Cut to the chase."

"I was afraid you would say that." He put his hand back on the wheel. "You're a smart, determined woman who knows what she wants."

"Would it help if I promise not be angry?"

He shook his head. "I find that hard to believe. Okay. I'll take it. You can be the tiniest bit bossy."

"Me? Bossy?" Her voice went up as she splayed her hand against her chest. "You must be joking."

Instead of answering, Mark's brow furrowed as confusion chased across his face. She could well imagine what he was thinking. Something along the lines of damned if you do and damned if you don't.

"Breathe easy. I know I'm bossy. I consider it one of my better characteristics, especially since I'm always right."

A choking sound came from the driver's side of the car.

"Get over it."

"You're not always right."

"Most of the time."

"Some of the time."

Her lips twisted into a moue of distaste. Mark was probably the only person who could get away with telling her she wasn't always right, and she could accept that, but not with grace. "I've forgotten what we were talking about."

"That you're nothing like a wedding planner."

"Exactly." Her phone chimed, interrupting a rerun of the point-less conversation. "Hello?"

"It's me, Tennyson. I assume you're on your way back."

"We are."

"There's some women who want to come and check out the front parlor. They may want to have a meeting or something. No food is involved. I wanted to know if that is a go for you?"

While she expected to hit the ground running once, she got back to Legacy, she hadn't expected guests in the inn already. "They aren't staying overnight, or are they?"

"No. No one mentioned it. Just want to check out the inn. Some-thing about they heard about you having your wedding here and wanted to see the place. Congratulations by the way. Tell Mark, way to go."

Her employee's enthusiasm on their upcoming nuptials made her smile. "How did anyone know about the wedding?"

"Maria called me. Not sure if she called anyone else yet."

"It's not important." Her money was still on Heloise. "Make sure the place is swept and dusted. If there are any fresh flowers that look halfway decent, move them into the parlor."

"Will do."

"How's Jasper?"

"He had the type of depression only scrambled eggs with cheese could cure."

"Sounds about right." She was ready to hang up when she real-ized she hadn't asked who was coming. It could be that snobby book club trying to get their foot in the door while her back was turned. "Who's coming?"

"Not sure about the name, just some wedding planners. See ya."

"Bye."

All of a sudden, she couldn't turn around without running into a wedding planner.

Chapter Three

THE GRACEFUL LINES of the inn came into view as Mark turned the corner. The grass needed to be cut, but it wasn't horrible. The purple asters she'd planted in the porch flower boxes before leaving were still blooming. She'd have to credit Tennyson for watering them.

The magnolia tree shade shadowed a few unfamiliar cars clumped together at the end of the parking lot. Donna pointed to the cars, noticing they were all more expensive than her own humble sedan. "Must be the wedding planners' cars. Looks to be a profitable business."

"Yep. Why wouldn't it be?" He gave a small snort and continued, not allowing her to answer. "Weddings nowadays are three ring circuses. You need a non-relative to bark orders to avoid people getting their feelings hurt."

"Spoken like a true man. Every bride wants to feel like a princess on her special day." She parroted the words she'd heard so many times from co-workers, mothers of the bride, and from one battered caterer she'd met in the emergency room, when 'Bride-zilla' had had a strong reaction when they ran out of crab puffs.

"Pleeeeease. Don't tell me you believe that. Are you going to go all out and get a wedding planner?"

The way he said it made it sound like the most ridiculous thing in the world. She'd been planning on something simple and tasteful with her old neighbor, Herman, presiding over the nuptials. Wasn't her besotted fiancé supposed to declare anything she wanted would be fine?

Nothing made her want to do something more than being told she couldn't. In this case, it wasn't exactly being told she couldn't, but an implication that it would be foolish to do so. "I wasn't planning on it, but maybe I should see what services they offer. After all, they are in regular contact with wedding vendors. They could advise me who have the best cakes, most extravagant caterer, cheapest rental."

"Come on now. Be the practical down-to-earth woman I love. I'm afraid putting a ring on your finger transformed you into someone else."

His laughter didn't ease Donna's irritation. She stuck her tongue out at him, which only made him laugh harder.

"You have no clue what is involved in weddings. I will need the help when you consider I'm still working second shift at the hospital *and* running the inn. I don't have time to plan a wedding."

"Then don't do it. All we have to do is go downtown, stand before a judge, and say our I do's."

"I refuse to do that. It smells likes a hurry-up wedding, the type of thing people do when the girl is already in labor or some guy must be married to inherit. No, thank you. Our wedding would be an excellent opportunity to showcase the inn."

A dramatic groan filled the car as Mark parked and switched off the ignition. "I thought our wedding was about us declaring our love and devotion to each other."

"Of course, it is." She smiled at Mark who gave her a disbelieving look as he swung his car door open. She waited until he had made it to her side and opened her door before continuing. "I'm not sure why it couldn't showcase the inn and declare our love at the same time."

"Who do we need to showcase the inn to? I'm sure everyone we know has already been in the inn already. Legacy's finest have tromped through the halls on various occasions."

The memory of the police being in her inn more than once to investigate murders made her wrinkle her nose. While Mark had managed to get the inn out of the paper on a few occasions, it hadn't stopped people from whispering. She'd like a better reputation for the inn than a place you'd most likely end up dead.

"That's all well and good. You can invite some of your cop friends, but I thought it might be nice to invite your police commissioner and the mayor."

"The mayor? That slimy dirt bag who came here from Maryland and knows nothing about what Legacy needs?"

"That's the one. How can he know what the locals need if they don't invite him to events?"

Mark moved toward the trunk, making Donna assume he hadn't heard her question or was giving her his famous silent treatment that usually had novice criminals breaking and confessing all. It wasn't going to work on her. Besides, she had nothing to confess.

He swung one bag out of the trunk, then another, before answering. "Go ahead and invite him. He won't come. The man has no clue who I am."

"I beg to differ. You've solved so many murders in the past that you're practically a folk hero."

"I'd be more of one if I could prevent them from happening to begin with."

He did have a point there. Still, it was harder to predict when a murder would happen since most that had happened in Legacy had been impulse murders caused by too much emotions, or liquor, and sometimes both. "You do what you can, and people appreciate it."

The side screen door slammed shut as Jasper shot down the porch steps, barking up a storm. Tennyson followed slower and without the need to announce his arrival. Donna squatted to scratch her puggle's head and have her face bathed with his extra-long tongue.

"How's my baby been?"

Tennyson answered since Jasper had never mastered English.

"Pretty good, although the dog had me cooking for him every night. He refused to eat his dog food."

She gave Jasper a censorious look, which he ignored as he wagged his tail. "Should I ask?"

"The usual. Scrambled eggs, cheeseburgers, and he has a surprising fondness for macaroni and cheese."

She gave her pooch one more pat before rocking back on her heels to stand. "At least I won't be the only one to have put on weight due to the cruise."

Neither of the men rushed to reassure her it didn't look like she'd put on any weight. While still being a lie, it would have soothed her ego enough for a Dove ice cream bar. Now she'd have to make do with some unsweetened iced tea.

"Since you're here, Ten, you can help carry in my luggage."

He shook his head, causing his bangs to flop back into his eyes. "I came out here to avoid the wedding planners."

"What's wrong?"

"It would be easier to ask what's right. To answer that question, nothing. I thought wedding planners would get along. They don't. The one named Charmaine thinks you should re-paper the parlor in peachy pink floral that would be more flattering to her brides. She refuses to think of your place as a venue until you do."

One hand found purchase on Donna's hip. "I went to a great deal of trouble to be period correct as far as the colors. Maybe we can do without Charmaine. She sounds like a bully."

Mark chuckled as he slammed the trunk. "Still want a wedding planner?"

"Obviously not Charmaine."

"I'm sure the other ladies are fine."

Tennyson shrugged his thin shoulders. "Depends on what *fine* means. Two of them, who both have that old lady blonde hair going, are in some type of feud declaring one of them stole a wedding that should have been hers. Then there's the man wedding planner."

"There's a man?" The idea shocked her, although there was no reason men couldn't be wedding planners. It was just that Legacy wasn't progressive. They hadn't gotten any women police officers until the last decade.

"Yeah. He's no trouble. He dresses all in black and does this a lot." Tennyson crossed his arms and jutted his nose up into the air.

"Male wedding planner. Is he from here?"

"Donna?" Mark interrupted "Did you miss the part about him being dressed all in black and having a superior air?"

"I see what you mean. Maybe he's a recent transplant or up from Charleston." Donna shouldered her purse and tote bag and led the way to the house with Jasper at her heels. He felt the need to yip the entire way. He could be complaining about her absence, but she'd pretend it was a welcome home ballad.

Once inside the inn, she could hear the raised voices.

"It's not my problem you can't contract any marriages after your last wedding implosion. Too bad no one was filming when the bride's veil caught the candelabra and pulled it down, setting fire to the veil and her waist length long hair."

"That's not what happened!" an irate voice answered.

A sound of nervous tittering followed the declaration.

The mental image of a flaming bride made Donna wince. Even she could see that a floor length veil could be problematic. She placed her tote bag and purse on the island and moved closer to the pass-through door. After all, this was her house, and she should be able to go where she pleased.

Mark and Tennyson made a noisy entrance that caused Donna to whirl around and hold her finger up to her mouth. The boys immediately quieted down. Tennyson pantomimed *wedding planner* by brushing a hand over his head to indicate a veil, then held out his left hand and waved it in a haughty fashion, then he opened up his hands as if a date book and consulted it for dates.

Mark's face reddened as he tried not to crack up at the antics. Okay, Ten was a little bit funny, but she did not walk around with her left hand on display. Her eyes flickered down to see where her left hand was. It was propped on the door mantle higher than her right hand, but it wasn't in-your-face out there. She allowed it to drop, knowing some people might argue the point. Silence reigned on the other side of the door, making her wonder if the wedding planners were eavesdropping on them or had already left.

All she needed to do was open the door the tiniest sliver. She pressed lightly on the door, opening it a few inches. The four of them stood near her Pembroke table, staring at something one of them held out. What was it? She eased the door opened a few inches more. If she opened the door any farther, she'd be noticed.

A dog barking outside resulted in Jasper pushing through her legs and racing to the front parlor window to bark back. The unexpected movement threw her off balance. Donna wind milled for brief seconds before she made full contact with the hardwood floor. *Oomph!*

The four wedding planners that had been having a silent stand-off turned their attention her way.

"Mercy me!" One of the hide-your-gray-with-ash blonde women moved crossed the room in short high heeled steps and offered her a hand.

Donna hesitated in taking it, sure she would knock the stick thin woman off her stilettoes. It didn't help that Jasper kept licking her, considering he was the orchestrator of this embarrassment. The male wedding planner had his index finger at his temple. It was hard to say if he had his nose elevated from this angle, but she felt judged. The other women appeared baffled but had made no offer to help.

She'd pushed up to her knees by the time Mark rushed out of the kitchen to help her.

"Allow me."

He hauled her to her feet with more vigor than necessary. Donna grabbed his arm with her left hand to balance herself and prevent another humiliating incident. A conversational murmur enveloped her. There was the tiniest tinge of excitement in it, which puzzled her. What could the four of them be so excited about?

Did they consider hoisting her to her feet noteworthy? The buffet line might not have done her any favors, but it wasn't the same as airlifting an orca whale. When she glanced at them, she noticed all four pairs of their eyes were fixed her left hand.

Her would be lifter spoke first with a high wattage smile. "You must be the bride."

Ding! The metaphorical light bulb glowing above her head just lit. As a future bride, she was the equivalent of a steak dinner to wedding planners. Make that several steak dinners.

"Yes, I am." She tried to gather her dignity around her, which was difficult since she'd already taken a face splat at their feet, which also alluded to her eavesdropping. It didn't help she was wearing a souvenir cruise t-shirt that read *I Like Big Boats and I Cannot Lie.* When she bought it, it'd seemed playful. Not so much now.

Mark volunteered additional information. "I'm the groom."

"Perfect!" A woman topping six foot in her sensible flats held out her hand and moved closer. "I'm Charmaine Sanders, Wedding Planner to the Stars."

The woman moving beside her gave a reproving sniff while the male wedding planner looked even more put out, if that was possible.

Donna took the outstretched hand and shook it. "Pleased to meet you."

Her lips tipped up in what she thought was an appropriate expression while reminding herself this was the woman who wanted to change the décor of the inn. If she needed a wedding planner, obviously, they'd all make a play for her business. So far, she recognized Charmaine's smoky contralto voice defending herself against the veil incident. It could mean the woman might give her a discount, but there would be no changing the wallpaper.

"Yes," the woman agreed, displaying a large array of teeth reminiscent of a shark.

"I'm Evelynn." A woman beside Charmaine waved. "You might have seen me at the Bergman-Sanders wedding or the Thornapple-Bassinger union. I do all the *important* weddings."

Since she'd dropped Charmaine's hand, Donna reached out for Evelynn's, pretending to ignore the flurry of coughing from the wedding planners that occurred when Evelynn emphasized the word *important.* If the four of them couldn't stand each other, why were they even here together?

As she expected, the third woman, who offered to help her, introduced herself. "I'm Grace Cummings, local mom and part-time wedding planner. After marrying off all six of my daughters and assisting with countless shirttail relatives' weddings, I decided I might as well get paid for it."

Honesty. She liked that in a person. Evelynn politely stepped back, releasing her hand, allowing Donna to grasp Grace's hand. Charmaine might be good for a discount, but she had a feeling Grace would be more her style. Her eyes cut to the man, who hadn't bothered to introduce himself yet.

He stayed in place and gave an apologetic shrug. "I'm Keith. I only came because I heard a new wedding venue was opening up. There's a limited number of acceptable venues in this area. Too many people think they can host a wedding in their backyard." He gave a heavy sigh.

Mark, who still stood at her back, asked the obvious question. "They can't?"

Keith blinked twice, then drew in a deep breath, as if preparing himself to deal with an unpleasant task. Donna hated him already. No one treated her sweetie that way.

"Technically, they can if they want a low-class wedding. Imagine wedding photos with a jungle gym in the background."

If someone had children old enough to marry, they'd probably gotten rid of the jungle gym long ago. Keith kept talking, not allowing her a chance to mention her insight.

"Think of the wedding guests in their finery trying to pick their way through the chickweed and fescue grass."

Donna's lips twisted as she debated that point. She had attended some weddings where her heels had sunk into the grass. Most of the guests had opted for more casual flats or dressy sandals. He had a point with that one.

"Then, there's the weather, so changeable."

Crud. Another reasonable point, and personally, she always wondered why people insisted on an outdoor wedding when pop-up showers could send everyone scampering for cover. It was getting hard to defend her sweetie when Keith had logical reasons. Still, she launched into what she thought would be a good rebuttal.

"People have weddings in botanical gardens all the time."

Her nemesis gave her the slightest of head nods, giving her the point, or so she thought.

"True, but botanical gardens have an indoor facility filled with water features, fountains, and plants. They also have walkways so the guests don't ruin their shoes. I suppose a botanical garden would be suitable, depending on the season. Unfortunately, there are none in this locale."

Donna wasn't sure how he did it, but somehow Keith had agreed with her while pointing out a botanical garden had nothing in common with a backyard.

Mark leaned forward to whisper in her ear. "Give it up. Tell him about the venue opening. You've been advertising the wedding chapel forever."

Not exactly forever, but as long as the inn had been opened. As much as she hated to do it, she'd have to give Keith an *attaboy* to get the unbiased information she needed. "When did you hear about the inn as a venue?"

"Early this morning."

"Me, too," Evelynn added while the other two women nodded.

"What made the four of you decide to come look at the place together?" Even though they were all in the same business, she couldn't imagine any of them socializing.

Keith wrinkled his nose and cut his hands to Charmaine, who spoke.

"I figured as a group we'd have a better chance of getting in. I even called and asked about having an informal meeting, then I posted it on a social media." She gestured to the other wedding planners. "These three were the only ones who could come at such late notice. The inn would be perfect for a wedding. The bride could stay here and get dressed without wrinkling her gown that so often happens in traveling. There's also a good-sized area for the reception with no more than fifty if a sit-down was ordered. More, if it was buffet style since people could also eat in the other parlor or even on the porch if the weather cooperated."

Grace gestured to the staircase. "That would make an excellent photo backdrop. The windows and fireplace would be another good shot. The couple framed in the main doorway would be nice as if they were welcoming you. I haven't been up to the bedrooms yet, but you probably have a Queen Anne style cheval mirror."

Well, she did, but it was in her bedroom where she liked it. Even though Maria had added the wedding chapel to the website and a wedding package to the price menu, they'd had no takers. Now suddenly, there were all these wedding planners inspecting her dining room to see how many guests they could squeeze into it and focusing on the best photo backgrounds.

"The front parlor does have a movable wall that opens up to the second parlor," she told them.

The VFW had taken out the wall to make the place bigger. With the use of plants and lightweight mirrors, she'd worked hard to direct attention away from the temporary wall. A few guests might notice it was a removable wall and somehow downgrade the inn in their reviews for it. People could be weird about the smallest things. One reviewer claimed the juice glasses were too small.

Evelynn and Grace appeared excited but tried to tamp it down. Keith lifted an eyebrow, while Charmaine clapped her hands together and declared, "Excellent. With appropriate furniture arrangement, we could get a hundred guests in."

A hundred. They'd have to be very small guests. Would her floorboards be able to stand that much weight?

A slight creak of the pass-through door meant Tennyson had joined them.

Evelynn grabbed her purse and waved at them. "Got to go."

Grace followed suit with an apologetic smile.

Charmaine pointed in the direction the two went. "Did you see that?"

Was this a trick question? "Two wedding planners left?"

Keith laughed. "Charmaine is mad because those two took off. They have weddings they want to stage here. They have to talk to the interested parties and nail down a date before anyone else gets there first."

"Oh." There really didn't seem to be anything else to say.

Charmaine grabbed her suitcase sized bag and made her way to the door. She turned slightly and called back to Donna. "I'll be in touch with booking dates."

As the only one left, Keith dropped his bored air and gestured to the window. "I'd like to see the grounds. Some of my clients might want outdoor photo ops. So predictable."

Tennyson volunteered to show him around while Mark and Donna followed at a distance, conversing.

Donna gestured to the man in front of them. "Did you see that? How he changed his attitude?"

"Yep. Wouldn't worry about it. It's probably all part of the wedding planner business. Apparently, people go to wedding planners to get information about where to have a wedding if they aren't using their local church. Maybe you should contact more wedding planners, maybe even host a luncheon for them."

She entangled his fingers with his. Overnight, the man was coming up with better strategies for running her inn than she had. Not a biggie since it would be their inn. It wouldn't hurt to release some of the control and let other people assist once in a while.

Wedding planners brought weddings your way and associated guests. "A luncheon sounds perfect."

"Your mother could help. That sort of thing is right down her alley."

Her mother? No reason to go crazy with allowing other people to help.

"I'll think about it."

Which, if he knew her as well as he thought, meant no.

Chapter Four

THE DAY AFTER vacation was always the worst. Not that Donna was an expert on vacations or days after the vacation, but people talked, especially her co-workers. They usually complained about being at work and not lounging on a tropical beach. Although, now that summer had arrived, North Carolina's coast boasted its own array of bask-worthy beaches.

Not exactly the same, since it was here and not there, away from piles of laundry and dirty dishes. Today wasn't a bad day since it was Sunday and few surgeons, if any, scheduled surgery on a Sunday. Most avoided weekends altogether. The fortunate patients managed to get released before the weekend, otherwise they'd have two more expensive days, watching games shows in a hospital bed, added to their bill. Insurance took a dim view of paying unnecessary time in the hospital.

It resulted in very little work being done while her colleagues demanded details of the vacation and proposal. Since she might still be called to testify in the cruise murder, she skipped over mentioning anything about it. Besides, it did nothing to enhance her story of sun, surf, and romance.

By eleven that night, she was heading for her car, exhausted not so much from the work, but forcing herself back into work mode. It amazed her how fast she had got used to doing nothing. No wonder people loved vacations. Her phone chimed in her pocket as she walked across the darkened parking garage.

No way would she answer it. Enough movies featured distracted characters who were killed, maimed, or kidnapped because of that one second of inattention. Who would call her so late at night? Mark usually texted her good night or left a voice message if he could call. So, it couldn't be him.

There were very few cars in the garage, just the employees. She spotted hers but waited to use the fob until she was right up on the car. Newspapers carried accounts of people being attacked by opening their car door too soon, allowing the attacker the needed time and access into the car unnoticed. It was hard to imagine someone opening her car door with the automatic interior light spotlighting the action. How would that not be noticed?

Maybe the parking garages in question were much bigger and fuller. She took a break from her worst-case scenarios to speculate on who might be calling her. It could be a sales call from someone wanting to tell her she'd won a free vacation that only required her to pay a couple hundred to enjoy it, or maybe she'd been chosen to receive replacement windows at a greatly reduced price. No. Even they wouldn't call this late.

That left wrong number or family as possible callers. What if something had happened to the newest member of the family, Baby Cici?

Her thumb pressed the fob, and she swung into action. It took her approximately five seconds to get into her car, lock the door, and check her phone.

Mother. Maybe it was Baby Cici.

Using speed dial, she'd called her mother and switched it to blue tooth while it was still ringing. No need to linger in the garage.

People who stayed too long in parking garages checking their voice mail or some other trivial thing often became crime victims, at least in the movies. She pulled out of the parking space, slowly checking for cars and a possible lurker in the shadows.

Her mother finally picked up the phone. "Donna, is that you?"

"Yes, of course it's me." She was tempted to ask if her mother had seen her number come up on the display, but since she was no technology wiz, she couldn't poke fun at her mom. "Is Baby Cici okay?"

"I'm sure she is. I haven't heard from Maria or Daniel, but it's hardly been a day. Wouldn't be surprised if the happy family is sleeping. That's not why I called."

Donna exited the garage and used the fast route home. The one good thing about second shift was the roads were usually clear most of the time. A slew of cars with something written on them followed in a loose line, honking at each other, and a few had people hanging out the windows yelling. *What in the world?*

Her curiosity prompted her to investigate the unusual occurrence, but she was much too tired to do so. She turned off on a side street to bypass the noisy group. Could be just tourists traveling in a convoy.

"Sorry about that. Did you say something?"

"There's been a murder." Her mother confided in a dramatic whisper.

The warm feeling she'd enjoyed due to vacation and a proposal, that had been slowly slipping away, disappeared completely all at once. "At the inn?"

"No. It was at the Swenson-Roberts wedding."

She heaved a sigh realizing her inn wouldn't be involved in whatever happened. Her mother's voice continued sounding more robust, blasting through her car speakers. "This isn't a Heloise's story. I was at the wedding."

She'd heard plenty of stories of brides and grooms turning on each other, but they usually waited until the honeymoon. "What happened?"

"Simon and I headed over to the reception early. We were in the back of the church so we slipped out."

"Simon?"

"Oh, you met him on the cruise. He was my plus one."

"I know who he is. Tell me more about the murder."

Her mother cleared her throat. "Well, they haven't exactly declared it murder, but…"

"Please. I need details."

"Simon and I arrived at Belmont Hall where the reception was being held. We were the first people on scene that weren't involved with the wedding. When we walked in, I noticed how beautifully decorated it was. Some people had the nerve to say it was going to be one of those over the top gypsy weddings. It wasn't. They had the cutest centerpieces on the tables with a white pillar candle, mirror, and calla lilies."

"Mother." Only her parent would lead with, there's been a murder, then describe the centerpieces. "Dead person. Who died? How?"

"Oh yes, that. Everything was so beautiful we couldn't figure out why the caterer was melting down. Screaming and babbling about being locked in her truck from the outside. She couldn't get out, which put her behind schedule, and about the cake being ruined."

She drove home mainly out of habit, too busy in unwrapping the ribbons of the story. "Who was it?"

"Millie Soames. Soames and Soames catering."

"One of the caterers died?"

"No, of course not. Why would you even think such a thing?"

"Thunderation. I'm tired, and I'm doing the best to make sense of your story. Who's dead?"

"Oh, that." Her mother emitted a tinkling laughter. "The wedding planner, of course."

The way she said it made it sound like everyone should automatically know, rather like the butler did it. "Do you know which wedding planner?"

"Charmaine Sanders, the one they hired. She was the cheapest and specializes in over the top gypsy weddings. The couple wasn't gypsy, but they liked things big and flashy. She became known for that along with the wedding veil incident."

My word, she'd just talked to the woman yesterday. She could be a little opinionated when it came to wallpaper, but that wasn't a killing offense. "How did she die?"

"Fell into the wedding cake."

"What?" She must have misheard. "Did you say fell into the wedding cake?"

"I did. It was a huge affair, as big as a person. I think if it was something smaller, she could have easily pushed herself out. We saw only her lower body sticking out the back. The cake from the front looked fine."

"What happened then?"

"I told them to lock the doors, and Simon would tell the guests there was a slight delay when they arrived."

"Did you call the police?"

"I did and the paramedics."

"I'll assume they took Charmaine away in the ambulance."

"They did. The police handled it quietly, taking photos, then shuttled the cake off to another room. It's assumed she had a heart attack due to the stress of handling an over demanding bride."

"It could happen."

"I agree, but it seems too coincidental that the woman fell into the cake."

"It does sound peculiar. Did Mark arrive with the police?"

"No. I managed to take a discreet photo when the caterer wasn't looking. Everyone assumed it was an inconvenient death. Only I thought it could be murder."

"It could still be an inconvenient death." The phrase always baffled her since death was seldom convenient. "I'm glad you called me. I met Charmaine yesterday, and she didn't strike me as a person on the verge of a heart attack. It was more likely she'd inspired those feelings in someone else. Makes you wonder."

"Exactly."

"Glad you called. I'll mention this to Mark."

"I knew you would."

"Bye now."

"Bye, sweetie."

She hung up the call, aware she wouldn't get any sleep tonight turning over the possibilities of what happened. If she had been there, maybe she'd have noticed something, but she hadn't. She didn't even know the Swensons or the Roberts, so there'd be no reason to receive an invite. On the other hand, her mother knew everyone in Legacy.

At the inn, she turned off the ignition and stepped out of the car. Once she'd put her home on the market she'd stopped living there. Strange that in less than thirty days a new family would move in, and another chapter would open in her life. She wondered how Mark would like living at the inn.

Her slow stroll across the parking lot abruptly halted. She realized they had never talked about it. Before the cruise, putting her house on the market before discussing it with him had upset him. If the man would have told her he was going to propose, his actions would have made more sense. At the time, she thought he was a wee bit over-controlling. Yes, she needed to definitely talk to Mark about where they would live as a married couple.

"The picture!" Her impromptu outburst reminded her she hadn't asked her mother to send the picture. Her fingers delved inside her purse searching for the cell phone. Even though she had just finished speaking with her mother, would it be too late to call back?

A blinking light on her phone indicated she had received a text. No way she could see it in the low illumination of the security light. Donna hurried to the porch and used the number lock while debating if she should get rid of it. Plenty of crime shows had people figuring out combinations by how worn certain numbers were. With real keys you had to worry about people copying them, keeping them after they left, or losing them, which is what happened when she had used regular keys.

Forget changing the code all the time. She tried that, and she was the one who kept forgetting which number to use and setting off the alarm. The last thing she needed was police cars in front of the inn. The bed and breakfast's reputation among the neighborhood set could use a bit more polish. Most viewed her as not genteel enough to live among them, and so far, she hadn't demonstrated otherwise.

Inside, she switched on the light, waking a sleepy Jasper, who blinked at her and pushed to his feet.

"Wanna go outside, boy?"

He ignored the request and flopped back down on his bed. "Yeah, I know buddy. It's late. I might have to bother you a little more though." She flipped on the counter light where she kept her coffeemaker and espresso machine. Donna made two cups of coffee using the French press coffee maker, which she thought would make less noise. No guests in the inn tonight, but Tennyson's room bordered the kitchen.

By the time the coffee was ready, Tennyson wandered into the room still dressed in his everyday clothes. The message turned out to be a video file her mother had sent. It could have been sent immediately after she took it, but sometimes it took forever for them to arrive. The image filled her phone screen.

Ten glanced at it. "Awkward. Who'd want that for a cake? What is it anyway? A Wizard of Oz theme or something for someone who loves shoes."

His comment made her take another look at the photo. The shoes were red and glittery. How did she miss that the first time? It's not every day you see a grown woman wearing shoes better suited for a five-year-old. Where did someone buy shoes like those?

Not receiving a fast response, Ten gestured to the phone. "Are you looking at possible wedding cakes? Forget about that one."

"It's not about Mark and my wedding. My mother, your pretend grandmother, believes this may be a murder site."

"I take back that pretend part. I chose your mother as my grandmother because she's so cool and kind to me. I like to think she chose me, too."

"I'm sure she did." Cecilia usually took to most people but had a kind heart for anyone she regarded as an underdog.

"That's right. Don't forget it." Ten reached for a cup and poured himself a cup of the freshly made coffee. "As for the picture, what's the deal? I've heard of death by chocolate, but never murder by cake. It looks like the cake swallowed her."

"I'm not sure. No one is at this point." She reached for her own cup and poured the remaining coffee into it, glad she'd made two cups as opposed to one. "Mother was there and took this picture. They think she had a heart attack and fell into the cake."

"Don't most heart attack victims fall backward?"

"It depends on what they were doing at the time. If she were leaning or kneeling, inspecting the cake, she could have fallen forward."

Her college student employee, who had become more like a son to her, sipped his coffee with a furrowed brow, a sign he was pondering the matter.

"Did someone see her fall into the cake?"

"No. The wedding party and the guests were still at the church. The caterer was apparently locked up tight in her truck. At least that's the story she gave Mother."

"Murdering someone in a public place is the same as asking to be locked up."

Donna hadn't really decided if it was murder yet. The person nearest a dead body tends to become someone of interest. "The caterer is dependent on Charmaine for referrals. No reason for her to kill the goose that lays the golden egg."

Something about the whole thing bothered her, besides someone dying during a wedding. She'd heard from her co-workers that wedding planners could be as somber as generals declaring war. They bark out orders about who should do what and were constantly consulting their clipboard.

Her hand when up to touch the base of her neck as she verbalized her thoughts. "Why was she at the reception hall and not at the church? There would have been plenty for her to do at the church along with lining up everyone for the reception line and making sure the right photos were taken."

Ten raised one eyebrow, confirming she'd hit on the one thing that wasn't quite as it should be. That was, if you discounted a dead wedding planner in a huge monstrosity of a cake.

Chapter Five

AFTER TENNYSON RETURNED to his room at half past midnight, Donna turned off the kitchen light. Her gait slowed, allowing Jasper to catch up with her as she turned out the hallway lights behind her. If there were guests at the inn, she normally left a few lights on so no one would pitch down the stairs in the dark.

Whoo boy, she was tired. Sleep couldn't come soon enough. It didn't help she'd spent an hour trying to figure out what happened to Charmaine. What she needed was more info. Maybe Mark could help her.

Oh my! She'd forgotten to say goodnight to her sweetie. Donna pulled her cell out and squinted her eyes at the tiny font in the dim light. Mark had sent a text, but her eyes were too tired to focus. "This is ridiculous. I remember when I used to be able to read under the covers with just a penlight. Getting old is for the dogs!" Jasper looked up at her as if to comment.

"Not you," Donna corrected, well aware her pooch already had a bit of white on his muzzle. "Those other dogs." Jasper kept his censorious gaze on her, making her feel that somehow, she erred in her choice of words.

"I meant cats. Getting old is for the cats."

Jasper gave a short bark in what she'd assumed was agreement.

Inside her bedroom, Donna flicked on the bedside lamp to read Mark's message better. Jasper padded toward his second bed to finish his interrupted sleep. Even though Jasper was a male dog, his bed was a pink and green floral to match the rest of the feminine décor.

The bedside light illuminated the phone, making it much easier to read, which made no sense considering the phone had its own light. Instead of overthinking it, as she usually did, she stared at her phone message.

Hadn't heard from you. Went to bed. Love you.

It wasn't a love letter, but it did sound like Mark. Why hadn't she heard the phone chime? A quick inspection revealed the sound had been switched off. She must have done it accidentally while talking to her mother.

She sat on the bed and considered what she should text him. As a practical woman, she hadn't been given to a great deal of emotion. She'd done her best all her adult life to stomp out that side of herself, never wanting to be labeled an over emotional female by one of the male doctors who somehow thought they were better than her by the simple fact they'd been born male. Although, it could have been their degree, too.

Dear Sweetie

She erased that before she even sent it. Mark had no clue that she referred to him as *sweetie*. It was one step up from *baby*, which he wouldn't have liked, either. Her free hand tugged on her ear, dislodging a stud earring that was within the acceptable guidelines of what jewelry nurses could wear. "Oops."

She made a mental note to find the stud before it became vacuum fodder or ended up in her bare foot. Right now, she needed to text her fiancé.

Hi Handsome

Nope, that didn't work either. It sounded forced, not her. She exhaled, confused at how what used to be such a simple activity had now become so hard once her relationship status changed with Mark. Not knowing how to address him, she decided not to. After all, who starts a text message with a salutation?

Sorry I missed you. Will talk to you in the morning. Love you.

That sounded okay, but it didn't address the possible murder. Maybe Mark didn't know. Yes, that had to be it. He was somewhere else, and no one had told him. That meant she should, obviously.

Need to talk to you about suspicious death at wedding.
Have reason to believe it could be murder.

Her cell vibrated seconds after she pushed send. It was Mark.
"Hello?"
"Donna, go to sleep."
Mark sounded tired, which wasn't too surprising. He'd probably had as hard a time getting back into the grind as she had. "I am. Getting ready right now."
"No, you're not."
Was he telling her what she was doing already? Her slumped shoulders went back. "Pardon me?"
"You're throwing out little tidbits about a possible murder to see if it might stir my interest. It's just like kids taunting one another with the fact that they have a secret no one else knows."
"I'm not taunting you."
"You are. Spit it out. Tell me what you think you know."
"You did know there was a death at the Swenson-Roberts wedding?"

"I heard there was a death, not a murder."

"I agree. You met Charmaine at the inn yesterday. Remember?"

"Not exactly, all I remember were four people eyeing me the way a starving dog eyes a half-eaten sandwich left on an outside café table as soon as we mentioned we were going to be married."

"They're wedding planners. We represented their target audience. Although, I'd assumed their ideal customer would be younger and given to fantasies of having a Cinderella-type wedding, complete with the carriage and six white horses. Charmaine was the tall one. Do you know who I'm talking about now?"

"Yes. I got the mental picture. Should I ask why you think it was murder?"

"It isn't exactly me. It was my mother who first suggested it. She was on the scene first and took a photo of the wedding planner planted in the cake." A hearty groan reached Donna's ear. "Don't be that way. I think Mother has a point. She also told me about some odd goings-on.

"Why?"

"We saw the woman yesterday, and she looked fine to me."

"How so?"

"Her color was good. When the others hot-footed it out of here to present the inn as a venue, she hustled out right after them with no shortness of breath or hesitation."

"That makes you think she didn't have a heart attack?"

"Not entirely, but an autopsy would cancel out accidental death. You need to push for an autopsy."

"It's not even my case."

"What?" She must have misheard him. "Everyone knows you're the best when it comes to murders."

"Thanks. At this point, it's a simple heart attack at the wrong place."

"It wasn't. Not only that, Charmaine was at the wrong place. A wedding planner should have been at the wedding. Mom mentioned the only person at the reception was the caterer who was setting up but went back to her truck to get a shrimp ring and got accidentally locked in from the outside. One of her servers arrived and let her out. That's when she discovered Charmaine stuck in the cake."

"Locked in the truck does sound peculiar. I might need to investigate then."

"We might need to," she corrected, knowing he meant *we* as opposed to *I*.

"All right, I'll check and make sure the body goes to the funeral home."

"If you're on the case, I can finally go to sleep." She toed off her shoes and pushed back against the pillows. A yawn caught her unaware as she dropped her shoulders, confident that if anything was out of whack, Mark would soon put it right.

"Tell me what you know. You do realize I won't get any sleep tonight."

"We can discuss it tomorrow."

He gave a heavy sigh. "You know better than that. Every day, even every hour, after a murder, there becomes less of a chance of apprehending the murderer. A few might stay in the vicinity convinced they'd gotten away with it. Most vanish, so, even if we do nail down the suspect, they're nowhere to be found."

Donna placed Mark on speaker as she forwarded the photo. "I hope I don't cut you off. I'm sending you the photo Mother took."

"Still here."

Her eyes rolled up as she tried to pull together any information, she had about the chance met wedding planner. "Before I fell into the foyer, I heard them heckling Charmaine about a previous wedding where the bride caught on fire."

"Excuse me?"

"The veil was too long, pulled a candelabra over, which burned the veil and the bride's long hair."

"It's possible someone could want to get back at Charmaine. Possibly hurt her business, but not necessarily kill her."

"She *is* dead." Even though she normally tried not to point out the obvious, she just did.

"I know. Sometimes people who want revenge only intend to scare the person, not kill them. The whole point of revenge is for the person to know who was delivering the beat down, which is hard to do when they're dead."

"So maybe someone hoped to just make her look bad as a wedding planner and pushed her into the cake. She could have smothered before she could get out."

"Strange, but possible. Smothered by wedding cake sounds like one of those mysteries you're so fond of reading."

"It does. If your murderer was more set on revenge, what are your chances of catching her?"

"I noticed you said *her* as opposed to him."

No one could accuse Mark of missing anything. "I did. Weddings are the domain of the bride. As you know, brides get very emotional about the whole thing."

"Is this a warning for me? You're going to go bonkers and off a wedding planner?" He chuckled as if he'd thought he'd just made a joke.

"Not funny. Besides, I'm not even sure I need a wedding planner. I considered Grace, the soft spoken one at the house. She's not over the top like the rest of them."

"Over the top?"

"You've heard the expression. Over the top wedding planners want everything big and showy to generate publicity for their services. If one wedding planner had a horse drawn carriage as part of a theme wedding, the next planner might have mounted knights in shiny armor or have the wedding party arrive in antique cars."

"Sounds expensive."

"It is."

"That's another thing to consider. If women get emotional about weddings, men get equally upset about spending large wads of money, especially if it didn't turn out as expected. What we need to do is check out Charmaine's previous customers, especially those who didn't have a perfect wedding."

Really, did he just say that? Now it was her turn to sigh, and she did. "It's not that easy. Something always goes wrong at a wedding. Part of the wedding party is late. Floral arrangements aren't the exact color as planned. The organist messes up a song. The ring bearer drops the ring. The flower girl refuses to walk down the aisle. The groom arrives drunk. The videographer starts filming at the wrong time. An ex-spouse or girlfriend shows up uninvited. The list is endless. I seriously doubt anyone has a perfect wedding. If you give people a chance to complain, they will."

"At this point, I'm not even sure a murder has been committed. If it has, I might need you to sound out the previous clients."

"Really? Me?"

Mark seldom asked for her help, explaining everything was police work. Even though she often unearthed clues the police missed, she usually put it down to their lack of female detectives. A woman saw things differently than a man. Often, a female could understand the feminine mind. Something no man, living or dead, had ever accomplished.

"I figured I should know what you're doing up front as opposed to wondering what you're doing behind my back."

Even though his tone stayed pleasant, his words dampened her sudden joy at being included in a possible case at the get go. "Gee, thanks."

"Rules are rules, as you well know. The department might consider you as a consultant, which is more than any other police department would do."

He was right, and she hated when he was right, but not as much as she used to. It would be foolish to marry a man who was wrong all the time. It would be tiresome having to correct him over and over. Thank goodness Mark wasn't like that. "I know. What's your schedule tomorrow?"

"Work as usual and we can speculate over morning coffee before I start the day."

She mentally planned her day. "I'd love to see you in the morning. Come on by. I won't leave for work until 1:30. If you swing back by, we can have an early lunch and discuss what you've found out." She smiled as she felt the combined tingle of seeing her sweetie and being on a new case. She'd not call it that, yet.

"Sounds great. See you then. Love you. Kiss, kiss."

Her eyebrows shot up. Did her somber fiancé just say kiss kiss? Good heavens, the rules were changing.

"Talk to you later. Love you, sweetie. Kiss, kiss."

Chapter Six

T HE COFFEE GRINDER whirled, filling the room with the rich aroma of dark roast Columbian beans and masking the sound of the back-door opening. Jasper noticed and gave a welcoming bark from his place on his kitchen bed. It wasn't enough to make him get up and greet the newcomer. Donna glanced over her shoulder expecting to see Mark but was surprised to see Maria with Baby Cici. The dark-haired cherub was snuggled against her mother's shoulder. The tiniest bit of yellow material showed above the infant blanket making Donna curious if it was the neutral play outfit, she'd gifted Maria.

"Good morning!" Maria called out.

Donna's feet carried her to her sister-in-law and her darling child. Unlike other women, she was no sucker for babies. They didn't draw her like a magnet. There were plenty of babies at the hospital to fuss over. What was one more? The nurse in her, however, reared its head.

"Do you think it's smart to have her out so soon?" Tradition recommended keeping the baby at home for a month to build up its immunity system.

The tinkling laugh Donna envied filled the kitchen. "Please, be serious. We just left a cruise ship of three thousand plus people, and Cici is fine. If she was going to get sick, it would have been then. Besides, I wanted her to meet Jasper."

Hearing his name, the dog lifted his head up.

Donna held out her arms, taking the infant whose dark eyes were open. She'd like to think the baby recognized her, but she knew better. She carefully cradled the baby against her body, surprised at how emotional she felt with Cici in her arms. It could be because she knew the parents or that she helped deliver the little one, but somehow the tiny human captured her heart with a fist smaller than an undersized apricot.

Jasper stood up and moved around the kitchen stiff legged, with his nose in the air. He recognized a different scent had entered the room.

"Since most people didn't bring newborns over to meet pets, why did you want Cici to meet Jasper?"

"I read online that babies who are exposed to pets or animals develop a better immunity system. Living out on a farm with dirt, plants, and pollen helps, too."

Donna bent at the waist to give Jasper a slightly better view. "Well, if you came here for dirt, I don't want to know about it. I imagine the place could use a thorough cleaning, which I'll do my first day off. I appreciate the visit, but it's hard for me to believe that as a new mother you're on a visiting tour with baby in tow."

"Not exactly."

The back door swung open, grabbing the dog's attention. Donna smiled in that direction, certain it would be her sweetie, but it was her mother. "Mom?"

"That would be me." Cecilia, attired in a floral dress with sensible shoes, looked tan and rested, the way a person was supposed to look after a cruise. She held out her arms in Donna's direction, signaling a transfer of the newest Tollhouse.

Donna gave up Cici, not because her mother held out her arms, but because she needed to get together the light breakfast, she originally planned for her and Mark. She should probably include the rest. "You hungry?"

Maria answered first. "Starving. I would have thought my appetite would drop off after delivering, but I honestly think it increased."

Her mother smiled at the baby in her arms as she spoke. "If you make something light, I could eat. Don't go to any trouble on my account. I see you have the coffee going already, but I wouldn't mind a cappuccino if you were going to make one for yourself."

Talk about a broad hint. "I can, sure. I was expecting Mark this morning and was just going to probably warm up a few things. Maybe a quiche and a couple of muffins."

Her mother stopped making faces at the baby long enough to ask, "Do you have any of those cranberry orange muffins left?"

"I can look." She glanced at her sister-in-law, expecting a similar request. "Maria?"

"Oh, those sound good. As do the zucchini lime ones you made before we left. The chocolate date ones would be good, too. Quite frankly, anything would be wonderful." She held up her watch. "Look, it's been almost two hours since I ate. No wonder I'm so hungry."

The coffee stopped brewing, and like clockwork, Tennyson entered the kitchen, waved to everyone, and made his way to the coffeepot. Maybe she should make a spread for five. "Tennyson, what are your plans today?"

He poured coffee into his cup, added an obscene amount of sugar, and spoke as he stirred. "I'm meeting my girlfriend for breakfast at the A Little Bit of Paris Café, but I'll be back to help you clean by ten."

"Sounds good." She would have preferred his help a little earlier but had no clue how long her family would be here. Since it was Monday, Ten could do the laundry while she was at the hospital.

The coffee aroma drew her to the pot where she poured herself a cup. She held up the pot, but Maria shook her head, while her mother gave an overly bright smile, which she interpreted to mean she'd wait on the cappuccino. Since her mother had graciously gifted her with the machine, she should use it.

"Should I ask what brings you here this morning, Mother? I doubt you've arrived to soak up any of the bacteria and dog hair Jasper is so thoughtfully providing to boost your immune system."

"Nope. I already get plenty of that from my own dog, Loralee, that you so thoughtfully offloaded on me."

"Hey, that wasn't me. It was Mark."

"Did I hear my name?"

Her sweetie walked in with a huge smile and an armful of flowers. He handed the flowers to her with a kiss on the cheek.

"What's all this then?" The show of flowers usually came with an apology. As far as she knew, no forgiveness was needed.

Mark's shoulders went up in a shrug. "Some woman on the corner of Main and Pearl was selling flowers out of her car. They were colorful, and I thought you'd like them."

Maria and her mother cooed in unison. Donna agreed with the sentiment. It was a pretty sweet thing to do. "Thank you."

She took the flowers and proceeded to look for a vase as Mark helped himself to coffee.

Cecilia chattered as Donna stuck her head deep into the cabinet, looking for one of the bigger vases she knew she had in there. Her body blocked out most of the light, making it more difficult to see, but she could still hear.

"Have you heard anything else about the wedding planner in the cake?" Good gravy, they were going to talk about Charmaine without her being present. Donna jerked upright and conked her head on the bottom of the counter. "Ouch!"

"Are you all right?" Mark asked as he knelt by the cabinet and placed his hand on her back.

"No. Tell my mother if she is going to wiggle information out of you while I am otherwise occupied, she'll have to do without her cappuccino."

"I'll tell her you play hardball, and my lips are sealed. It doesn't matter all that much since I have nothing to report." He chuckled at his own wit.

Her fingers wrapped around the vase, and she backed out just in time to hear her mother's comment.

"No worries, I can make my own cappuccino. Eventually, you'll tell me what's going on."

She had three people in her kitchen expecting breakfast soon. A quick survey of her upright freezer contents netted her the needed items. As she defrosted the containers, she considered why each person had shown up on her doorstep. Mark was the easiest. Engaged people tried to spend as much time together as possible, unless they didn't get along that well, which begged the question why they got engaged in the first place.

Her mother didn't try to hide her interest in the possible case. To be fair, she was at the epicenter of the whole thing. Without her photo and questions, Donna wouldn't even have told Mark about it. That left Maria.

While she knew her sister-in-law was more fit than most, having a newborn baby still took a great deal out of you. Most nurses, who took off for maternity leave, stated they came back to work for the rest. Maria popping over for a visit after they had just spent a week together on a ship, didn't add up. It had to be something else.

The microwave dinged letting her know her items were sufficiently thawed for the next step. She transferred the quiches to the toaster oven, but the muffins sat on the top for just a touch of heat. No one really liked soggy, microwaved muffins or quiches. The only thing the microwave was good for, besides thawing things in a hurry, was reheating cold coffee.

A loud whirling noise signaled her mother had made her own cappuccino as threatened. The coffee carafe was already halfway gone, too. Donna's lips pursed as she considered making another pot. The group's laughter drew her.

"What's so funny?"

Somehow, she'd missed out on something humorous. Mark turned and smiled at her. "Cecilia was regaling us with the meeting between Heloise and Simon."

Her eyes rolled upward on her own as she imagined the outspoken town gossip and her mother's latest beau. "Go ahead and tell me."

Mark held up one finger as he inhaled trying to control his merriment. "Heloise told Simon about us getting married."

Her shoulders went up in a shrug since nothing struck her as being even slightly laughable so far, but Mark continued his recitation.

"She pointed out that Cecilia and Simon weren't getting any younger and maybe they should make it a double wedding."

Yep, that sounded like something Heloise would say. "What did Simon say?"

Her mother jumped into the conversation as she rocked the baby. "That was the best part. The man appeared in shock. I thought he was going to pass out. He glanced over his shoulder as if there might be another couple behind us and asked if Heloise was talking to us. I told him it was a joke, which set our favorite gossip on a tear."

"Not my favorite gossip!" The tiny woman with the oversized mouth and her need to spread rumors whether they were true or not had stung Donna on more than one occasion. "I'm not sure why you even invited her on the cruise."

"Truthfully, I can't remember now. It was more like she invited herself, and I didn't have the heart to refuse."

"Speaking of weddings," Maria interjected as she pulled a carton of milk out of the fridge and poured some into a waiting glass on the counter.

"We weren't talking about weddings, but rather Heloise and her gossip factory."

Her sister-in-law chugged the milk and put it down hard on the counter, similar to the way those television Cowboys always slammed down a glass on the bar. "You were, in a roundabout way. I'm here to talk weddings."

The statement puzzled Donna at first, since obviously, Maria was already married. "Do you mean the wedding where the planner ended up in the cake?"

"How awful. I hope it didn't ruin the entire reception."

"No," her mother interjected. "The bridal party arrived later due to taking photos. It was the rest of us who milled around in front of the reception hall. I did my best to entertain them by recalling various funny wedding traditions. Simon directed the police to the side door, so something being wrong wasn't too obvious. The paramedics rolling Charmaine out in a body bag was harder to miss, though."

Maria made a sad sound. "How did you explain that?"

"I didn't. Simon referred to it as an unfortunate incident. He reminded everyone that it was the bride's day and to not mention anything about it would spoil it."

Donna could see the dignified silver headed Simon making such a speech. Most would try to follow his directions, but there had to be more than a few who would be anxious to share the news with the new bride. Instead of sadness, the woman might feel angry that someone dared died on her special day.

"I wonder if the bride could get her money back since the planner didn't deliver the whole package."

Her mother shook her head emphatically. "Most of the planners have a no-refund policy. Turns out most in the wedding industry do not do refunds. All too often a wedding doesn't go off as planned. It rains on an outdoor wedding. The bridesmaids' dresses are the wrong color."

Good heavens, it sounded like she was describing Donna's own failed wedding to Thomas. They never even got to the marriage part. Even though she'd told Mark about the situation—especially when Thomas ended up booking a room at the inn—it didn't make hearing about it any easier. She held up her hand, hoping to stop her mother from reciting everything that could go wrong at a wedding. Unfortunately, she kept talking.

"Then the groom could turn out to be a horse's rear-end and not even show up for the wedding."

She groaned. Yep, her mother went there. Interestingly enough, her mother still held onto her anger. Donna had allowed hers to slip away as the years passed. If she had any thwarted hopes of what her life would have been like if she'd married Thomas, meeting him and his dysfunctional family made her thankful she'd avoided that calamity.

The toaster oven buzzer had her moving in its direction with a large platter.

She hoped her mother was finished listing everything bad that could happen at a wedding. When Cecilia made the mistake of pausing for a breath, Maria addressed Mark. "Have you decided on a theme for your wedding?"

A sputtered "What?" followed by coughing meant Mark must have been drinking when she posed the question. It didn't matter since Donna could field this one.

"A theme for what? Weddings are weddings. People say some words. They're married, then everyone has cake."

Baby Cici chose that moment to smile. "Look. She smiled," Cecilia announced with glee.

Everyone crowded around the baby, smiling and cooing at her, trying to coax out another smile without luck.

Maria crossed her arms and pouted. "It's not fair. She smiled at you first. After all, I did all the work."

"Ah, sweetie." Her mother comforted her daughter-in-law. "She wasn't smiling at me. Instead, I think it was the sheer ridiculousness of Donna thinking weddings have no themes. She doesn't even remember her almost wedding had a Hawaiian luau theme."

Mark's bushy eyebrows went up at the pronouncement. "Luau?"

"Don't ask." She wasn't sure why a dead wedding planner brought up memories from so long ago when she was incredibly stupid and naïve.

Too bad no one else in the room felt a similar reluctance not to discuss it. Maria, who now cuddled her baby, looked up in interest. "Tell me more about the luau theme. I've heard of hippie weddings, beach ones, even Renaissance ones complete with costumes."

Mark groaned on that one and even paled the tiniest bit as Maria continued.

"There're destination weddings, including some on cruise ships, underwater settings, and even a few in hot air balloons."

With a quick glance at her fiancé, she could tell by the pallor of his skin that one of the mentioned themes didn't agree with him. Good gravy, were they going to beat this to death?

She held up her hands. "Enough! It was more of a luau reception. We had birds of paradise flower arrangements on the table. The servers all had on Hawaiian shirts, and there was pulled pork."

"And fruit kabobs," her mother added. "Your father thought they were overpriced for cut up fruit on a stick."

Now her mother was bringing her father into it? Would it ever end? She placed the platter on the island, then turned away to the fridge to get the butter she should have put out to soften if she'd been thinking straight. Mark slipped up behind her and put his arm around her.

"I'm sorry all this talk about weddings has upset you." He gave her a one-armed hug. "You know, we could elope. Get married by Elvis or on a ship. We don't have to do anything you don't want."

She leaned back against him as a tear slipped down her cheek. She half-whispered the words. "I know, but I want a wedding. I deserve one. I've already been cheated out of one, but nothing weird such as the hot air balloon idea. Something that suits you and me and who we are."

"Hmm, that must mean there would be a murder involved since we initially met because of a dead stranger at your inn."

A chill danced up her arms. "No, thank you. We already have one dead wedding planner. That's more than enough."

He dusted a kiss on her head. "Got it. No murder themed weddings. No hot air balloon take-offs. Any other requirements?"

"Yeah, you need to be there." Her aggravation that her previous wedding had been brought up dissipated like soap bubbles in the air. Secure in the fact that her fiancé would be there this time, she could joke about it.

"I will be. Nothing can keep me from your side."

Chapter Seven

THE MORNING SUN illuminated the room with a rosy glow. The stove and toaster oven added some warmth, but not enough to cause the air conditioner to kick on. Jasper's raspy snore mingled with the burr of a lawn mower in the distance. Donna breathed in the slight tang of the cranberries and lime along with the understated cinnamon. While the cruise had been fun, especially after she and Mark had a chance to relax, it wasn't home. It was hard to put her finger on when the inn had become home to her, but it had, which had made it easier to let go of her house.

It could have been that the inn kitchen welcomed her family, Mark, and the occasional guest who marched into the kitchen without invitation. Donna used to consider herself more of an introvert but discovered she didn't mind social interaction in appropriate chunks. No reason to go all crazy and be surrounded by people twenty-four-seven, though. Still, family worked, especially when she included Mark and Ten.

Maria and Cecilia, continued to discuss possible themes as they munched on muffins.

Her sister-in-law smiled down at her child, hoping to have a re-occurrence of the sought-after baby grin. "How about a black and white wedding?"

Donna answered. "That sounds more like some art project. Should I ask?"

"It's where you ask everyone to only wear black and white. You put it in the invitation, and it looks good in the photos later."

"Maybe if you're trying to make it look like it took place before the invention of color film. Besides, I don't think Herman would care for being told what to wear."

Her mother looked up at the mention of Herman. "Have you contacted him yet?"

"I've been home an entire day. No, I haven't contacted him."

"Don't make the mistake of thinking seniors have no social life." She wagged a finger at her. "He'll have to make plans for the trip from Indiana. I imagine he won't come alone, either. His friends will need to have time to make arrangements, too."

Her nose wrinkled. She hated it when her mother was right. "I'll call him today. I never would have known he was a justice of the peace if his heartbreaker of a granddaughter hadn't mentioned it in passing. Apparently, he presided at his son's second marriage."

"Do that." Her mother popped the last bit of muffin into her mouth and slid off her stool. She shouldered her handbag and added, "I gotta run. Simon and I have a French class to attend this morning."

Donna kissed her mother goodbye and waited for her to leave before turning to Maria. "When did mother start taking French?"

Her sister-in-law shrugged and held out Baby Cici for Donna to take. Maria straightened her clothes and grabbed the baby knapsack. "I need to go, too. Right now, this little darling is contented, but she'll be screaming for her second breakfast soon enough."

Mark accompanied her to the door to see off the new mother and child. They both waved until Maria pulled out into the street, and then they returned to the kitchen. It was a little weird the two of them waving from the inn doorstep as if they were already a couple who happened to live at an inn. Before the cruise, she and Mark had argued about her selling her house. That was before she knew he was going to propose. He hadn't wanted her to sell her house if it were simply a matter of raising enough money to install an elevator. How was she to know their income would be combined?

"So, when we're married, what are you going to do about your house?" Her natural assumption was that he'd move into the inn, and she'd redecorate the master bedroom to be less girly. Maybe something in burgundy and forest green with some light oak touches and gold throw pillows to keep it from being too dark.

"I'm planning on keeping my house."

Did she hear him right? "You're planning on keeping your house?"

"Yes." He uttered the words in his usual calm manner as he moved toward the coffee pot for a refill.

Something wasn't right. Maybe, he wasn't seeing the big picture. One of the reasons she put her house on the market was that it was hard to run an inn and not be on site. There was only so much Tennyson could do and most of it involved a panicky phone call, detailing the latest disaster. While the boy was good with children and animals, he didn't stand a chance when it came to persnickety guests.

She waited until Mark returned to his stool and picked up one of the leftover muffins to say her piece. "You do know I sold my house." Her hand splayed against her chest as if he might need a reminder.

"I know. I wish you weren't in such an all-fired hurry about that and would have told me."

Her eyes closed briefly as she drew in a breath. Not this discussion again. "If I knew your intentions, it might not have made that big of a difference. I want to make a go of the inn, and I can't run back and forth across town. I need to be here. That means when we marry you need to be here, too."

His furrowed brow indicated that he might not be getting it, but maybe he might be thinking about it, which was a plus. Now, all she had to do was point out the obvious. Men tended to need that in her experience. "You need to put your house on the market. It might take some work to get that smoke smell out of it. It would be good for you to move out of it for your own health."

The lines in his forehead deepened as he sipped his coffee. Donna recognized a stalling technique when she saw it. "You gonna nurse that coffee all day?"

"Nope. I'll drink it until it's gone, and then I'll leave."

Leave. That sounded ominous. "Are you going to sell your house or not?"

Mark stood up with the cup still in hand. "Not. I didn't want you to sell your house. You had it fixed up the way you liked it. The neighborhood was good. We could have both lived there comfortably. You always have to rush into everything."

What did he mean by that? Occasionally, she had made a few impulsive assumptions and had a few overpriced auction items to show for it, but that didn't make her into a rusher. One fist found a perch on her hip. "That's how I get things done."

Mark took a final sip and placed the cup on the island. "Yeah, I know that's what you think. I need to check out our dead wedding planner. The coroner was gone over the weekend. They did manage to reach Charmaine's son, and informed him about the autopsy."

"That's good." The change in subject allowed them both to cool down a bit, in her opinion. Murder may have drawn them together, but they couldn't deal in crime cases all the time. "Will you be back for lunch?"

"Of course, I will." He gave her a quizzical look, then headed for the door.

Donna followed, unsure if their flare-up disagreement had blown over or was only tabled for the time being. At the door, Mark gave a swift kiss, reassuring her some. He told her, "People disagree, but it isn't the end of the world."

On an average day, she disagreed a great deal with people, but never anyone who mattered to her as much as Mark. She managed a wobbly smile for him and muttered, "I know."

She really didn't know. Who hadn't heard the old saw about the road to true love never being smooth? Having passed the big five-0, she didn't have the mindset of the younger set that someone better would come along. She knew better. As for the two of them, they could deal with each other's' idiosyncrasies and possibly find them adoring. Still, a house was a very big issue. Would they end up living apart? Her in the inn to be ready to fix an early morning breakfast and him in his house so he could watch television as loud as he wanted.

It could be the elephant in the room, and for once, Donna had no clue how to deal with it. Her fiancé couldn't be faulted for wanting privacy. It made sense after a long day of dealing with people. Still, she had no intention of getting married if she wasn't going to sleep in the same bed as her husband. The possibility made her stomach turn sour.

She exhaled and borrowed a coping technique from one of her favorite fictional characters, Scarlett O'Hara, from *Gone with the Wind*.

"I'll think about it tomorrow."

Chapter Eight

T HE RADIO TUNED to the oldies station played in the background as Donna called Herman. Even though the number she had was supposed to go directly to her former neighbor, she had to talk to two different people, explaining who she wanted to talk to and the nature of their relationship. Was Herman in a witness protection or prison? Maybe they thought Donna was the issue. Finally, she reached him.

"Hello, Herman. It's Donna, your former neighbor." Realizing the man could have had numerous former neighbors she tacked on, "In Legacy. Across the street. In the converted VFW/ Victorian."

"Morning, Donna. I do remember who you are. I'm just old, not senile. What's up?"

"Exciting news!" She knew the cryptic phrase would pique his interest.

"You finally found the lost jewels."

"No but Tennyson did a little more research, and we might be able to claim the jewels if we ever find them, since I bought the house in good faith and all its contents."

"I should have looked a little harder when I was there."

Donna laughed because she knew Herman expected it. Ripped up floor boards, holes in plaster walls, as well as a yard punched full of holes didn't normally amuse her. Her hand went back to her neck, rubbing it. She was almost certain Herman wouldn't tear her house apart. Probably ninety-nine percent certain. There was that one percent that kept her on edge when the man started talking about stolen jewelry. Herman, however, was past the age of treasure hunts. Good chance he didn't even believe in the stashed loot, but someone could.

"Yeah, you could have, but I've been through the house several times from top and bottom without any luck. Ten and a friend have knocked on all the walls, hoping to discover a hidden panel or passage without discovering any."

"If you didn't call about the jewels, what then? This isn't one of those charity calls where you feel sorry for the old geezer?"

"Get real." She snorted into the phone. Now and then, even though she did something nice, she would never qualify as a do-gooder. "Mark and I are getting married."

"Well, I swan! I thought it would happen the way you two colored up around each other, but I certainly didn't expect it while I was on the right side of the ground. Congratulations! Are you inviting me to the wedding?"

"Well, I am, in a way."

"You're not making me the flower girl, are you? My legs wouldn't look none too pretty in a frilly dress."

"You're not the flower girl. Hadn't even planned on having one. Gwen mentioned when she was here that you are a justice of the peace. Are you still?"

"I am. Not sure why I keep renewing my license, but I must be holding out for all those oaths and depositions I need to witness. I can even rule on small claims in Texas. You're in luck. I can marry you, since you're not in Rhode Island."

"What does Rhode Island have to do with anything?"

"They don't allow JPs to officiate at weddings. The state always had an ornery streak if you ask me. Probably afraid money might escape the state coffers. Have you decided on a date?"

Her lips twisted to one side as she pondered the question. No, they hadn't decided. Mark declared anything was fine, but implied sooner was better than later since they could get a call to testify. She wasn't sure why their depositions weren't good enough. How long would she need to pull things together? A month, six weeks? There was a calendar near the phone that she usually consulted when making reservations.

"How about June twenty-fourth? This year."

"Good. I couldn't guarantee I'd be here next year. Are you going to put me up in that fancy bed and breakfast of yours?"

"I am. I thought you might want to bring along a few friends for the drive."

"Woo hoo, a road trip! Gus and Jake will be very happy. Just the other day they were talking about we should make a break for it."

"My goodness, is it really that bad there?"

"My suite is a little crowded since I brought so much, but it's still nice. It faces east, so I get the morning sun whether I want it or not."

His husky laugh reassured her a little. "Are you making any more friends?"

"I am. There's a lovely lady cop here that's letting us help with cold cases, which is more than I remember Mark letting us do."

"I don't remember you asking."

Here in Legacy, Herman could have been a huge help, since he knew so much about the town over the years. Still, he'd shown interest in the cases but seldom contributed useful information. He might not know as much about the area as she'd given him credit for. In the end, the lady cop was probably just keeping their minds engaged and not expecting any break throughs.

"Fair enough. I'll be there even if I have to ask Gwen to drive me. My night vision is completely gone."

The name of his niece, Gwen, caused her teeth to click together. The last thing she needed was that homewrecker stirring things up again with Ten. Their brief association that consisted of shared conversation, walks, and Donna didn't know what else, convinced her vulnerable employee that he was in L-O-V-E. Too bad the girl forgot to mention her boyfriend back home until she was ready to leave. It took a good two months of moping before Ten returned to normal. Overly dramatic teenage girls had nothing on him when it came to unrequited love.

"You don't have to drive at night."

"I'll try to remember that."

"I'll pencil you and your friends on my guest calendar."

"Good. Bingo is in five minutes. I need to go. If I don't get the prime seat close to the caller, I'll never have a clue of what's being said. Bye."

"Bye."

A smile tugged at her lips as she hung up the landline phone. A soft spot existed in her heart just for Herman. Would driving across states be too hard on him with his night blindness and compromised hearing? If he really did have issues hearing, it might make the wedding ceremony challenging.

Herman's friends would gobble up more than a third of her rooms. Mark's sister and mother might be willing to take a suite, but that would only leave three rooms. She had no long-distance friends or family she wanted to invite. Her goal was to keep it quiet and simple with no over the top theatrics. No horse-drawn carriage, no releasing of doves, no children's choirs, no Irish dancers. Just a simple exchange of vows and a dining room server loaded with food.

No wonder brides turned into a screaming bunch of emotions. Here she hadn't even planned anything, and she was already having doubts. When Mark arrived, she'd have to remember to tell him the wedding date.

Tennyson returned on time to help her with the rooms as she debated with herself if she should make the wedding food or have it catered. Having someone else make it made the most sense. She wouldn't have the bother of preparation or clean-up, but how could she be sure they'd do it right?

In the kitchen, pulled pork simmered in a small slow cooker for sandwiches for lunch. All her inner dialogues focused on food. Should she go with traditional? She saw some very cute dipped strawberries with wedding sprinkles online, but would they hold up? She'd have to make them the night before and she doubted she have the time or the patience.

"Honey, I'm home."

Mark's voice silenced her mental discussion as she hurried down the stairs. "Is it that late already?"

The fact that her fiancé grinned up at her from the base of the stairs meant their earlier sparring had been forgotten. Obviously, her practical suggestion of selling his house had taken root. He'd not want to mention it just yet. In a few days, he'd announce it as if it was his plan all along. She'd give him that.

"Hey there, handsome." She brushed his hand with hers as she passed, and he entangled his fingers with hers as she hoped he would. "I just have pulled pork for sandwiches. We could have some chips and dill wedges to go with it."

"Sounds yummy."

"It does. I don't always have to have a fancy meal or even make one for that matter. Smoked meat and salty food is our family tradition."

"Ours, too."

"Probably most Southern families, if not all." Donna led the way into the kitchen and pulled the buns out of the cabinet. She had to tiptoe to reach the chips but spoke as she was doing so. "Hear anything about the dead wedding planner?"

"I figured I would at least get to eat before the third degree, but I should have known better. The bride's mother came to file charges against Charmaine for not providing all the services she paid for. I tried to explain there wasn't much we could do since the wedding planner was dead, and she was her own company. There were no partners to hit up, and from what I've heard, she had no assets to attach a financial ruling against, either."

Chips reached, she dropped back to her heels with the bag in hand. "That's what I heard, too. Apparently, she was flying close to the wind, not getting the notable weddings. What did you tell the woman to calm her down?"

"Told her there was no use suing a dead woman. She'd be stuck in court for at least a year with lawyer fees costing her more than anything she might have lost."

Mark reached into the cabinets and withdrew the plates for lunch. "Do we need a plate for Tennyson?"

"Might as well. He'll show up eventually. He may be on the third floor."

A third plate was added to the stack and carried to the crockpot. "As you know we left the body for inspection to see if any foul play was involved. Once the cake and frosting had been scrubbed off, we found bruising around the neck and shoulders. There were fingertip impressions with tiny cuts at the end of each one."

She opened the buns on the plates and loaded meat on top.

"Could you get the condiments out of the fridge and whatever you want to drink?"

"I'm on it."

Arms over-burdened with barbecue sauce, mustard, and dill pickles, Mark ferried the items to the table. "I kinda expected you to make some comment about the coroner's findings."

"I'm thinking about it. Did he say it was strangulation?"

"No. Whoever it was may have tried to strangle her, but Charmaine went into the cake with her mouth open. It was suffocation since her entire head was inside the cake. She even had frosting in her lungs."

"A wedding planner with wedding cake in her lungs gave the whole thing an ironic twist. Whoever it was probably had a definite desire to put an end to Charmaine, and the cake just assisted."

"That's one way to look at it. I was more curious about the cuts and the fingerprint bruises."

"Fingernails. Long ones. The better question would be if they were artificial or natural. See if the coroner can scrape anything out of the cuts. You do realize that most of the women at the wedding probably have their nails done specifically for the wedding."

"True, but you're assuming the killer was a wedding guest *and* a female."

Tennyson walked into the kitchen and grinned when he saw an extra loaded plate. "Is that for me?"

"Of course." Donna knew her employee could earn more money elsewhere, but he'd miss out on the free room and board. Besides having grown fond of Ten, she didn't want to have to break in anyone new.

After selecting a dill pickle spear and loading down his sandwich with sauce, Ten looked up. "What are ya'all talking about?"

"Strangulation versus suffocation as a method of murder." Mark answered, as Donna bit into a chip to quell her urge to giggle at Ten's expression.

"Okay, then. I'll take my food to the dining room." His actions suited his words.

"Ah, look at that. You traumatized our boy," she teased.

"No, he'll be fine. So, I want your opinion on the possible motivation. Who kills a wedding planner?"

"My first assumption is anyone who had a bad wedding. You already heard my mother's laundry list of things the wedding planner could be blamed for. Everybody is sue-happy nowadays. It's the first thing that comes out of their mouth. At the hospital, we even have parents sue the obstetrician years later because their child didn't turn out cute or smart enough."

Mark chewed thoughtfully as he tried to talk with his eyes. It wasn't working. He swallowed. "I was trying to convey that people may threaten to sue, but not kill. As for the babies, that's crazy. Do any of them win?"

"Most are thrown out before they even get to court, but all the same, it causes mal-practice insurance premiums to go up. Doctors used to be credited with bringing new life into the world. Not so much now. As for people threatening to kill, they do it all the time. Still, I believe if someone had planned to kill someone, they wouldn't be foolish enough to announce it."

He held up his finger. "I know it's off topic, but I almost forgot. I talked to my mother and sister to tell them about the wedding, and…"

He trailed off making her wonder if they would forbid the marriage or something equally archaic. "Are they going to make me pay four goats and a milk cow for you?"

"No, nothing that dramatic. My sister, Eileen, was wondering if she could help with the wedding."

"I'm not sure I understand. There isn't anything that involved that needs assistance. I buy a dress. You rent a tux. Herman says the words. That's about it."

"Surely there are other things. Helping out would be a great way for her to get to know you."

Then your sister is crazy. Strange, she seemed normal when they had met in the hospital after Mark had been shot. Already, she had the feeling she'd have to avoid the helpful suggestions of both her own mother and sister-in-law. "Um, how does she suggest we communicate since we don't even live close?"

"Skype."

"I don't Skype."

"It's time you learn. I'm sure Tennyson could teach you."

"Yippee. That's another thing on my don't-want-to-do list. Why is this important to you?"

"For a long time, my sister, Eileen, was estranged. At first, we thought there was some imagined wrong she felt existed, which was why she never talked to us. Later on, we discovered her husband prevented any interaction. He was very controlling. Thank goodness she got away from him. Anyhow, she has missed out on family functions all that time. I thought it might be a nice chance for you two to bond."

His explanation did tug at her heart strings, but it also demonstrated he knew nothing about women. "Did you suggest this?"

He grinned. "I did. Isn't it a great idea?"

Her mother had counseled her once that the secret to a good marriage wasn't saying everything she thought at the moment. At least wait for the right time to say it. "It should be interesting."

A phone call should smooth out the misunderstanding. Mark's sister would probably laugh about it and confess to not wanting to be troubled by the whole affair anyway. Donna would politely point out that all the sister would have to do is buy herself a new dress if she wanted and come to the wedding. Yeah, she could fix that. With a lot of luck, her family should be just as easy, but she had serious doubts since she already knew them.

"Do you think another wedding planner killed Charmaine?" he asked.

Some people would assume murder and marriage went together. Her first impulse was to say *no*, considering all the negative talk from the other planners. Still, that didn't mean anything. It could even indicate jealousy. Maybe Charmaine was getting the weddings they wanted. She could be undercutting prices just enough to make her services more inviting.

"I'd say no at first, but it's hard to say. It could be a vendor and not necessarily one she used, either. It could be someone she'd bad-mouthed. Then again, murder tends to be personal. It could have nothing to do with weddings but could be related to more intimate issues."

"I thought that, too, the personal angle, I mean. As much as people hate to hear it, the police usually examine the spouse and family first. They have more reasons to dislike or resent the victim. Then, the circle is widened to include friends, extended family, and co-workers."

Was there anyone who disliked Donna enough to kill her? There were a few doctors who resented her non-subservient manner. She saw no reason to bow down to a doctor just because he or she had more money and in turn could attend school longer than she had.

"I can see that, but when it comes to co-workers, that might only include the other wedding planners. Although, it could also include everyone from venue owners to cake decorators."

"You do realize you've just multiplied the suspect pool."

That thought had occurred to her. "I'm doing what I can to help."

"I know. About that, I should mention Captain Lowery is retiring."

"We should invite him to the wedding." Donna liked him. Instead of being a stuffed shirt about helping, Lowery was cool with her since she tended to get results, but then he also pulled in psychics for lost children.

"Okay. We can do that. Still, that's not what I was trying to say. They're going to replace him and..."

"They gave you the job!" She bounced off her stool and rushed around the island to hug her sweetie. This would probably mean longer hours if that were physically possible considering the time Mark already put into his profession. "How exciting! You deserve it."

Mark's chest moved as he struggled to inhale, causing Donna to loosen her grip so he could speak.

"I didn't get the job."

"They didn't offer it to you?"

Mark had probably been a part of LPD longer than anyone, and they overlooked the obvious choice, the hardest working man on the force. Her face reddened as she considered the various ways Mark had gone the second mile. No one disrespected her man.

"I didn't apply."

That made no sense. "Why didn't you?"

"Didn't need the headache of being blamed for every terrible thing that happens in the city. Besides, I knew we'd be getting married. I figured you'd keep me plenty busy."

Donna burst into laughter at his comment. "Oh, you!" She tapped his arm, then rested her hand on his forearm. "What were you trying to say before I went all crazy thinking you weren't being valued appropriately?"

"Jerome Billings, who is the front runner, is a real no-nonsense candidate. He's stated on more than one occasion that civilians should not meddle in police matters."

"I don't meddle. I help."

"I know that. For the time being, I think we should be low key about your helping. I thought you could pretend to need a wedding planner to get information."

"I thought your sister was my wedding planner."

"She is."

"I need to pretend to get into the wedding planner circle and retrieve vital information?"

"That's pretty much it."

"I hope this will convince the ignorant Jerome that I'm important to solving cases." Most people, when confronted with the obvious, would accept it.

"You can try. To start with, it might be good not to call him Ignorant Jerome."

"Oh." She rounded her mouth as if experiencing an insight. "You're right. Ignorant is too kind a word. It simply implies not knowing, but capable of learning. *Idiot* has a better ring to it."

Mark heaved a heavy sigh. "With any luck, the two of you will never meet."

"He better hope we never meet." Donna withdrew her hand and returned to her stool on the other side of the island. "Because I'd set him straight on a few things, such as all the roundabouts. How in the world is that supposed to help traffic? Just slows everybody down since the people going east and west never even get a chance to get into the circle."

"That's the street department and the city planners' area, mainly the planners."

She hit her forehead with her palm. "I know that. Well, there are other things I'd like to talk to Jerk Jerome about."

"Donna, I love you, but being on the force is very political. I've probably stayed as long as I have by not saying anything." He reached across the counter and clasped her hand. "Could you hold your opinion for my sake?"

"It's not right. Why should you have to hold your tongue when you know someone is being a pompous fool?" She allowed her hand to remain joined to his. It was hard to be indignant when Mark behaved this way.

"It is what it is. Usually, the pompous fool moves on to a new position."

"He's fired?"

"Yeah, I wish." Mark managed a weary smile. "Promoted, but not in my neighborhood anymore."

"I hear ya. Happens at the hospital, too. I'll keep my lips sealed. Perhaps he won't get the job. Who knows? He might have some dirty secret that might come out."

Mark had to release her hand to stand up and come around the island. His hands cupped Donna's shoulders. "The gleam in your eyes gives you away. I don't want to hear about you spreading any rumors about Jerome Billings."

"I won't." She opened her eyes as wide as she could without looking bug-eyed, believing that such an expression made her look innocent.

"It still counts if the rumor comes from your mother."

"All right, already."

Mark's shoulders dropped a little, but his eyes intensified the tiniest bit. "Or Heloise."

"Hey!" She held her hands as if surrendering and stood up, breaking his hold on her shoulders. "That woman is a rumor factory. She doesn't need any actual news. There's no way you can pin what she says on me. I've been a target of her tales more than once, as have you."

"Me?" He pointed back to himself with his thumb. "What did she say about me?"

She shrugged, not really wanting to say. She'd kind of resigned herself to the fact that Heloise was a lonely woman who used gossip as her calling card.

"Come on, you brought it up."

Her lips pursed as she considered how Mark might take his own rumor. She inhaled once, then slowly exhaled. "She called you the love-em-and-leave-em type, and because you were a cop, you had a string of women."

Instead of being angry, Mark stayed expressionless for a few seconds, then a chuckle emerged, followed swiftly by another one. He laughed so hard that a tear squeezed out of his eye and rolled down one cheek.

Finally, he leaned against the island counter as he caught his breath. "Well, if that's typical of her tales, then no one should believe her. Thanks for my laugh of the day. See what you can do about talking to the wedding planners."

Really. She needed to discuss invitations and venues with a wedding planner. "I'd like to do some real investigative work."

"This is real work. You can get the planners to gossip about

Charmaine, and they will, which is not something they'd do to the police. They'd be afraid anything they said might give them motive or at least make them a person of interest."

"Did you say planners with an *S*?"

"I did. Don't actually hire them. Tell them you want to interview them."

Her eyes rolled up in her head as she considered the planners' reaction after spending thirty minutes with them, having them trot out their various services, then leaving with a promise to call them. It made her sound like every bad date she'd ever had. "There's one problem with your plan."

"What?" His eyebrows lifted at her pronouncement.

He truly didn't know. How could he remain clueless after they've have spent so much time together about the demands on her time? Although to be fair, most of her colleagues thought she had oodles of time since she didn't have children to ferry around to multiple sports leagues or coordinate events with a mate. They also imagined she relaxed in front of the television with a bowl of cereal and a glass of wine after work, which was possibly what they wished they could do.

"Civil War re-enactors are coming for five days. They'll be here on Wednesday."

Mark stroked his chin. "That could be problematic because we need whatever rumors and conjectures are out there as soon as possible. Why would re-enactors be here? There were no battles here. Shouldn't they be camping out in a tent on a muddy field somewhere eating weevil-invested gruel?"

"The battle's in Charleston, South Carolina. That's the reason they're staying here. They don't want to be seen checking into a Holiday Inn or the Hilton by other re-enactors, and it's an easy drive to Charleston. I guess they're not dedicated to acting out the entire experience twenty-four-seven. I have an idea." The cloak and dagger aspect of re-enactors checking into out of the way hotels made her grin.

"I'm afraid to ask. Tell me anyhow."

"I could recruit my family to help. Maria could interview the out of towner planner since he has no clue she's already married. Mother could do the uppity one since she charms people so well. I could do the nice one named Grace. Then, we could talk to Heloise."

"What! She barely got off that cruise ship without a half dozen people wanting to strangle her."

"I agree, but the woman works harder than Homeland Security at gathering evidence."

"Mercy, I can see it now." He rubbed his hand over his face.

"Don't overreact. Most informants seldom give you the whole truth, just dribs and drabs that you have to piece together." She picked up their empty plates and put them in the dish washer. The clock above the sink warned her that she only had forty-five minutes before her shift started. For a change, she was anxious to get to work since her fellow nurses would fill her in on everything, she'd need to ask a planner. They probably knew what a decent price would be, too.

"You have a point. Well, I need to see if I can get anything from the caterer. Larson was originally assigned to this case, but I generously offered to take it over since your mother had already involved herself. Besides, he is going on vacation in three days."

"Give me the name of the caterer. I might need her for the wedding."

Mark pushed his sports jacket back enough to put his hands on his hips. "Are you going behind me and checking my work? Don't think I'll ask the right questions? Or get all the information?"

"What in tarnation are you talking about? I really might need a caterer for our wedding."

"Oh." His face flushed slightly. "I guess I'm on edge. No one is very happy with Lowery retiring and the possibility of Billings taking his place. Sorry." He dropped his arms and stepped closer to give her a quick kiss before he left.

Donna watched her fiancé leave, deciding he was much better at reading her than she initially assumed. She really might need a caterer, and why not question the one who had been at Legacy's latest murder venue.

Chapter Nine

THE HOSPITAL FLUORESCENT lights illuminated everything with yellow glare, making even the healthiest person appear slightly jaundiced. The overly strong odor of pine cleaner dominated the less pleasant smells. There was a rattle of a meds cart with one wheel that stubbornly stuck in one direction, making whoever was cursed with it involved in a battle to keep it going straight. Strange how this uninviting place had become Donna's home and her co-workers had become part of her world.

The patient load was light. Even though surgery could be scheduled on Mondays, not too many surgeons had. The plastic surgery rush was over since summer had officially started in Legacy with hot temps and skimpy summer wear. That meant she didn't have to assure bandage swathed patients that they'd look wonderful. Part of her did it because she felt they needed the encouragement after undergoing the ordeal. She never knew how they had looked since she never saw them before the surgery and never saw them after the swelling and bruising went away.

Shelley had unearthed a yellow legal tablet for her to write down the various wedding suggestions. Supper was served and picked up, which allowed a little lax time for the women to coach Donna through the intricacies of weddings.

"What are you going to do for favors?" Loretta asked. The aide had a hobby of making etched glass keepsake items. She usually brought them all etched Christmas ornaments as presents, with the year etched on them. Donna had so many she could now display a table top tree bedecked with all her crystal ornaments.

"What are they? And do I need them? It's only going to be a small wedding."

Loretta scoffed. "Girl, if you don't have favors, little gifts that the guest can take home with them, you might as well say your wedding isn't going to last."

She didn't want that. "What type of favors should I get?"

"Anything with your and Mark's name on it, along with the wedding date," Sydney, a new nurse, offered.

Loretta shook her head. "It needs to be classy." She held her index finger and directed it at Donna. "I know you're a classy person, which means you *do not* want to send anyone home with a box of mints with your names and date stamped on it."

Personally, she didn't want to send the guests home with anything, except maybe a full stomach and a pleasant memory. She'd heard weddings could be expensive, but she had no clue so many little things nickeled and dimed you.

When she'd contemplated marrying Thomas, she'd picked out whatever struck her fancy, never asking the price. Occasionally, her mother would redirect her saying something wasn't appropriate, which she now understood was code for *too expensive*.

"What would a classy person give as a favor?" Since she didn't expect to have more than thirty at the wedding, how expensive could it be?

"Candles." Kathy, the swing shift nurse, spoke up. "I had them at my first wedding and they were relatively inexpensive."

That could be a possibility since everyone like candles, with the exception being firemen who knew what a hazard they represented.

"Are you serious?" Loretta questioned Kathy's favor choice as if she'd suggested giving out vials of the Ebola virus. "Now, I know you're divorced."

"You know I am. Jason didn't want to get anything more expensive since we were paying for the wedding ourselves. He thought it would be funny to give out tiny bags of airline peanuts since our theme was Let's Fly Away."

Donna thought the airline peanuts was rather clever but was smart enough not to say so. "Are you saying the wrong favor will ruin a marriage?" she asked, feeling she was in the realm of superstition. Should she try to walk with a penny in her shoe? The point of that adage escaped her.

"No!" Loretta answered fast and held up her hand to let everyone know she wasn't through. "Marrying the wrong man will ruin your wedding and your life. Hand to God, I've done that." She nodded to Kathy.

"Okay. I'm good then. I've had my brush with the wrong man early on in life. I know I have the right one this time. It may have taken awhile, but I do know what to look for."

A help light lit up the board. Kathy glanced at it. "Oh, great, it's my patient." She moved off in the direction of the room but called back over her shoulder. "Don't talk about anything good while I'm gone."

"How come we never heard about the one who got away? You've always been close lipped about your romantic life." Shelley edged close enough to nudge her with her elbow, but since Donna was sitting, the elbow went into her ear.

"Stop that!" She pushed Shelley away from her. "I'll talk if you don't deafen me. It was a long time ago, when I was young and stupid. Instead of using my brains, I fell for a handsome head of hair and broad shoulders. The fact my father couldn't stand him should have told me something."

Shelley kept her arms close to her side as she sidled closer. "What happened?"

"He decided he preferred someone in the wedding party more than me. They took off together." Funny, the secret she held so close all these years no longer seemed important. Instead of the women appearing shocked, they wore similar sympathetic expressions.

"That happened to my cousin," another nurse confessed.

Shelley gave Donna an awkward pat on the back. "Sorry I asked."

"Don't be. It is what it is. Not too long ago, he and his family booked a room at the inn. Maria booked it since I would have lied and said the inn was full. Anyhow, I met the man he'd become, which was no prize. I felt sorry for his wife."

"Did he marry the woman he took off with?"

Donna couldn't place who asked the question, but it was an easy enough one to answer. "The woman he showed up with was unknown to me. Could be taking off was just a fast way to get out of a marriage he was ambivalent about. Even though my family was stuck with the expense of everything, my father claimed he got off cheap since he'd have paid anything to prevent a disastrous marriage."

Kathy strolled back with an aggrieved air. "I knew you were talking about something good, and I missed out."

Donna shrugged. "It wasn't that good. Just a tale about a potential groom leaving my family with the bill for a catered dinner for two hundred hungry guests."

"Oh, I knew it would be something juicy. Mrs. Aikens couldn't reach her remote."

"How did she call you then?"

Kathy jerked. "You're right. She played me. Well, like a lot of people I guess she just wants company. At least she doesn't make the mistake of marrying for it."

One of the aides, who had remained silent, spoke. Her previous silence made her words that more riveting because she so seldom said anything. "Don't go blaming yourself. At least she didn't marry every man who looked at her twice, like poor Charmaine Sanders."

Donna's sleuth antennae went up and pivoted in the aide's direction. What was her name? She should know it, but since she switched to second shift, she hadn't memorized everyone's name yet. Kathy glanced at the woman. "What are you talking about, Shirley? I never heard of Charmaine, uh, what's her name?"

"Charmaine Sanders. She was my cousin, shirt tail relation really. She'd show up whenever there was a big reunion, trolling for future brides. As a wedding planner, she implied she'd give family members a special discount. Not sure if she did or not. I know my Aunt Cora complained she charged plenty. Cora also said that Charmaine probably used her connections for her own weddings."

In very tiny print, Donna wrote *Charmaine married?* several times. *Husbands* – she put a question mark by. "How many times was she married?"

Shirley shoved her hands in her pockets and rocked back on her heels. "Every now and then, she'd drag to the reunion whatever man she was currently married to. I remember Jameson, kind of a quiet man who drank single malt liquor. Then there was Clark, who was loud and obnoxious. Not sure what Charmaine saw in him. I remember my mother telling me she was on husband number six, but I knew she was married when the accident happened. They were trying to track down relatives, and they called us. Thankfully, my mother had Treasure's—her daughter—phone number."

"Who'd name their daughter Treasure?"

"I've heard worse."

Her co-workers offered more ridiculous names people had actually given their kids as she wrote down *Jameson, Clark,* and *Treasure.* "Was Jameson's last name Sanders?"

"Oh, no, that was Charmaine's maiden name. I always thought she couldn't be serious about any of the men if she refused to change her name to theirs."

"That's so old-fashioned," one of the younger nurses commented.

Just maybe Mark could look up the wedding licenses under Charmaine's name. Although, it would be hard to know what beef an ex-husband could have against her, especially if they'd been divorced forever and a day. Still, around here, people often took pride in their grudge-holding abilities. It was right up there with re-enacting civil war battles and tracing your genealogy back to the first settlers. No one, however, would admit to holding a grudge. The very word had a taint of not being quite right. Perhaps they might refer to it as having strongly held opinions instead.

"Donna, are you going to change your name?"

Why would she do that? She'd been a Tollhouse all her life. "It's my name."

"Your fiancé," Shelley cleared her throat before continuing, "being of a certain era, might expect it."

"What you're saying is mature individuals always conform to the rules. I've never been much of a traditionalist."

"You aren't having wedding rings?"

The questions came at her as she was still caught up in the possibility that Mark would expect her to take his name.

"Of course, we'll have rings." What she didn't add was she'd been single so long that she refused to give up her one visible symbol that would denote she was now part of the married group.

"Then, you're a traditionalist," the young nurse announced.

Donna stood, the better to peer at the nurse-in-question's left hand. "I noticed you have a wedding ring. A big, shiny bauble that announces your status to the world. I guess that makes you a traditionalist."

The woman smirked and waved her ostentatious ring-clad hand in the air for everyone to see. "Everett did insist on a huge ring so there would be no doubt I was married. Even from a distance, a man could pick out the ring and not waste his time trying to impress me."

The women made some comments about the ring, but probably not as many as the ring holder would have liked. This wasn't the first time they'd seen her left hand.

"Where's your ring, Donna?"

The fact she'd been mentally thinking about her tasteful engagement ring at home and comparing it to snarky nurse's caused her to jerk and almost stumble, but Shelley caught her arm.

"It's at home. I didn't think it would be too hygienic to wear it to work. It would be hard to get the rubber gloves on. It's a beautiful sapphire that reminds me of Princess Diana's ring."

Without meaning to, she'd implied her ring was too large to fit a glove over. Before she could correct the assumption, Shelley answered for her.

"I don't blame you for not wearing it here. Sapphires are so valuable, especially one that size. Diamonds are as common as quartz. Mark did well to pick you out such a beautiful and unique ring."

It was always good to know who your friends were. "He did. I was even surprised it fit, but Maria, my sister-in-law, was in on the deal and lifted a ring from my jewelry box to make sure it was sized right."

"That's sweet." Shelley gave her a reassuring pat while snarky nurse lifted an eyebrow and muttered something about never seeing the ring.

As Nurse Snarky left for her lunch break, Donna leaned toward the head nurse, Shelley. "Can you make sure Nurse Bad Attitude never comes back?"

"Yeah, I feel you. She hasn't been on the post-op floor that long, but she has already rubbed everyone the wrong way. Word has it she applied for maternity."

"They'll make her take off that big ring so she won't scratch the babies."

Shelley chuckled and tapped her index finger against her cheek. "I'm willing to bet the ring isn't real. Think about it. If it was real it would easily be over a hundred thousand dollars. First, who would wear something like that to a hospital? Secondly, if you had a man flush with money like that, why would you be working here?"

Donna whistled long, surprised at her co-worker's deductions. "You're one sharp cookie. How could you price a diamond so easily?"

"I used to work at a jewelry store on my off time to save up money for my daughter to make it through college. There's never enough money when it comes to children. I also noticed when Bad Attitude flashes her rings, she swings it around so you can never get a very close look. If I could get a good look, I could tell."

"How?" The idea intrigued her. Here was a skill she didn't have. It might be useful in some way.

"Tons of ways, but most would involve me having the ring off her finger to examine. I could breathe on the ring. Diamonds immediately disperse the fog, while a fake diamond takes longer. If she had her hand accidentally X-rayed, a real diamond doesn't show. If it's moissanite, it sparkles more. Of course, if you have an expensive ring, you should have an equally nice setting. Cheap setting equals fake diamond."

"Sounds like a great deal of work, and I can't imagine you breathing on the ring would go unnoticed. You could be reported for harassment."

"I wasn't going to. You asked how I could tell."

"I did. If it is fake, I'm not sure of the purpose behind wearing it or pretending she had a doting husband who gave it to her. She may not even be married."

"I've thought of that." Shelley stretched her hands above her head. "Often, people aren't who they pretend to be. They could be someone else altogether."

"Seen it. Makes me feel sorry for Nurse Snarky, even if she did get her jabs in. Once the false exterior is stripped away, what is there?"

A clucking sound that reminded Donna of a crazed chicken floated down the hall. It was Dr. Aleman, who was probably unaware that his rubber soled shoes made such a noise. It served as an early warning signal, causing both nurses to busy themselves. It didn't matter that the doctors spent time in the lounge drinking coffee and chit-chatting, Nurses and aides had to give some semblance of doing something hospital related all the time. Donna picked up the tablet to record vitals as she slipped around the station gate.

Shelley grinned at her, leaning forward enough to whisper, "Have you bought Mark's ring?"

She was supposed to buy a ring for Mark? It made sense. Did she ask him about his preferences or present it as if a done deal? So much to consider along with everything else.

Her opened mouth must have served as an answer. Shelley turned to the keyboard and started to type in patient notes. Oh well, she might as well check on her patients. She'd have plenty of time after work to fret about his ring.

Inside room 311, a bored female patient flipped through the television channels, giving a tiny moan with the appearance of game shows, news, or talk shows.

"Day time television is the worst. On the upside, you should get out today."

"Really?" The patient appeared immensely cheered. "You're not just saying that?"

"Nope. The orders have been signed. I can get an aide in here to help you pack. Do you have a ride home?"

"I can get one even if I have to call a taxi. You just made my day. What can I do for you?"

Truthfully, patients never asked to do anything for her, which made it hard to come up with a suggestion. "Well, you can give me your opinion. I have some Civil War re-enactors who will be staying with me. They told me they want whatever the troops ate, such as watery oatmeal and hard biscuits, but I have a hard time believing that. What do you think?"

"A friend's husband did that stuff for a while. My friend told me they used to sneak out to fast food places to get something to eat. Then, they usually smoked a cigar, passing it around to rid themselves of fast food smells."

"That's a no to the oatmeal and biscuits, then?"

"Go ahead and serve it anyway. That way they can tell the other re-enactors that they did eat original, and they can commiserate together. Make sure to have something extra like scrambled eggs and bacon, though. The soldiers had to eat the food they did because there was nothing else."

Donna glanced at the name on her tablet. "Thank you, Mrs. Fitzwilliam. You've given me very good advice."

Loretta appeared in the doorway with a cart. "Shelley sent me down to help her pack up."

"Yes. Our friend gets to leave today. Just waiting for her paper-work and ride."

Mrs. Fitzwilliam held up her phone. "Let me call first, then you can take my vitals. Seems a little silly to have to do all that when I'm going home."

Donna nodded as the woman spoke into the phone. She took a couple steps back to give her privacy. Loretta moved flowers onto the cart "Such nice flower arrangements. Quality stuff. That's what I do. Quality Keepsakes. I can make you some favors etched on glass teardrops for only three dollars a charm."

Since she had no experience with favors, Donna had no clue if it was a good price. Still, tear drops didn't bode well. Why not something happier like hearts or circles for that matter?

It looked like she had a lot to learn about weddings and wedding planners. Thanks to Charmaine, she'd be learning a lot fast. As she waited for the call to end, the image of Charmaine as she been the only time, she'd seen her came to mind. The tall woman struck her as friendly, a little pushy though, in the way salespeople anxious to make a sale push for a decision before you're ready to commit. Was she really like that? Was that who she was? Would there be enough evidence to find out? Part of her felt like she owed it to the woman. She wasn't a nameless statistic. For a moment, they were face to face, eye to eye.

It might be easy for other people to forget her as they did most sensationalized news, but Donna couldn't and wouldn't.

Chapter Ten

AN UNEXPECTED QUEASY feeling pushed her breakfast of yogurt around in her stomach, making her regret bypassing the croissant and bacon. Donna was already regretting her actions when she'd popped the top off the plain yogurt. Still, if she wanted to drop eight pounds by her wedding day, there'd need to be sacrifices.

She took the questions Shelley had written for her, typed them out, and added a few more of her own. Thank goodness for her co-workers since she would have been clueless on what to ask. When she showed the list to Mark, he stared at it for two seconds before saying, "It looks awesome."

She knew good and well he hadn't read it. Just like she knew her goal was to get the woman to gossip. Stuck in the side cushion of the hedge rose wing chair was a tiny tape recorder she'd hidden. She wasn't too sure how well it would pick up, but it was better than trying to remember everything. Knowing anything recorded without the person's consent couldn't be used in court, her goal was to scare up some possible suspects.

Her fingers worried the edge of the paper as she glanced up at the clock for the fourth time. It wasn't quite nine-thirty, their agreed upon time. She wasn't late. Maybe her nervousness came from being given an actual job in a case. Before, she'd eavesdropped, followed possible suspects, and even photographed incriminating evidence in their rooms while cleaning. She did all this despite Mark telling her not to. This was the very first time he'd asked for help.

Most men were lost in the world of wedding planning and pageantry. It would be natural for a bride to enter the hallowed sanctum. Both her mother and Maria were very excited about their roles. Her sister-in-law acted out her persona as the woman who was finally getting her boyfriend to make an honest woman out of her. As she pretended outrage at her slacker boyfriend, her husband grimaced. Baby Cici would go along, making her tale more convincing.

Her mother's enthusiasm was a little more reserved, but she had clapped her hands together. "This will be such fun!"

Right about then, Donna didn't feel fun, but rather regretted that she'd called Grace, the nice wedding planner. Her original motivation was Grace would be easy to fool since she was so open and honest. People usually expect the same characteristics in others that they themselves had. That's why liars expected others to lie about everything.

She had made a lovely tray of snacks with sugar dusted cookies and eclairs plump with cream. Both hot water for tea and coffee waited since she didn't know what Grace preferred. There were cold drinks in the fridge, too. If nothing else, she could get the woman some refreshments.

A tap on the kitchen window startled her, almost knocking her off her stool. A smiling Grace stood outside the window waving and mouthing some indecipherable words. Donna unhooked her feet from the counter stool and stood, pointing toward the front door. On her way, she picked up the tray of yummies.

She swung the front door open. "Hello," she announced to an empty porch.

Grace was on the sidewalk, wiping the mulch off her classic

pumps. Half-bent with a tissue in hand, she called back. "Just a minute!"

After tucking the used tissue in her purse, Grace climbed the porch steps. "Sorry for my unorthodox behavior. I wasn't sure what door to use, but then I saw you sitting in the kitchen."

"You're here now. Come in." Donna stepped back to allow her guest to enter. Grace did with a few short steps, then she stood awkwardly next to the foyer wall until Donna led the way to the parlor. "Would you like some tea or coffee?"

"Either one is good, but if you have it made, coffee would be great."

"Coffee it is." She sat the tray on the little drum table that separated the wing chairs. "I'll only be a second. Make yourself at home."

In the kitchen, she poured the hot coffee into the pot and placed matching cups and saucers on the tray, along with a cream pitcher and a delicate crystal bowl full of sugar cubes with silver tongs. As she assembled the needed items, she spotted her list. She had to have that. Donna picked up the list with intentions of sticking it in her pocket only to discover the summer dress she decided to don in deference to the occasion had no pockets. Couldn't leave it on the tray since it would ruin the look. She folded up the list and stuck it underneath the strap of her bra. Once she put the tray down, a turn toward the window would allow her to retrieve the paper without anyone being the wiser.

Mentally, she ran through how she'd casually mention Charmaine and what a shame it was she died so young. There would be no mention of murder since only the killer would know or at least that is what she thought.

Inside the parlor, there was a slight hint of lemon wax since she'd recently dusted the furniture. The drapes looped gracefully against their satin rope pulls. The fresh flowers Mark had brought her added a nice touch on a long foyer table pushed up against the wall. Grace was half-bent in her chair, patting Jasper.

When did he get out? She was pretty sure her pooch had been with Ten, but he must have left, leaving the puggle loose to seek out his own entertainment. Jasper could charm dog lovers and usually turned into a terrible mooch.

Grace lifted her head and straightened in the chair, the rose chair, the one with the tape recorder. Sheesh, this was a predicament Donna hadn't planned for. In her mind, she would have immediately taken the rose chair, leaving the hibiscus strewn chair for Grace.

What to do? What to do? Somehow, she had to get Grace out of that chair.

Donna placed the coffee on the Pembroke table on the other side of the room. She swiped the sweet tray just as Grace's hand hovered over a cookie and moved it also to the far table. Donna gestured to the relocated tray. "I think it looks nice over here. Aren't weddings all about appearances?"

Her wedding planner's forehead furrowed the tiniest bit as she forced a smile. "Some are. I tend to think you can have both a beautiful and meaningful wedding."

"Yes, you're so right. Help yourself. The coffee's caffeinated, which I hope is okay." Donna sidled closer, trying not to look as if she needed to be in a position to snag the chair as soon as Grace left it.

"I could always use a little boost. Not a morning person." She stood and strolled to the table.

As soon as her back was turned, Donna sunk into the chair. *Victory!* A folded white square of paper stood out against the oriental carpet. Her list had fallen, which was probably six giant steps away from her current location. If she tried to retrieve it, Grace might return to the chair she originally occupied. Without the list, she had nothing to talk about.

Grace turned with a cup in one hand and plate of treats in the other. If she was surprised that Donna had taken her seat, she didn't show it. She calmly took the facing wing chair, placing her items on the drum table. "This is such a nice room. Is it the one you want to use for the wedding?"

Donna stared at her dropped list. The paper mocked her from it's out of reach position. Since Grace was already seated, surely, she wouldn't take her seat if Donna retrieved the paper.

Jasper, with the attention no longer directed his way, headed in the direction of the kitchen. As a pup, he had a tendency to shred anything that had the misfortune to be in reach. Her dog had gone through newspapers, magazines, toilet paper, and even library books. Once, she had to ask for a new paycheck since he had destroyed hers. The paymaster was not a fan of Jasper.

The years had caught up with her dog, turning an ordinary walk into something an artistic cinematographer might film with stops for no reason, as he stared at something no one else could see. Jasper had almost passed the paper on the floor. He'd leave it alone. Before they left for the cruise, she'd taken him to the vet, concerned about his health level that had varied between hyperdrive and barely breathing. The vet confirmed his behavior was normal for an aging dog. She commented, with a grin, that dogs could be like people and occasionally, for a few seconds, he would think he was a pup again. The outburst of energy was usually followed by a long nap.

If they had a psychic connection, maybe he could hear her thoughts that there was a hidden treat in the kitchen. No sudden increase in his pace, which meant they didn't have a connection, despite what the television dog expert said, or Jasper knew she was lying. That was probably it.

Just as she looked away to see how Grace was, she heard the playgrowl and the ripping of paper. "Oh, no!" She slapped both hands on her cheeks as she sprang up.

"Don't worry about it. My dog is much, much worse."

"Well, I, ah…" She stalled, not knowing what to say. All her plans were going south in a hurry. The tape player wasn't even on yet. "That was my list of all the wedding questions on it. My friends at work helped me to put it together."

Grace reached for her oversized purse and pulled out a white binder decorated with golden outlines of wedding bells and doves. "I probably have the answer to most of your questions in this book. Trust me, there has been another bride who has asked the same question." She offered the manual to Donna.

She reached for the book with one hand but found she had to use two to hold the heavy binder. "Goodness, you must have a lot crammed in here."

"I do."

Donna sat and opened the binder. The oversized cover allowed her to slip her hand into the cushion to click the device to record. The delay was just as well. No need for Mark to hear the dog fiasco when she played it for him.

"Have you done a lot of weddings?"

"Enough. I haven't really kept count. I know some people will tell you they have staged a thousand weddings or something like. I might be getting close to fifty. I don't even like the word, staged. It sounds too much like a theatrical production. How do you feel about it?"

"I don't really want to stage anything. It sounds like too much work. Wedding, here, in the parlor." She gestured to the room and continued speaking. "The back wall is removable. This used to be a VFW hall, and they wanted it to be big to get as many veterans in as possible."

This wasn't getting her where she needed to go, but she didn't know how to segue into dead wedding planner in a cake.

"I remember that. Not that I was ever inside. I imagine you did a great deal of work to get it looking so nice. I was very excited when I heard the inn was opening up as a wedding venue."

You would have thought the mention of weddings and justice of the peace on the website would have gotten that done before, but no, it hadn't. A chance call Tennyson fielded ended up with the inn being on the wedding planner radar. To think she'd spend an entire weekend in a hotel conference room learning how to be a justice of the peace two years ago. She could have been marrying people right and left in all that wasted time. At least a few, if not dozens, could have been married in this parlor.

"Have you walked through the rooms?"

"We had a pretty full tour when you…ah…" Grace dropped her chin, unable to complete her sentence.

"When I dropped in on you?"

"Yes."

"That was humiliating. I wanted to see if anyone was still here, and Jasper pushed the door out that I was leaning against. He may be man's best friend, but I have doubts he's mine."

"No worries, especially if you weren't hurt."

"Just my pride." Donna managed a sheepish grin that took no effort at all.

"I know what you mean. What is the fire marshal standard on maximum capacity for your front parlor and then your combined parlors?"

"Fire marshal standards?" She said the words as if she'd never heard them since she was pretty sure she hadn't. Every now and then she'd see signs for maximum occupancy in elevators that included a number that would make everyone entirely too close. Those posted by swimming pools would have everyone standing side by side like tin soldiers in an uncomfortable communal bath.

"Your inn was inspected by a fire marshal?"

"It was. It passed. I had to change out some curtains and a few electrical switches, but everything else was okay."

"You should have a report that states the limit of people you can have inside the room before it becomes a hazard. Personally, I think the number is always too high and tell my clients to go under, not over."

"I do have a report, but I'll have to ask my brother. He handled the fire marshal since I was at my day job at the hospital." Even though her mouth was moving, she kept returning to *maximum number of occupancy*, as listed by the fire marshal. Had she ever exceeded it? She hoped not. Maybe, she was supposed to have those little signs everywhere. "I was only expecting to have thirty people."

"That's good. I'm sure it wouldn't exceed the limit. You sound like a very busy lady with the inn and your job at the hospital. I'm not sure when you'll have time to plan a wedding."

"That's why you're here."

"Of course." The woman gave a nervous laugh. "I'm sure you'll want to talk to other wedding planners, too."

No need since her family had that covered. "Are there many wedding planners?

Grace smoothed her hand down her thighs, then one fluttered up to her neck, betraying her nervousness. "I understand that you might want to go with a better-known wedding planner. Evelynn handles all the important weddings."

"I have heard from Evelynn."

The remark made Grace's hand drop to her lap as she continued to speak. "Then there's Keith." She leaned a little closer to whisper. "He's a Yankee. I think he's from New York, but I'm not sure."

Donna gave a short nod, not too sure how shocked she should act. "I didn't think he was a local."

"He likes everything cutting edge artistic."

"What does that mean?" He may have said the same thing himself, but she was rather rattled after making a public fall.

"Less is more. A strawberry on a kale leaf with three blueberries and a snow pea pod serves as an entrée. That kind of stuff. In one ceremony, where the couple had divorced and wanted to remarry, he made them walk down the aisle in reverse, symbolizing undoing their separation."

"I could never walk down an aisle backward."

"Apparently, the bride couldn't either. Then, there's Charmaine. She usually handles the showier weddings. You know the ones you see on television, where the bride wants the wedding cake to be a life-size replica of herself. Although she'd do backyard ceremonies, too. She's good at…" Grace stumbled to a stop. A tear slipped down her cheek. "I can't believe she's dead. We were just here the other day, talking to you."

"Was it normal for the four of you to do things together?"

"Absolutely not. Keith and Evelynn are always trying to out snob each other. I think Evelynn is even worried that Keith is cutting into her market. Those with money don't necessarily have any taste and need to be told how a wedding should be. If Keith tells them they need to be serving the food out of coconuts husks because it's the in-thing, you'll have people in black tie dress eating out of coconuts."

"Goodness, it sounds like that children's story, The Emperor's New Clothes."

"Yeah, I remember that one. The con artists told everyone that only the intelligent can see the clothes so no one will admit to not seeing them." She managed a wobbly smile that collapsed. "Charmaine was the only one who was nice to me. She encouraged me, even threw business my way when she had more than she could handle. We'd become friends."

Bingo. Although she hated taken advantage of Grace's distress, if it helped find her killer, it would be beneficial. "I heard she died at a wedding, but not much more than that. Was she suffering from any illness?"

"I know people are saying she had a heart attack, but I don't believe it. A couple of months ago, she went through one of those involved medical tests. She confided to me her mother had died of ALS. Her doctor wanted to be sure she didn't have any of the symptoms. He found nothing. Declared her healthy as a horse. If Charmaine had any issues, I'd say she was too romantic. She'd married a number of times and divorced just as many. All she ever said was she left when the magic did. It must have fizzled fairly fast."

"No reason for her to suddenly pitch into a cake." Donna cringed the tiniest bit, wondering if she had just revealed more than she should have known.

"Can't think of any. Charmaine had recently become a vegan. She complained to me that she couldn't taste most of what the caterer made since it interfered with her vegan philosophy. I'd say it was more likely Keith or Evelynn pushed her."

"Why is that?"

Grace placed a hand over her mouth. "I'm running off at the

mouth. Forgive me. You must think I'm a catty person to say such things."

She was going to stop just when they were at a possible motivation. She needed to do something to prod her along. Donna sauntered over to where the coffee and cookies sat, picked up the tray of treats, and brought it back. Sugar may not work the same as alcohol, but it might loosen Grace's lips.

"Cookie? Éclair? I made them myself."

"I really shouldn't." Despite her assertion, she picked up a gooey éclair.

Donna picked up the other remaining éclair since she read people tend to like it when you mirror them. It had nothing to do with the bland yogurt she'd had earlier. Sometimes, undercover work demanded sacrifices. She bit into the pastry and covertly watched Grace consume hers. She was almost finished, the perfect time.

"I really have no interest in using Evelynn or Keith. It wasn't hard for me to tell they had no interest in a small wedding of a middle-aged couple."

"That's not true. Detective Taber is rather well known. After solving a string of murders, he's a regular hero."

You'd think they'd make him captain. *Focus, Donna.* "Why did you think Evelynn or Keith would push Charmaine?"

"Maybe I was being overly emotional with Charmaine dead, but the two of them never had a nice word to say to Charmaine. Still, people flocked to her."

"Even after the veil fire?"

Grace shook her head. "Even you heard about that. I bet you heard the bride was on fire and had to stop, drop, and roll."

"Something along those lines."

Grace's right hand went up as if she were ready to testify. "I was at that wedding. Knew the folks. Charmaine was mentoring me at that point. Anyhow, she told the bride no cathedral length veil or no candles. The bride wouldn't listen. Charmaine said not to light the candles. Someone did, not sure who, probably some well-meaning individual. Her veil caught the first candelabra and pulled it down. Most of the candles went out with the fall, but one ignited the veil, which was stomped out by her father. The bride didn't get burned, though."

"What happened then?"

"They stopped the wedding. They went into the narthex where the bride removed her veil, repeated the processional, and the wedding went off without a hitch after that. All those rumors of a burning bride and a general disaster were started by the toxic two, as I refer to Keith and Evelynn."

It gave her a great deal to think about. Had she found out anything useful? The wedding business could be cutthroat, and the coroner had established the death was not from natural causes. Her co-worker informed her that Charmaine did like her weddings, including her own. As for Charmaine's financial situation, it might be better than she suspected, which meant a look at the will would be in order.

"When are you getting married?"

She automatically repeated the date she'd told Herman. "June twenty-fourth."

"Sweet Jesus! Are you out of your mind?"

What had happened to her soft-spoken mother of six? "No. We might be called to testify at a murder trial, and I thought a quick wedding would be better. We have the venue here." She used her hand to indicate the room as if either one of them could have forgotten they were sitting in the sometimes-wedding parlor.

"There's so much to do." Grace shook her head, apparently more upset about the idea than Donna.

"I have the officiate."

"That's good, but what about the food, the cake, the flowers? Even the invitations won't be ready in time. You're supposed to give a month notice to people."

Donna found herself patting Grace's hand. "It's not that big of a deal. Those who want to come, show up. If they've got something else to do, it's not a problem."

"What about your dress?"

She hadn't given much thought to that. "I may need your help. Would you mind working with my future sister-in-law who might want to help? It's supposed to create some type of bond between us."

Calmer, Grace steepled her fingers, hiding her mouth, but not the amusement in her eyes. "It wouldn't be the first time I served as a buffer between family members."

Chapter Eleven

*B*UFFER? WHAT WAS that supposed to mean? Donna sat in the parlor long after Grace had left. A restful silence descended upon the house. She thought Tennyson's departure had something to do with school, but it probably had to do more with his latest girlfriend. She couldn't remember. There was so much to do, too much really. It reminded her of that performer at the circus that kept all the plates spinning on sticks.

Instead of plates, she had to go through her current furnishings at her house and decide what to keep and what could be hauled away by a local charity. The place would have to be cleaned, too. Maybe she could hire that out. There was her job at the hospital and contacting the elevator company as soon as possible. With any luck, she could get the elevator in before Columbus Days. Oh, yeah, and she had to plan a wedding and now a dress to find.

When she accepted Mark's proposal, she had no clue what an additional workload she was agreeing to. Why hadn't she gone along with Mark's idea to be married at sea? She heaved a sigh. Even though shipboard weddings would have a certain panache, she'd still be married on the cruise where a man had been murdered. Not exactly how she wanted to remember her wedding day.

Now, she had to worry about a dress. There weren't that many formal shops in Legacy. This would require a trip to Charleston, for which she didn't have time. Mark would probably base his tux on her dress. So, she'd have to get it soon. Her lips twisted as she mulled over the possibility that Mark's sister, Eileen, might be expected to accompany her dress shopping.

"Sugar. That's the last thing I need."

Women tended to be stereotyped as clothes horses and shopaholics. Donna was neither. The idea of shopping for a formal dress had about the same appeal as oral surgery. Having company while shopping moved it right up there as oral surgery without anesthesia. Add in a total stranger, which is exactly what Mark's sister was, then she might as well let the blacksmith do her dental work. Not something she looked forward to.

A strange rattling noise along with footsteps on the front porch ended her woe-is-me attitude. She had a lot of good things in her life and even more to look forward to, but right now she'd better investigate what was going on in the front.

The kids in the neighborhood were not the type to ring your doorbell and run off. For the most part, the children stayed behind closed doors playing with game consoles. The only time she'd spotted a child was when they were being driven somewhere in mom's upscale SUV. Sometimes, a stiff white-wrapped top indicated karate, while a ball cap, possibly baseball. Then there was the occasional beret which she surmised meant scouts or a junior militia group.

If she was outside with Jasper when the car passed, she often held her hand up in greeting. The SUV usually slid by without any real acknowledgment. The kids usually were looking down at a cell phone or portable game unit. Every now and then, one would look up and place their hand on the glass.

Donna would imagine them saying, "Help me. Get me out of here. I want a normal childhood where I can play into the woods and wade in the creek."

Of course, a child would want to be outside to enjoy the summer. Maybe some of the children had escaped from their over scheduled lives and sought sanctuary on her porch. If she slipped into the kitchen, she could peek out the window without any of them seeing her. Contemplating the upset a rebellious child would cause in one of the very proper households that surrounded her, she managed to shake off the funk that had descended upon her earlier.

Working thirty years in the hospital allowed her to discover things weren't often what they appeared on the outside. Still, they had it all over her, because she didn't even try to pretend to be proper and superior. Donna was neither. She sneaked into the kitchen without making a sound. By flattening herself against the wall, she could see a portion of the porch through the sheers.

Instead of dirt smudged children, three adults milled on her front porch, looking like refugees from a low budget historical movie. A fourth walked up to the porch brandishing a rifle as big as he was. What in tarnation was going on? She kept her place by the wall, wishing she wasn't dealing with the dilemma all by herself.

The foursome conversed loud enough for her to hear snippets of the conversation.

"I don't think this is a good idea."

Donna nodded her head in agreement, and she had no clue what they were talking about.

"The boy I talked to said it was okay," a man's voice asserted.

What boy?

"Our reservations aren't good until tomorrow. The worst that can happen is we have to bunk elsewhere."

They had reservations? She was expecting the re-enactors tomorrow, with the operative word being *tomorrow*. Donna took another peek at the group. Their clothes were a mish mash with a bit of Confederate Gray here and there, but not too much. At the start of the Civil War, the different regiments had various colored uniforms. One even had red and white striped pants and wore fezzes. Near the end of what many referred to as The Battle of Northern Aggression, people wore whatever they could cobble together, which was sometimes uniforms combined of both Union Blue and Confederate Gray. The woman in the group toted a cauldron or was that a cooking kettle? They had to be part of the second battle of Charleston's re-enactment.

She might as well answer the door. They might be grown-ups in costumes playing at war, but still, paying customers all the same. At least the rooms were clean. Mentally, she checked her cupboards. Her goal had been to go to the grocery before they arrived. Obviously, she'd need an alternative plan.

Donna swung the door open before they could knock, startling her guests. "Hello. Can I help you?"

The woman in the cambric dress with a flour sack apron nudged the man sporting a battered cavalry hat. "You do it."

He removed his hat and nodded his bearded head. "Why, yes ma'am, you can. We seem to be travelers with no place to lay our heads this evening. We'd be beholden to you if we could drop our rucksacks here and catch some shuteye."

Her re-enactors, of course, and already in the spirit of things. She could act as well as the next person. "Well, now," She stalled not totally sure what to say. "If you be God fearin' folks that won't cause me any grief, I can let you stay."

Feeling like she found her voice, Donna put one fist on her hip as she tried to take on the demeanor of no-nonsense innkeeper. "After that, you'll have to be on your way because my rooms are reserved for the McDougal and Warren families."

"That's us," the woman volunteered. She gestured to the man who spoke, "My husband, Zachariah. I'm Susannah."

Susannah half-turned to indicate the man with the rifle. "That's my brother, Beauregard."

Surely those couldn't be their real names. Donna only hoped the name on the credit card worked. The man Susannah gestured to tugged on his hat and nodded in Donna's direction. The male beside him couldn't be more than a teen, a young one at that with his baby smooth skin.

Continuing her introduction, Susannah smiled at the young man as she spoke. "This is my nephew, Thaddeus. This is his first battle.

Around the corner of the house, a feminine voice carried.

"You won't believe what lame thing my family has me doing now!"

A slender female appeared, garbed in a period dress with a simple flounce on the bottom, but none of the numerous petticoats to puff it out that made movement such a trial for antebellum belles. The family must be representing the lower rank of Southern society during the Civil War period, possibly share croppers.

The soft-spoken Zachariah whipped around and startled Donna by shouting at the approaching girl. "Liza Anne, you put that phone up! You know what the rules for this trip are!"

Instead of complying, she held up her hand and continued talking. "Super lame. I have to go now." She remained silent as if listening, then laughed. "Yeah, right. I guess I'll have to send you a message with smoke signals. Bye now."

The annoyed man on her porch, which she assumed was the parent, flushed as he stared down the unconcerned Liza Anne as she sauntered down the walk. The phone vanished to an unseen pocket and the hand dropped to her skirt. She grabbed a handful of fabric and swished playfully.

Zachariah turned to Susannah. "You do something about her. She's your daughter."

The woman gave a massive sigh. "Liza Anne, honey, you know how much this event means to your father and I."

The girl snorted. "Do I! It's all you ever talked about for the last six months. Why can't you be like Jenny's parents who are such big sci-fi fans. They actually took a sci-fi cruise. At least she got to do shore excursions, hang out at the pool, and flirt with the cute guys, which has to be better than wearing this dress," she held out the wide skirt and lifted it to display heavy brown boots.

"Liza Anne, we'll talk in private."

The girl glanced at Donna briefly, wrinkled her nose at her parents, then glanced back at Donna. "You look normal, and you're letting my family stay here?"

Considering some of her previous guests and a few uninvited ones, these folks were closer to average than the daughter might expect. "You'd be surprised at the people who show up for the Columbus Days re-enactment and festival, Liza Anne."

The girl's eyebrows went up at the use of her name. "That's not my real name. It's for the re-enactment. My dad thought it would be a clever idea to be a historical person."

The father fired an annoyed look that had Liza Anne bristling and crossing her arms. Before she could say anything, Donna interrupted in what she hoped would be a conciliatory measure.

"Why don't you come in, and I can show you to your rooms." Donna stepped back to allow them to enter. The girl pushed in front of the adults, entering first. She smiled at Donna and arched one eyebrow.

"My real name is Giselle, which reminds me of gazelle. At least I'm used to it."

"It's a lovely name, too." But since Giselle mentioned it, she'd be forever thinking of gazelle and would have to work hard not to call her that.

After passing on this information, the bored teenager strolled down the hallway, peeking into any rooms with open doors.

Zachariah stepped into the foyer next. His gaze ran over the walls, artwork, and even dropped to the carpet. "I suspect everything isn't period."

Well, it wasn't. Even decent reproduction cost money. "It's close though, especially the paint and window glass. It's Victorian, which is post-Civil War." As soon as she uttered the last comment, she regretted speaking out loud. It could be construed as a dig at his history knowledge or lack of it. If she learned anything from Legacy's Columbus Days was that re-enactors never like any implication that they might be incorrect when it came to anything historical. If he was hoping to stay in an authentic place, then he probably needed to camp out in the fields with the other re-enactors.

Susannah and Thaddeus squeezed in while Zachariah stood in the way, mentally cataloging her time inappropriate furnishing, or at least, she assumed he was. Donna blocked Beauregard's entrance with his extra-long rifle.

"This is a no weapon zone."

The combination of worn uniform pants, scruffy beard, and what she was sure had to be Daniel Boone's original fringed buckskin jacket still didn't hide the appearance of a possible accountant or bean counter. Instead of making him look rugged, Beauregard appeared as awkward as his name.

"It's not loaded." A tiny whine of grumpiness colored his words.

"Doesn't matter. It's my inn. Weapons are not permitted. You can lock it in your vehicle if you wish." Mentally, she decided she needed one of those circle decals with a line through a gun on her front glass. It could go right beside the credit card ones. Your credit card is welcome, but not your weapon. Her fiancé and soon to be husband could get away with a firearm since it was part of his business apparel, although he very seldom drew it.

A mulish pull of his lips indicated the man might fight about it. Instead, he made a low guttural sound of disapproval. He placed the gun on the porch, which wasn't much better. It would be the perfect enticement for those neighborhood children she'd hoped would escape from the watchful care of their parents.

"That's not an option, either. Are you all from around here?"

"No. We drove down from Kentucky."

Fantastic. That meant she could take a page from Maria's handbook and create fake regulations. "The city of Legacy doesn't permit the public display of any firearm, be they traditional or reproductions."

His eyebrows went up, announcing without a word how he felt about the matter. "Let me get my son settled. You can stand guard over my rifle since you're so worried. I was planning to camp out under that big oak tonight."

"You paid for a room."

"My son can use it. He's soft. As for me, I couldn't meet the eyes of the other re-enactors tomorrow if I slept on a modern mattress."

The thought of him camping out in the backyard when her surrounding neighbors didn't even let their children play outside stunned her into silence. She was almost certain there wasn't a law against it. Since she'd already failed to endear herself to most of her neighbors, she doubted she wouldn't do anything else to set them off. Still, a small tent in the shade of her oversized oak shouldn't attract much attention.

"Okay. It might be better to place the gun on the floor porch as opposed to standing it up against the wall. You certainly wouldn't want to take a chance of it falling and being damaged before the battle."

No reason to have it going off, either, when it fell. She wasn't thoroughly convinced about the not loaded status. That's what most of the gunshot victims admitted to the emergency room claimed when attempting to explain their injuries. They thought the weapon wasn't loaded. One good shot would not only end up with her neighbors calling the police but could take out her beautiful pottery pots filled with bright pink geraniums.

The man knelt and lovingly placed his rifle on the wooden porch. He even removed a handkerchief from his pocket and wrapped it around the barrel with the white cambric cloth only covering a portion. His bare left hand rested against the barrel as he fussed with it. If the man showed the same care for a woman that he showed for the rifle, he'd probably not be doing these re-enactments with only his son. More likely, most women would have the wits to suggest something everyone might like, such as a theme park or the beach.

Inside, the group had split up examining the various parlors and dining room. A feminine squeal of delight and, "All right!" came from what Donna had designated as the entertainment room. She'd abandoned *music room* since no one arrived with musical instruments and instead had installed a wide screen television, comfy seating, a game console, and a somewhat limited movie library.

Thaddeus stuck his head out the door. "There's game console

and games. A little retro, but it might be fun to play the games you liked as a kid, Dad."

Retro, huh? She knew the word served as a euphemism for dated, which explained why everything had been on sale. Only people who knew nothing about games, like her, would buy them. Her previous visitors had no complaints, though. Was she so dissimilar from her neighbors in how she was providing ways to keep children inside? Most vacationing parents didn't want their kids wandering strange neighborhoods. Besides, she'd found more than one adult couple playing the games.

Zachariah came to life and hurried down the hallway to where his nephew was. "No games, no television. This is our return to a simpler way."

Gisele's sigh carried all the way down the foyer.

At first, Donna thought her newest guests couldn't be any worse than previous ones, but she was beginning to have her doubts. However, something wonderful happened next.

The front door bell rang as her mother let herself in and entered talking. "I met with the wedding planner you suggested—" She stopped when she realized Donna wasn't alone. "Oh, hello." She gave a slight wave.

The side door slammed, and Jasper gave a joyous yip. Tennyson was back. Maybe she *would* get to the grocery today. "Mother, the McDougal and Warren families are staying at the inn for the Battle of Charleston."

Her mother placed her fingertips together and managed a nod, while her eyes clearly asked, *What battle?*

With the entrance of her mother, Zachariah turned away from reprimanding the children for the use of modern entertainment and tugged on his hat. "My pleasure, ma'am. It's no surprise that a lovely woman like yourself is getting married."

Her mother giggled and used her hand as if she were batting away the heavy flattery. "It's my daughter who is getting married, not me."

The kitchen door swung open, and Tennyson, spotting Donna, announced, "Did you know there's a big truck in the parking lot with a big rebel flag on it?"

No, but she did now. Even though North Carolina did fight for the Confederacy, most weren't enamored about talking about it since the South lost. Occasionally, they looked upon those who insisted the South would rise again with indulgence. Other times, they were annoyed. It just depended on the person or the neighborhood. Her cheeks hurt as she held her forced smile even wider, hoping her employee would get a clue that he was in the presence of the truck owner.

Tennyson turned his head, taking in everyone who was in the room. "Ah, you must be the people I talked to on the phone."

"We are." Susannah volunteered for the group.

It would help if Donna could get everybody in their rooms and Beauregard fixed up out back, although, she'd have to insist he use the inside facilities. Legacy did have a law against that.

"Tennyson, you can help with the rooms." Donna moved behind the narrow table they used as a registration desk. It's thin table top boasted two drawers, used for keys and pens.

She turned the roster around and provided a pen. "Could you sign in please?"

Enough true crime shows had highlighted how much easier it would be to track down a criminal if only the desk clerk had asked them to sign in. Anything, from their handwriting to their fingerprints could be left on the roster.

"You reserved four rooms. Will you be needing four?" She wasn't exactly sure who to address, throwing it out to the general group.

Susannah held up three fingers and added, "My sister was coming, but she had a sudden change in plans."

Donna could well imagine what other things might override spending a summer weekend in period clothing. Yep, in her mind, just about anything would supersede.

Giselle decided to peek out the parlor at that moment. She looked in Donna's direction and blinked, then grinned. The interest in her eyes wasn't for her, she knew, since Giselle was moving in Ten's direction.

"Hi. I'm Giselle. Do you work here?"

"I do."

"Cool. This trip just got better."

Zachariah's brows drew together, none too pleased at his daughter's reaction. Yeah, she missed out on this kind of thing by not being a parent. She had never pictured Tennyson as a heart throb, but she tried to imagine him as a teen girl would. He had bulked out a little, which took him from alley cat scrawny to thin. His shaggy hair could be the current hot style, and on the upside, he usually had an easy manner with all the guests.

Donna gave Tennyson the keys while deciding to oversee her outside guest and the setup of his tent. Her mother stood on the sidelines, trying to decide who to follow. She ended up trailing Donna as she eyeballed her backyard being turning into a campground.

Her mother nudged her. "It looks like it's going to be an interesting weekend."

It felt that way to her, too.

Chapter Twelve

MOTHER FOLLOWED HER into the kitchen where Donna ended up pulling out her laptop. She booted it up and scrolled through site listings trying to find out which grocery had delivery service. "Mom, do you know of any grocery that has a delivery service?"

"Jameson picks out your groceries, but you have to pick it up."

It wasn't exactly what she wanted, but it would help. "Maybe I could ask Ten to pick it up if I paid online?"

Her mother shrugged her shoulders. "It's worth a try. Do you want to hear what I found out from Evelynn?"

With the confusion of her unexpected guests, she had forgotten all about the case she was trying to solve. "Do tell."

She kept scrolling until she found the right site and clicked on it. Her mother spoke as she speculated on what she needed to restock the pantry and fridge. Would her guests expect breakfast tomorrow? Probably.

A hand was waved in front of her face. "Donna, are you listening to me?"

"Sure. Of course, I am."

"What did I just say?"

Not that question. The one that would highlight her inattention. "Ah, could you repeat what you just said? I was debating between white or pasture raised brown eggs."

"Go with the brown eggs, so much trendier. Let me tell you about Evelynn. She has some decent caterers with good appetizers.

"What was your impression of Evelynn?" She clicked on the fresh fruit section. Anything she had before the cruise would have gone bad by now. *Apples.* Yes. *Bananas.* Yes. A mental cash register compiled the numbers in her head.

Mother's brow furrowed as she grimaced, then spoke. "You know I don't like to speak badly about people, but Evelynn doesn't deserve my reluctance."

"I can imagine. Did she have anything to say about Charmaine?"

"Plenty. She basically implied that Charmaine had it coming. I didn't even mention that it could be murder. It was odd how I got the impression she knew. It could be me assuming a great deal. Seeing what wasn't there."

Possible motivation was replaced by the thought of how many pears she needed. "Did she say why Charmaine had it coming?"

Placing her nose up in the air, Cecilia imitated the thin, arrogant tone of Evelynn. "Charmaine couldn't even do low-class weddings well, which is saying a great deal."

"Did she give specifics?"

"The bride who caught on fire."

"She didn't. Grace explained that to me. The bride didn't catch on fire at all. The whole tale about her catching on fire was courtesy of Evelynn and Keith. The family wasn't upset with Charmaine that the long veil pulled over a candelabra. Charmaine had insisted if they were going to go through with the veil after she told them not to and the candelabras, not to light the candles. Oddly, someone did. Although, no one will admit to it."

"Well, if that is true, I didn't learn anything. Except that Evelynn's wedding planning is way overpriced for what she does."

Her mother cocked her head, much the same way a robin does when listening for a worm.

"What is it?" Donna asked. "I can see that light bulb over your head light up."

"As if. What if someone didn't wish Charmaine well?"

"The fact she ended up face first in a wedding cake proves it."

"I mean before that. You stated that Charmaine warned the bride against the veil and lit candles. If she could see it could be a problem, maybe someone else could, too." She held up her index finger ready to continue, but Donna interrupted.

"That same person lit the candles themselves, told someone, or possibly paid someone to light the candles. A young relative, catering help, anyone who should have been at the church could have done it. After the accident, no one would admit to it."

"Evelynn made sure to point out there had been a history of such mishaps with any wedding Charmaine handled."

Donna spoke. "If you heard there were accidents or mishaps at weddings, would you hire that wedding planner?"

"You got a point. They even have sites of reviews for wedding personnel. Everything from venues, officials, even wedding planning."

Since she already had the computer on, it wouldn't be that hard to look that up. "Do you have a name?"

Her mother skirted the island and headed for the fridge. "Do you have any of that Italian soda left?"

"Your guess is as good as mine." A few clicks moved her out of the grocery site to a search engine as her mother pawed through the fridge. "You never told me the name of the site."

"Ah-ha, I found one. Obviously, Tennyson doesn't like peach-mandarin."

"The name?"

A few quick steps took Cecilia to the bottle opener on the wall left from the days the inn served as the local VFW. "I'll know it when I hear it. I thought it was adorable. So right. So cute. So perfect."

"It is?"

Her mother held her hand up. "Don't rush me. It had something to do with weddings." Three fingers and her thumb folded down leaving her with an index finger still pointed upward. "The last part was *reviews-dot-com.*"

"Weddings, bride and groom, happy day, wedding day?" Donna threw out suggestions, but her mother kept shaking her head. "Obscene expenses, bridesmaid drama, honeymoon regrets?"

"Be serious. No one would name a site after obscene expenses. Bridesmaid drama and honeymoon regrets sound like a reality show. Think Donna, something to do with weddings."

As she tried to think of anything associated with the wedding, Tennyson pushed open the swinging door. "Are you playing charades?"

Cecilia laughed and patted Ten on the cheek. "You're such a clever boy. Maybe you can help. I forgot the name of a wedding planner review site. Actually, they review anything associated with weddings. I can't remember the name. Something clever and it has *review* at the end."

Did her mother think Ten could help? True, she thought of him as her grandson and probably had higher expectations of him than his own parents. Why would a college age boy know anything about weddings?

"Bouquets?" Ten offered.

Her mother looked disappointed he hadn't gotten it right off, but he continued guessing.

"Rice? Rings? I do?"

"That's it!" She clapped her hands together. "You always were my favorite grandson."

His happy expression touched something inside Donna. It amazed her how well Tennyson fit into their family. "Is it rings? Rice? I do?"

"Yes." Her mother patted her pseudo grandson on the back and moved over to Donna's side. "It's called *Say I Do Reviews*. It would be interesting to see if there were any negative reviews."

A few quick taps and a fast speed connection brought up the site. The home page had a montage of happy couples staring into each other's eyes. It asked for a zip code, which Donna typed in. There were five listed wedding planners including Charmaine, Keith, Evelynn, Grace, and Ramona Edwards. "Have you ever heard of Ramona Edwards?"

"I have. She's the daughter of one of my friends. More than a few years behind you in school."

"Thanks, Mom. Somehow with that one remark, you make me sound ancient."

Tennyson curled his hand like a cat and make an angry cat noise. "I better leave before the claws come out."

"You better. Put on your head phones to drown out the screaming."

"Hush, Donna. He might take you seriously." Her mother pulled up a stool to read the reviews. She pointed to one. "Look at the date."

The review underneath Ramona's name was dated two years ago. It wasn't exactly glowing praise, but not terrible either. *Services delivered as requested without any additional expenses.*

"I assume the date is important."

"Somewhat. I thought I remembered Ramona had left town. Not sure why. Her mother and I aren't that close, but I do remember it was an overnight thing. One day she was here. Then she was gone."

"While that's peculiar behavior, it doesn't exactly finger the woman for Charmaine's death."

"I wasn't talking about her death. I think it's more curious that we are losing wedding planners. First Ramona, now Charmaine." An elbow in Donna's rib cage drove the point home.

Someone leaving town wasn't that unusual. Legacy drew seasonal visitors with its pretty coastal views, restaurants, and unique shops. Still, there wasn't enough of a permanent population in Legacy. Ramona must have looked elsewhere for a job. "She could have moved to Charlotte or even Charleston. Much bigger cities have more of a need for wedding planners."

"It's a possibility, but her mother has said nothing. You know how parents are. They're proud of their children. They even relate non-information just to remind people they have a child, as if they'd fulfilled some cosmic mission." Her shoulders went up in a shrug.

"Thought you weren't that great of friends."

"My friends know her friends. It's like social media without the Internet. There's nothing out there about Ramona, which means she has truly vanished from the face of the Earth, or her mother is hiding something."

Her hand shot through her straight blonde hair wondering why they were spending so much time discussing a woman who was clearly not Charmaine but *was* a wedding planner. "So, do you think I need a wedding planner?"

Her mother laughed, tapping her chest. "Please, darling. I've been waiting for this moment ever since your first wedding imploded."

Donna groaned. Here she thought Eileen, Mark's sister, might be an issue. Now, it was her mother. "I was thinking about asking Grace to help. She could probably use the money. Unlike Keith and Evelynn, she's not aggressive about going after the brides. Charmaine even gave her weddings when she had more business than she could handle."

"Aw, that was nice. Seems like the more I find out about Charmaine Sanders, it makes me wish I'd taken the time to get to know her better."

"Me, too. The least we can do is find her killer. The wedding planner angle is at a dead end unless Maria shows up with a signed confession from Keith, which would be nice. Everyone likes it so much better when the killer is an out of towner."

"We all do," Cecilia agreed, lifting her soda for a quick drink, then putting it down on the island. "It would be hard to have the killer be someone she knew or even trusted. That would be much worse. I'd feel like I wasn't a good judge of human kind."

The thought needled Donna, but she knew better than to worry. Somehow, she had a radar of sorts when it came to murders and murderers. So far, it hadn't gone off.

Chapter Thirteen

D ONNA PLACED HER grocery order and convinced Tennyson to go pick it up, not that he needed too much convincing. Giselle had decided to follow him around and flirt with him. Before he left, he shrugged his shoulders and commented, "I had no clue I was catnip to teenage girls."

Cecilia raised her eyebrows at his latest pronouncement. The slam of the screen door along with Jasper padding back to the kitchen meant Ten was on his way.

Donna shook her head. "I should have warned him to go easy on any teenage girls who might be working the grocery pickup line."

Her mother smirked. "Don't ruin his moment."

The kitchen clock showed it was close to lunch time. She wondered if her newest guests would expect refreshments. Without groceries, she didn't have much to offer. "I can warm up some frozen appetizers and even thaw some mini key lime pies. Sound interesting?"

"It does. Make enough for four, though."

Heading halfway to the upright freezer, she questioned the number. "Four?"

"Ten will come back, and Maria is on her way over. She texted me to make sure you'd be here."

"Oh." Why hadn't she texted her? She may have, though. It would involve going to her bedroom and retrieving her phone. With

Grace showing up to explain the wedding planner business and her early guests, things had been a little left of normal.

She busied herself with selecting rosemary and garlic meatballs, mini-pizzas, and cheese-filled phyllo cigars. Her sister-in-law enjoyed the cigars because it gave her chance to do her best Groucho Marx impression. The man had probably died before Maria was even born.

"Simon is so patient. I took him along with me when I went to talk to Evelynn. He pretended to be the besotted bridegroom to be. Of course, Evelynn seized on the lack of an engagement ring. Simon replied that he was having one specially created for me because someone as unique as I was shouldn't have a ring like anyone else."

Sweet, but she wondered if it was all acting. Donna stopped arranging appetizers on the cookie sheet to glance back at her mother, who had upended her soda. "Did you think for a moment he could be absolutely serious?"

Her mother choked on the soda and had to put it down. She patted her chest with her open palm. "Mercy. Could you not make those wild statements while I'm drinking? I could have choked to death. I'm not sure where you get your wild ideas."

"Simon. I got them from him. When he asked Mark and I about you, his heart was in his eyes. He adores you."

A small snort escaped her mother's lipstick enhanced lips. "Get serious. He loves the girl I was or possibly the girl he wants me to be, but not me."

"Do you think you're so unlovable?"

A knock at the window had them both glancing in that direction. Maria waved with one hand while trying to balance Baby Cici, her purse, and an oversized baby bag. Cecilia slipped off her stool. "I need to help her."

Translated, it meant she'd carry the baby while Maria dealt with everything else. Donna couldn't begrudge her mother's absolute adoration of the newest Tollhouse. She was pretty besotted with her niece, too.

A tall glass of milk waited on the counter for Maria. Her mother might suck down the rest of her soda, but Donna needed coffee to make it through her shift tonight. She started on a fresh pot as the two women entered the kitchen talking. Maria's amused tone carried over whatever her mother was saying.

"It was so obvious he was mad that I brought the baby. Then, he started saying all this crazy stuff."

That sounded intriguing. "What kind of crazy stuff? Anything like, I push the competition into cakes?"

"No, afraid not. He thought I should wear a red dress since white would be wasted on me. When I asked him what he meant, he tried to back pedal by telling me my skin tone could take the color better."

"True." Donna agreed as she pulled out the mini key lime pies. The toaster oven was already heated, but instead of putting the pies in the oven, she put them on top. It would just take the chill off and leave the pie firm and cool.

Before she could ask anything else, her mother did for her. "What else did he say?"

Maria wrapped her fingers around her glass and took a long sip before replying. "He did say half a dozen times that he was a professional, not a babysitting service. He usually trotted that one out whenever Cici made any type of noise. Keep in mind, she did not have a full out crying fit. Just an occasional fussy whimper now and then."

"Obviously not used to being around babies." Donna had to smirk, knowing she herself was no expert when it came to tiny humans, but somehow, she had no issue when pointing this out about someone else.

Her mother cooed over her new grandchild, but still kept her hand in the conversation. "Get any pertinent wedding tips?"

"Depends." Maria boosted herself up on the stool. "He trotted out the whole less-is-more concept. I should carry a single flower. As for music, we should have a harpist or a flutist. If we chose to light a candle, there could only be one. Daniel and I would have to light it at the exact same time."

"That would involve using two matches," Donna was quick to point out.

"If I wasn't trying to keep Cici calm, I would have thought of that. It was more of the same. My thirteen-year-old cousin could come up with better wedding ideas. In fact, she has. I assumed due to not being local and dressing in unrelieved black, people imagine he has some type of grasp on wedding trends."

"He may. I haven't considered wedding trends. Maybe the single flower is a thing."

"Could be," her mother added. "I do know the cookie table is a new wedding thing. I've been to enough weddings in the last year to realize it might even be a competition to have the biggest and most varied one, too."

Cookies, while yummy, did nothing to further the investigation. Did her sister-in-law even ask about Charmaine? Did the man's snooty attitude make her forget? Maria, unaware of Donna's mental debate, chatted casually with her mother-in-law.

"Did they still have a huge cake with the cookie table?"

"Most didn't. Those cakes can cost up to a thousand dollars. You can get grandma and a host of other relatives to make cookies for almost nothing."

A thousand dollars? Did she hear her mother right? Maybe she could do without a cake. "Goodness, you must get a whole lot of cake for a thousand dollars."

Her mother wrinkled her nose. "You'd think so, but some of the price is for decorating along with the delivery of the cake. I think an average cake runs six dollars a slice."

"Good heavens! I can get an entire layer cake at the Piggly Wiggly for that, especially if it's been marked down, which makes it less than a dollar a slice."

"Yeah," Maria nodded and spoke, "but do you really want 'Happy Bar Mitzvah Jacob!' on your wedding cake?"

"They don't all have writing on them. It's a ridiculous price meant to take advantage of people planning a special event."

"People might say that about the inn prices," her mother declared with a devilish glint in her eyes.

"They'd be wrong. This is a business, not a charity. I have expenses. I'm barely making a profit as it is. That's the whole reason for me having the inn open seven days a week and renting out for parties and weddings."

Her mother gave a sage nod, probably realizing she'd made her point. If that were true, wedding cake designers must have incredible overhead expenses. More likely they were more like high-end car salesmen, able to live for a while off the massive commission of each sold car. Well, she couldn't, which explained her new seven days a week philosophy.

"Have you talked to Mark about this?"

Maria's question delved into that touchy area where Donna didn't want to go presently. "I think I mentioned it. The better question is, did you manage to mention Charmaine, and what was Keith's reaction?"

"I did." She blew out an audible breath. "You're not going to like it."

"Tell."

"I thought I was being subtle when I mentioned what a shame it was that the huge wedding cake was ruined when Charmaine fell into it. You'd think I mentioned the anti-Christ. He threw up his hands, stood, and told me not to mention her name. He paced for a couple minutes before he sat down and continued with wedding suggestions."

The buzzer sounded on the stove as she turned over Keith's reaction in her head. Maria's general description indicated anxiety. Maybe it was irritation. Everybody and their cousin could be asking for details about Charmaine's demise in a wedding cake. People he thought were potential customers just wanted gossip. That could be annoying.

The smell of warm tomato sauce and cheese wafted from the oven as she opened it. "I made your favorite, Maria. Phyllo dough cigars."

"That's my reward for putting up with Mr. Superior. He acts like he's all East Coast Hipster. I wouldn't be surprised if he wasn't from the Midwest. All the same, it's a pretty sweet gig when all he does is give ridiculous suggestions he may have harvested from bridal sites or wedding magazines and charge folks big bucks for it."

Donna plated the appetizers and carried them to the table. Her mother handed the baby back to Maria and helped gather the small plates, napkins, and flatware.

While the wedding planner did seem like a big expense, she didn't think it was a total waste. "Grace explained to me that wedding planners pick out the most trusted vendors. They arrange cake tastings and can often have potential caterers bring the food to you. They also have the clout to get into certain venues that an individual doesn't have on their own. Their connections can rush an item like a dress or invitations."

"Sounds like you got a great deal of practical advice from Grace." Her mother shot her a knowing smile.

"I did."

"Did you tell her a date?"

"June twenty-fourth."

Maria exclaimed, "This year!" which started Baby Cici crying. She tried to calm the baby by jostling her with no luck. "Donna, can I use your bedroom to feed Cici?"

"Go ahead, it's unlocked. With everything that's been happening this morning, I never had a chance to go back and lock it."

Before she left, she locked eyes with Cecilia. "I want details."

The baby wails grew fainter as Maria made her way down the hallway. Cecilia picked up her fork and stared at the food. "It looks good. It's a shame Maria's will get cold."

"We can warm it up in the oven."

Her mother chewed but tried to talk with her eyes. Most people could do that in books or action movies. Her mother's intense look probably didn't mean there was an assassin in the next room or possibly hit the floor when I signal.

Donna brought the tiny pies over, deciding they had thawed enough. "I know you're dying to tell me why I can't have a wedding that soon, but I checked the calendar, and there are no guests then. If we're going to marry this year, we need to make it soon since the busy season is just starting. Then, there's the possibility that Mark might have to go to Miami to testify. I doubt they'll call me because they don't consider me a professional crime solver."

She poured herself a cup of coffee and waited for her mother's reply since she knew there would be one.

"Donnnnaaaaa," Her mother lengthened her name almost making it into a wail. "You can't do it in a month."

"Grace thinks it will be hard, but she didn't say it couldn't be done."

Her mother stabbed her food with her fork with a little more energy than needed. The tines of the fork skittered across the stoneware plate. "All of a sudden, it's Grace this, Grace that. You do have a family to help you."

I will not be sucked in. This must be how bridezillas were created. Everybody had an opinion on the wedding. "You do know Mark and I could have been married by the captain. It's starting to look attractive with everybody suddenly wanting to put their two cents into the wedding."

Her mother picked up the phyllo cigar and shook it in Donna's direction. "A ceremony at sea has its own mystique, but you won't be able to smoke out a wedding planner killer by pretending to plan a ceremony."

"I'm not pretending. I had to tell Herman a date, and the inn was free then."

"Just how much do you and your good friend Grace have planned so far?"

Why did family have to be this way? She picked up her miniature pizza and bit into it. Maybe if she chewed slowly some great insight might happen. Donna slowed her jaws, trying to prolong the destruction of the sauce and dough.

"What are you doing? You look like you're taking part in one of those dental hygiene movies we were forced to watch in school."

"Trying to think of a way to make the wedding less stressful and have everyone get along at the same time."

"Not going to happen."

"Thanks, Mom."

"I thought you appreciated my honesty."

"Only sometimes."

"What are your plans so far?"

"Seriously, do you think I've had time to make plans?"

Her mother straightened her posture until ramrod stiff, which meant Donna had created the opening the mother had been looking for. *Whoopee.*

"Exactly. If you don't have time to make decisions, how can you pull off a wedding in a month?"

"I was thinking about working part time." The words were out of her mouth before she had fully thought out her career change. Her ultimate goal was to quit the hospital and run the inn full time. She might as well start by cutting back hours.

"You can't walk in there today and tell them you want more days off. These things take time."

"Not as much as you might think. Plenty of nurses are looking for some extra time and there are nurses wanting to return to the field but don't want full time." Her mother folded her arms and acted unconvinced. Donna had made it up on the fly. There may be a few nurses who'd like to pick up more time, but the hospital was never a fan of paying overtime.

"What are we going to start on as far as the wedding?"

She knew her mother meant the two of them, but she couldn't resist teasing her and releasing some of the tension "I'm not sure what you and Simon are up to, but the next things on my list is to get a dress. I have the venue. Secured the official. Apparently, I need to have my dress in order for Mark to pick out his tuxedo."

Cecilia steepled her fingers together. "Makes sense."

"Mark also wants me to include his sister in the wedding planning, but she doesn't live nearby. Do you think I should invite her for dress shopping?"

"Absolutely not. You have tomorrow off. We can get on the road tomorrow after you feed your guests."

Donna felt like she should protest her life spiraling out of control, but she did need to get a dress. The door creaking signaled Maria was returning without the baby.

"Cici fell asleep. I put her down in the center of your bed and surrounded her with pillows."

Donna leaned over the island to pick up her sister-in-law's plate for reheating. Maria put her hand over hers. "Don't bother. I have a feeling I will be eating quite a few cold meals in the upcoming years. Might as well start now. Tell me instead what you did discuss while I was gone?"

Cecilia waved her hands and announced, "Road trip tomorrow to get Donna a wedding dress. It's going to be such fun!"

Why didn't she share the same enthusiasm as her mother? Donna never considered herself much of a shopper, but even she would like to have a nice dress. No reason they couldn't mix wedding business with a little skullduggery.

"Maybe we might run into Ramona Edwards while we're there?"

The doubtful looks Cecilia and Maria shared meant they thought the possibility highly unlikely, but Donna refused to share their negative attitude. Ramona might provide some answers.

Chapter Fourteen

EN HAD RESTOCKED the snack pantries for her with sodas, bottled water, and iced tea along with familiar nibbles, which included cookies and personal-sized bags of pretzels and chips. Donna made a final check before heading off to fix breakfast and discovered her guests had made headway into her supplies. They had no issue with eating non-Civil War food, which was too bad since all they were getting for breakfast was an apple, oatmeal, biscuits, and bacon. She decided against eggs since she felt the troops would have had difficulty carrying them.

She sent Ten outside with Jasper to notify her camping guest that breakfast would be ready soon. Unfortunately, Ten wasn't as fast as Jasper when he spotted the tent located in what he considered his territory. Not only did he bark his discontent, but he left a liquid calling card.

Beauregard was still muttering about her dog when he entered the dining room.

Even though she was probably meant to hear, Donna centered a basket of red delicious apples on the table while pretending not to hear about the "maggoty hound". It was even harder to keep her lips from tipping up. The best thing she could do was absent herself and finish breakfast.

Her mother insisted on driving to Charleston later this morning, which could be an adventure in itself. Her mother sometimes could have a surprising lead foot for someone her age. Since she knew everyone in Legacy, including the police officers, she never, ever received a ticket, just warnings. Not only would Donna be pushing the invisible brake pedal that wouldn't work, but she'd be on everyone else's time table. If her mother wanted to pop into just one more darling shop, they would.

If her mother and Maria hadn't seemed so excited about the prospect, she'd have called it off. There were plenty of online sites where she could order dresses. It wasn't uncommon to order several and send the rejects back. It had to take less time than driving down to Charleston.

The side door opened, and she could hear voices, masculine ones. Evidently, it was someone she knew. The biscuits were almost done, while the crisp bacon waited in the microwave for a thirty-second heating. The oatmeal could use another stir. She prided herself on the steel cut oats, but not everyone was a fan. She had her back to the foyer, but she strained her ears to hear who had come in through the side entry.

The pounding of boots on the interior staircase drowned everything else out and meant her guests were ready for breakfast.

A slight lift of her hair was the only warning she received before a kiss was dusted on her neck. Her arms swung up in alarm. Her right hand still clutching the oatmeal spoon.

"Ouch! Donna!"

She turned around slowly, well aware she'd just nailed her beloved with a serving spoon. "Oops."

Mark rubbed the side of his face and worked his jaw back and forth. "That will teach me to avoid spontaneous affectionate gestures."

She hurried over to him, ready to make her apology in the form of kisses. His out stretched hand held her off.

"Put the spoon down first."

She did. Then covered his face with tiny kisses. "I so didn't mean to do that, but you should know I startle easy."

He chuckled. "I do know. The funny thing is how much I worry about you. Give you a fully stocked kitchen and you're dangerous."

Her index finger tapped his nose. "You're a comedian now? I didn't expect you this morning. What brings you?"

"Daniel told me you ladies were going out dress shopping today." He kept his arms around her in a light embrace and grinned at her. "Figure this is the only time I might see you today."

"Well, I hope not, but it could be. Mother likes to shop. No, make that, she loves to shop. Even wants to take her car, which has a huge trunk. That should tell you something."

He laughed. "Enough! I was wondering if you heard anything else from your wedding planner inquiries."

"Goodness, I already told you all I knew last night when you called. If you're here, you might as well help me get the food out."

He dropped his arms, allowing Donna to turn back to the stove. "I'm serving everything family style. I'm not sure if that's how it was done during the Battle of Northern Aggression, but it is today."

She reached for a bread basket and a checkered cloth for the biscuits. The filled basket along with honey, apple butter, and regular butter went on a tray. "You go on and take that out."

A microwave warm up readied the bacon for the table. She flourished the platter with a smile. Bacon always seemed to receive a warm welcome except for the few times vegans booked a room. Then, all she received for her efforts was judgment. After that incident, Maria put in a disclaimer on the website stating any food preferences had to be noted at least two weeks before arrival. It gave her enough time to visit the expensive organic market in the next city.

The bacon garnered smiles, but the oatmeal had Zachariah staring into his bowl as if he'd never seen such a thing before. "Oatmeal? A soldier in the Confederacy would eat grits."

Already a little frazzled at their early wake-up and the upcoming trip, she placed a balled fist on her hip and held the tray by the handle, allowing it to hang by her side. "A soldier in any army has no control over what food he gets and is happy to get any."

Beauregard talked around a mouthful of biscuit, dribbling crumbs in the process. "She's right. Our job is to follow orders, not give them."

That shut the man up quick. Giselle waved her down, forcing her to move around the table. "What can I do for you?"

"It would be wonderful if I could have a cappuccino."

The words drew a thunderous glare from her father, which made Donna determined to make the girl one even if it dirtied her machine. The man rubbed her the wrong way. He could go out and play pretend soldier, but why force his family to do it? It was obvious the daughter was not on board, and made Donna wonder about the mother's attitude.

After fixing the beverage, she carried it out and placed it in front of Giselle who gave her a genuine smile.

"Is your mother coming down later for breakfast?"

Before the girl could answer, her father did in a brisk tone. "Says she's too sick to take part in the battle."

Giselle turned just enough to wink at her. It made Donna wonder why she hadn't done the same.

"Is Tennyson around?" The teen-age girl inquired with a hopeful simper.

Should she throw her college helper in for another round of practice flirting? Nope, she'd need him in her good graces. He'd have to handle the re-enactors if she didn't get back in time. "I haven't seen him." Which was technically the truth. She'd heard him in the back hallway but hadn't laid eyes him.

"Oh, well," Giselle shrugged her thin shoulders. "I'm sure there will be plenty of young guys at the battle. My job is to bring the weary soldiers a dipper of cool water."

"That's an important one." Inwardly, Donna cringed, thinking of all the different germy mouths touching the same dipper. The promise of young men also explained the reluctant daughter's change in attitude. No reason to mention that, unlike the actual battle, most of the actor/soldiers would be middle-aged.

Back in the kitchen, Maria had arrived with the baby. Her mother fiddled with the cappuccino machine without much luck.

"Oh, please, I know good and well you know how to use it. You made yourself a cappuccino the other day when you were tired of waiting on me."

Her mother stopped fiddling and pivoted. "I did, but it was more by accident than intention, and it wasn't as good as yours."

Mark laughed, aware of the machination of her family. He had a biscuit in his hand and popped it open. Instead of asking her for butter or jam, he made his way to the fridge and helped himself. She appreciated that trait in him. It probably came from living alone, but she could hope it wouldn't change. If he turned into one of those men who waited for his wife to stand up to ask for something since she was up, words would be exchanged.

Stop that. They hadn't even exchanged I do's, and she was already concocting worst case scenarios. Might as well get things done and leave. Her mother sat as Donna made her drink. There was a flurry of boots and the *ding* of her front door bell as her guests left. A deep throated cough of the F-250 meant the troops were heading southward. It had to be a tight fit in the truck.

Maria drifted to the window just in time to witness the exit and the truck horn playing a tinny version of 'Dixie' as the Confederate battle flag belled behind it. "I bet your neighbors are loving this."

"It's not that unusual." Mark gestured to the window with a coffee tumbler he'd brought in. "The traffic unit reported an entire stream of similar vehicles heading to Charleston. A few of them are enriching the county with their rush to get to the battlefield. With any luck, you ladies won't get caught in the traffic."

Traffic. That was another thing she hated. It was the reason she combined her errands and ordered everything possible online. The idea of the upcoming trip was becoming more and more undesirable. She glanced back at her fiancé who was topping off his coffee.

"You need me to stick around and do some investigative work?"

"You already have."

"I didn't get anything good. Keith was afraid of just talking about Charmaine, as if thinking that would create bad vibes like she was a mythical creature. Evelynn had nothing good to say about her either, but I'm fairly sure that's true of everyone she talks about. Then, there's Grace who paints a picture of Charmaine as a thoughtful romantic, who would throw jobs her way. None of them paint a very thorough or accurate image. My co-workers pointed out she'd been married numerous times, which does show endless optimism or stupidity."

His eyebrows drew together at the last word which made Donna backtrack. "I didn't mean us. We're not stupid. We're mature individuals who have..." She stumbled to a stop at Mark's upraised hand. Might as well quit while ahead.

"Got it." He capped his coffee and pecked her on the cheek. "You girls have fun."

Fun. He had no clue. She watched him walk out, then realized she should have walked out with him. A few large steps brought her to the hallway, but the slam of the screen door meant he was already gone. Got to do better in the future. Somehow, she needed to revisit the issue of him holding onto his house. There never seemed to be a right time, as it wasn't a conversation she wanted to have on the phone or in front of her family.

Maria returned to her seat. "I noticed your litigious neighbor was outside when your colorful guests left."

"Wouldn't be surprised if I get an anonymous note about it." A pecking at the kitchen door caused the three of them to glance at the pass-through door. It opened the tiniest bit to reveal the pale face of Susannah, the mother.

"Are they gone?"

Donna assumed they meant her family. "Yes."

"Do you have any breakfast left?"

That depended on what the family hadn't gobbled. "I have some oatmeal left." That she knew. "And coffee. I could make you toast or warm up a croissant."

"That would be nice." She glanced in Cecilia's direction who was sipping her coffee beverage with a reverent expression. "Could I possibly have a cappuccino, too?"

"Sure. Would you like that in the dining room or the parlor?" She added the last part aware she hadn't cleared the dining room yet.

"Could I eat in here with you?" Susannah pushed open the door, revealing a floral blouse and khaki capris along with a whimsical pair of sandals adorned with colorful butterflies.

Somehow, Donna had a feeling Zachariah hadn't approved her

attire.

At her nod, Susannah, who informed them she'd prefer to be called Sue or Suzie, grabbed a stool and started chatting with her mother and sister-in-law. Donna tried to recall anything within walking distance the woman might like to do as she put together her breakfast.

Tennyson drifted in, greeted everyone, and poured himself a cup of coffee. He timed that just right. Sue probably hadn't been the only person waiting for the family to leave.

"Ten, could you clear the tables in the dining room? I can get the dishwasher going, and I'd appreciate it if you make up the beds. Shouldn't be more than three. Although, before you do that..." She held up a finger to Ten and turned to address Sue. "You aren't going back to bed, are you?"

"No, of course not. Your mother just invited me to come along on your wedding dress shopping trip. It should be such fun."

Ten nodded. "Okay, I'll make up all the beds and empty the trash."

"Wipe down the fixtures also. You'll need to restock the snack pantry on the second level. Try to stay around the house starting at three. Not sure when they'll be back."

Sue shrugged her shoulders. "This is their first time. So, it's hard to say."

Donna stored that nugget away, remembering Beauregard's attitude toward his son who was soft because he was a newbie. Could be the man had been born in the wrong century.

Twenty minutes later, everyone had settled into Cecilia's new luxury sedan that her brother had nicknamed *highway yacht*. Charleston was a straight shot from Legacy and at the rate her mother drove, they should be passing Sue's family anytime now.

Maria kept a constant stream of chatter in the back with Sue while Donna sat silently beside her mother in the front seat. Her mother tried to put a CD in the player with one hand while speeding down the highway.

"Let me do it." She took the CD and inserted it.

"What has you so cranky?"

"I'm not cranky." She was—just the tiniest little bit. Okay, more than a tiny bit. She wanted to know when her life went screaming out of control.

"You are."

Her mother whipped around a motor home she'd been tailgating, then floored it. Donna pushed back in her seat, repressing anything she might want to say so as not to distract her mother. As much as she might resent the trip, she'd still like to arrive alive. Once her mother had passed the RV, two semis, and a minivan, she returned to the slow lane, allowing Donna to release the breath she'd been holding.

"Truth is," she lowered her voice, "I was hoping to find out more about Ramona Edwards while we're in Charleston."

Her mother took her eyes off the road to deliver a somber look.

"Eyes on the road!"

"Please. I've been driving longer than you've been alive."

The car drifted to the shoulder flinging gravel for a few seconds before Cecilia guided it back without blinking. She continued speaking as if nothing noteworthy had happened. "You might as well give up on Ramona. Her mother hasn't heard anything from her in over a year. Rumor is she took off with a carnie, which makes you understand why her mother is so close mouthed."

"You know this how?"

"Her hairdresser. We both have the same one. Kelly at Betty's

Beauty Box. Anyhow, I just had my hair done for the case, of course. Had a rinse with some red in it. You didn't even say anything when I came in. Maria noticed."

"It looks great. The sun really brings the red out. If you remember, I was busy feeding the guests."

"I'll give you that. Anyhow, Ramona's mother gets her hair done every week. Hairdressers are like bartenders due to the fact they hear all the stories. Kelly tries to be nice and asks about Ramona every now and then, just to show she remembers the name of her daughter. One day, Melanie, the mother, snaps at Kelly. Tells her she doesn't ever want to talk about her daughter again, that ignoramus who took off with a carnival worker."

If that had happened, it would ruin Donna's theory that an embittered psycho was taking out wedding planners. *Darn.* She was sure that one had movie-of-the-week all over it. A smart director might ask her and Mark to appear in the movie, even if only at the end. That would be dependent on solving the case, of course.

"Melanie heard a rumor that her daughter ran away with a carnie." She mentally placed the idea under possibilities as opposed to evidence.

"That's what I said." Her mother directed her a questioning glance.

Donna tapped her imaginary brake and gestured for her mother to pay attention to the road. "I'm not going to talk to you if you can't keep your eyes on the road."

Her mother snorted. "I doubt that. My eyes are on the road."

For now. "All I was saying is a rumor is not the truth. We both know Legacy is full of rumors. Remember Edith Ann McGill went to go take care of her ailing aunt, and people said she'd joined the circus as a tight wire walker?"

"I never believed that one. Edith never had any type of balance, which is why she never wears heels."

"My point is it could be a rumor. If so, there has to be another explanation for the disappearance of a wedding planner." Done talking, she pressed the play button to allow the mellow voice of Frank Sinatra to sing about doing it his way.

The man must not have had bossy family members who insisted on doing it their way.

Chapter Fifteen

FORTY MINUTES INTO the ride, they did encounter the traffic Mark had warned them about. Men in both blue and gray uniforms were yelling out of their truck windows, campers, and RVs as they weaved through traffic, acting more like teenagers than seasoned adults as they called out what they were going to do to the other side. They epitomized an accident waiting to happen. When her mother suggested stopping at a textile mills outlet, she heartily agreed, wanting to get out of the accident zone.

Sue, in the back seat, had a little more to say. "Just look at those fools. At least their wives had sense enough to stay home."

Maria asked the question Donna wanted to. "Why did you come?"

"Once he saw the ad on television about the battle and the need for additional soldiers, he went bonkers as if it were his patriotic duty or something. He called my brother, who's a history nut, and got him riled up. The next day they were online trying to figure out what they needed to order. A couple of weeks later, they were assigned to the unit. That's when the trouble started."

Donna would assume paying hundreds of dollars for uniform and props you'd only use once would have been where the trouble started. "Okay," She half-turned, making no bones that she had been listening to the conversation. "What trouble?"

"Whoever oversees this re-enactment stuff stated they really needed families. Women, teens, but not very young children, since they wouldn't have been in battle, but you would have had flag boys, drummer boys, nurses, wives, even camp followers. Zach convinced me it would be a fun activity for the entire family. He booked at your inn thinking it would make me like the idea better. He even called it a second honeymoon." She snorted in response to the idea of spending an entire summer day dressed in period clothing as romantic.

"Well, your husband appears to be very into it."

"Too into it. He's a middle manager back home with a fondness for history. Now, he's yelling everything and expects us to jump. I'm surprised Giselle agreed to go, but he promised there would be tons of young men there. She could work on her historical flirting. It would be something fun to share with her friends back home."

"He knows this how?"

Sue gave her a long look, which basically shouted *Are you kidding me?*

Oh yeah, he lied. She knew that and had figured as much when Giselle mentioned at the breakfast table about the young men at the battle. Lying as a form of parenting might be workable. After all, people made up stories about Santa Claus, the Easter Bunny, and the Tooth Fairy. It was surprising that kids trusted their parents at all.

A good hour later and armed with five hundred count sheets for the inn, Donna got into the front passenger seat and buckled her seatbelt. As Cecilia opened her door, Donna offered to drive.

"This is my car. I'll drive unless it gets dark before we leave, then I'll let you drive. My night vision isn't as good as it used to be."

At least the drive back would be non-eventful. "Will do."

The navigational system flared to life, warning of a crash on the highway, which ended up with them navigating the back roads, which were surprisingly littered with adorable shops and restaurants. They made another stop at a drive-in restaurant named the Root'n Toot'n Root Beer Stand. Her mother was a sucker for nostalgia. The frosty mugs brought back memories of when she could only lift the junior mug.

When they finally made it to the first dress shop, a sixtyish woman dressed in a severe black dress appeared and blocked the doorway as she asked if they had reservations. *You had to make an appointment?* In Donna's experience, people went into a store and tried on a dress. If they liked it, they bought it. Simple.

Maria answered as she jostled a fussy Baby Cici. The infant loved the car ride, but not so much the stops that interrupted it. "Tollhouse. We called ahead. Traffic was heavy, but we still made it within our time window."

The woman pursed her lips as obvious distaste passed over her face. "You only have fifteen minutes. Missy, your attendant, has been cooling her heels waiting for you to show up."

She needed an attendant? What in the world was going on? Miss Pursed Lips guided them through racks of dresses in anonymous white dress bags. How could people look at stuff if they couldn't see it?

Finally, they reached a series of dressing rooms surrounding an island with a stage containing a three-panel mirror. There were chairs scattered about. A weary looking middle-aged woman sat on one chair. She glanced up as they approached and managed a smile. Her attention focused on Maria.

"I bet you're the happy bride. I'm waiting for my daughter who is trying on her twelfth gown."

Before Donna could correct the woman's wrong impression, an excited girl popped out of the dressing room in a billowy dress with another dark garbed employee followed behind, straightening the train as she walked.

"This is it. I love it!" The girl tried to twirl, almost pulling the employee off her feet.

The mother pushed to her feet and asked a low-voiced question. Whatever the employee said certainly colored the mother's face. She spoke to her daughter in a clipped tone, "Go get changed. We're going elsewhere."

The disappointed girl moved slowly back to the dressing room, her eyes glassy. The mother cleared her throat as the attendant left to help the daughter. Once the employee had left, the woman held her hand up to the side of her face. "They wanted eight thousand for that dress. Can you believe it? They start you out with something reasonable, around seven or eight hundred, but those happen to be ugly, then the dresses get better looking as the price goes up. Hope ya'all have the big bucks. We're heading over to the Bridal and Formal Warehouse."

Warehouse sounded good to Donna and eight hundred dollars did not sound reasonable for a gorgeous dress, let alone an ugly one. "Do you need an appointment at the warehouse?"

"Heck, no. It's not a fancy schmancy place like here, but they do have nice dresses at affordable prices."

Donna got the address while Sue wandered off to finger the accessories. Their attendant appeared with a tiny smudge of catsup near her lips. It was easy to see that she had her meal interrupted as opposed to languishing because they hadn't arrived on time.

"I placed the dresses I pulled for your party in dressing rooms three, four, and five. Room three is for the bride. Room four is the mother of the bride, and room five is the maid of honor."

Maria threw her a strained smile on the last pronouncement.

"How did you pick out clothes for us?" No one had picked out her clothes since she'd been in grade school, and to be fair, only then did her mother had some latitude.

"The maid of honor gave me the sizes, price range, and possible preferences."

Well, that should be interesting to see what Maria thought she might like in bridal wear and to see Missy's interpretation. She entered room three, followed by Missy.

She pivoted fast and closed the door to prevent the attendant from entering with her. No need for a youngster with a firm body to gaze on Donna in her underwear. No, thank you.

The first gown wasn't white, but a blue-gray tea length gown that was probably meant more as a bridesmaid dress. It had a stiff skirt that held its own without needing a hoop or multitude of taffeta petticoats to do so. The small mirror did little to display the dress, which meant she'd have to use the mirrors on the platform.

If she hurried, she could scramble up on the platform, view the dress, and get back into the dressing room before either her mother or sister-in-law popped out. She wasn't in love with the color, which shouted somber, spinster aunt to her. If they still practice full mourning, the color would be labeled as acceptable for half-mourning. If the dress was available in a different color, the price *was* doable.

The unhappy mother and her daughter had left, which left the path clear except for Missy, who jumped up from the chair as soon as she saw her.

"That looks glorious on you. Makes you look, ah, sixty again."

Really, sixty again? Now, she knew the younger set viewed everyone over thirty in the same age group, as old as dirt, but sixty? She'd gained the platform to examine herself in the oversized mirrors when Sue came around the corner.

"Mercy sakes! You look like a bell. Liberty Bell or something like that." She placed her hand over her mouth as her eyes bugged out over her fingertips. A mumbled, "Sorry," worked its way out.

The mirrors did reflect a bell shape, which wasn't a good look for her. "Don't worry about it, Sue. You're more likely to give me an honest opinion as opposed to anyone else. No worries. I didn't like the dress, either."

When she returned to the dressing room, she discovered all the other dresses were simply the same dress in different fabrics. She could be a floral bell, a pink bell, even a white bell. She'd already given up the white dress idea, not due to her age, but her blonde hair and pale skin would end up with her resembling a ghost bride.

More than one woman comedian had found material in brides-maid dresses. Most dresses were made ridiculously over-the-top, just to make the bride look good. Superficial brides even picked the homelier relatives and friends as attendants to up the bride as a star image. Nothing here for her. Donna dressed and return to the waiting area where Maria was on the platform, checking out her view in a peach halter dress.

Her sister-in-law looked stunning. The graceful lines of the dress hid any post-baby bump, and Maria had to be the one person in the world who would look good in a bridesmaid dress. "You should get it. You look great."

Maria smoothed her hands down the material. "I don't know. I'm supposed to coordinate with you." She shot her a questioning look as she continued. "That is, if I am the maid of honor."

"Of course, you are." Donna hadn't given it much thought, but apparently Maria wanted the job. It worked for her.

"Yay!" Her sister-in-law clapped her hands together. "I want to try on the other dresses before I make my decision."

After thirty minutes over their allotted time, her mother not being able to decide if she wanted the spring green suit that had flowers embroidered on it in a darker green, only exacerbating Missy nervousness. The girl shifted her weight from one foot to the other.

"Go ahead and get it," Donna told her. "It looks good on you. If you don't wear it to the wedding, I'm sure Simon will take you somewhere you can show it off."

"You're right."

Missy heaved a sigh of relief. When they were ready to leave, Sue emerged from the racks of dress bags. "It's amazing how many distinctive styles of wedding gowns there are."

"Off to the next place!" her mother announced with glee.

She was halfway out the door with Sue following when Donna knelt to fix her sandal strap that had become twisted. Maria, in the process of paying, had to put Baby Cici down to withdraw her credit card.

"Donna, could you hold Cici?"

Before she could reply, the disapproving matron swept in to hold the child. She placed the baby on her shoulder and patted her back. A stream of white spit up oozed down the black uniform. Donna sucked in her lips, not wanting to say anything. Missy could have the joy of breaking the news to her boss.

THE BRIDAL WAREHOUSE didn't provide anything decent for Donna to wear, either. Women over forty didn't want to don strapless gowns or gowns cut through the front skirt meant to pull away whenever a bride took a step, revealing their gorgeous legs.

As they all loaded back into the car after the third store, her mother asked, "What did you have against the dresses in Gigi's?"

Her mother hadn't said it in so many words, but Donna was fairly sure her mother thought she was being too picky. Maybe she was. "All I had to choose from was white, off white, eggshell white, and ivory, which made me think of old white. None of the several versions of white were that flattering, either."

She expected some type of comment. *Nothing.* Thank Heavens.

Donna reviewed what she hadn't bought. If she had to choose from old lady, dowdy dresses that were boxy in shape or a form hugging dress created out of spandex, she was almost ready to opt for the purple dress she'd wore to her high school reunion a couple of years ago. Maybe she had something workable in her closet.

Ready to give up, a last-minute stop at an out-of-the-way boutique landed her a magical dress. The fluttery concoction was a cross between a medieval princess and a fairy queen. The rich green dress had delicate gold flowers worked into it. The Boleyn sleeves were cut at an angle so they hid her last two fingers when her hands were down by her side. The empire waistline didn't highlight her cruise weight gain. She would have bought the dress for just that reason alone.

Normally, she'd pass on something so not like anything she'd ever bought before, but Sue recommended she try it on since it suited her coloring. The one thing she'd discovered on the trip was that Sue could be brutally honest while family members tried to soften the blow of another awkward dress.

Sure, comments about a too short dress showing her knobby knees didn't make her happy, but it mirrored her own initial impression. It rated up there with Sue pointing out dresses that were too young for her. Noting her irritation, the woman was smart enough to change the words "too young" to "does not suit."

Chapter Sixteen

As DONNA STEERED the car home in the summer twilight, a snore came from the back. She wasn't sure if it was Maria or Sue, definitely not the baby. Her mother rested in the passenger seat with her eyes closed. Downing that espresso at the coffee bar in the shopping center had paid off for Donna in keeping alert. She was tempted to turn on the radio but resisted, afraid she might wake the drowsing shoppers.

At least the traffic had thinned out, due to the would-be soldiers getting where they needed to go. It made her wonder what they'd do tomorrow. The beach might be a nice change, and she'd make sure to mention Janice's restaurant, The Croaking Frog.

Without the traffic or any helpful instructions from the passengers, she made good time and pulled into the inn parking lot as the night sky shifted from a murky navy to indigo.

The big truck sat in the parking lot, minus the flag. Could be the troops needed it. Surprisingly, Mark and Daniel's respective vehicles were there, too. It made her speculate what could get them both over here. Tennyson calling them in a panic might be behind their appearance.

"Come on, ladies, time to get up. I don't have time for a slow awakening." Donna swung open the car door and raced to the back door without checking to see if everyone else was up. Her inn could be flooding for all she knew. The back door was unlocked, probably for Beauregard. Jasper investigated her arrival, moving slow and stiff, meaning he'd just scrambled out of bed. Nothing earth-shattering had happened to make him move, which meant all was well with the inn.

Underneath the yellow light of the kitchen overhead fixture, Daniel, Mark, and Ten sat with a couple open bags of kettle chips and sodas.

"Look who's back," Tennyson announced, causing Daniel to turn, but Mark stood, approached, and dusted a kiss on her cheek.

"Were you successful?"

"I think so. I did find a dress."

"Great. So, do I need a matching cummerbund in metallic silver or electric yellow?" he joked.

"Neither. A plain black tuxedo would suit unless you don't want to wear black. The dress is green, mostly. Can't imagine anyone even making green tuxes."

Daniel cleared his throat. "Sorry to interrupt your fashion commentary, but where is my wife?"

The door slammed, and Maria called out. "Right here! Why are you here and not home?"

Donna turned to watch her sibling answer since she was curious, too. His shoulders went up in a shrug. "The house was lonely without you and Cici there."

"Makes sense." Maria agreed, with her eyes going soft at her husband's admission. "Take us home. I can't speak for Cici, but I'm shopped out."

The two of them murmured their goodbyes as Baby Cici maintained the untroubled sleep that only the extremely young and innocent are capable of. Cecelia and Sue made their goodbyes in the hallway to the departing family.

Sue greeted Tennyson first, asking, "How's the family?"

"Dead on their feet. Today was only a muster and training day. Tomorrow is the actual battle or maybe it's the next day."

That meant another day of camp breakfasts. Since she found out Zachariah was a total jerk and only acted like what he thought a traditional man acted in that period, she'd make grits tomorrow.

Her dress judge groaned. "I'm not feeling well. It was nice of ya'all to let me tag along, but I better spend tomorrow in bed."

As Sue pushed out into the main foyer, Donna yelled after her. "The beach is nice!"

That left just Mark, Tennyson, and her in the kitchen. Her helper grinned at her. "I'm not sure if I was supposed to make the family dinner, but they dragged here half dead, muttering about how hungry they were. Dressed as they were, I thought it might worry any restaurant owner if they showed up. I made them sandwiches."

"No worries. I would have done the same. Sometimes it's a judgment call. You made a good one."

"All right then. Heading off to bed."

After Tennyson left, she smirked. "Heading off to bed is 'I'm going to call my girlfriend and we'll stay on the phone until we fall asleep.'"

"Did we ever do that?"

"Probably, but not out of sheer romance, but rather exhaustion. I'm surprised to see you tonight. It's sweet you waited up for me."

"I worried about you."

"You'd worry more if you saw my mom drive."

"I have, so that was part of it."

"Not all of it?" Donna opened the fridge and grabbed a drink and an apple.

Mark resumed his seat and rested his elbow on the counter.

"What were you saying this morning about a missing wedding planner?"

"Ramona Edwards. Rumor is she ran off with a carnie, but her mother has had no contact with her. Sounds off to me."

"I'll assume she had a car."

"Probably. Why are you so interested all of a sudden? I felt like my suggestion got the brush-off when I mentioned it."

He heaved a deep sigh. "I had the feeling you might make me eat crow. Okay, hand me a spoon, and I'll eat it."

"No need. Just tell me what's happening."

"Your favorite wedding planner—" Mark managed the words before being interrupted.

"Grace?"

"No, Evelynn. Her car blew up."

Donna's mouth dropped open. Maybe she could be a profiler. She had nailed the motive with embittered individual. Still, it could be someone stood up at the altar. "Was she in it?"

"Thankfully, no. The wedding planner business must pay well because the woman has three cars. She chose not to drive the exploding one today. I'm here to ask you if you think anyone might have it out for Evelynn."

"That would include anyone who ever met her or spent more than ten minutes in her company."

His right hand smoothed over his face. The gesture would sometimes hide a smile or any other expression he deemed not appropriate. "That's no help."

"It's true." She took a bite of her apple and chewed as she pondered the situation. "Where's Evelynn now?"

"Checked into a hotel since she considers her home unsafe."

"It probably is. I know we haven't really gotten anywhere with

Charmaine's case, but maybe it's not about Charmaine. Maybe it's about wedding planners as a group. The secret may be Ramona Edwards and what happened to her."

His hand slipped up to rub the back of his neck. "I don't like where this is heading. Accidental death is difficult. Manslaughter is worse, with premeditated murder being the absolute worst. Never in my life would I expect a serial killer in Legacy."

"Maybe not a serial killer, per se, some crazy person on a mission to stomp out weddings or something like that." She took another bite of her apple, hoping she was wrong about this.

"Somehow that makes it better?"

"No, I just don't think crazy people believe they are doing anything wrong."

Mark shook his head. "I so don't like this. I come for information, and you thrust this at me."

It sounded like she was the one out causing wedding issues. It had to be someone who had been hurt by a marriage gone wrong or hadn't married at all. "Before Herman left, he told me about the elderly woman down the street, the one who measures the parked cars to see if they're infringing on her property. She became bitter due to a lost love."

"While that could be true," he shot a hand through his already disordered salt and pepper hair, "I can't see that old lady shimmying underneath a car and attaching a bomb."

"She could have an accomplice. Ramona Edwards, for example?"

Mark raised one eyebrow. "Ha! I saw what you did there. Every time you involve another person, it multiplies the risk of being found out." He reached for the chip bag and rattled it. Hearing some noise, he dipped his hand into it.

"I'll keep that in mind next time I decide to commit a crime. Get real. Most criminals don't analyze the situation. They just do it. Despite the television shows and the movie portrayals of super smart criminals, there seldom are any. The only reason they succeed is they keep their cool and hide in plain sight." Donna knew she was right and part of her needed Mark to agree. So far, he hadn't really bought into her Ramona Edwards theory. Although, she wasn't sure if Ramona was the killer or possibly a victim.

Mark held up his hand. "Tell you what. I'll try to see where Ramona has run off to if it will make you happy. Shouldn't be too hard."

His suggestion pleased her, but the hall phone rang before she could say anything. Who could that be this time of night?

She ran and caught the phone on the third ring as she considered the antique cuckoo clock. When she bought it, she couldn't understand why anyone would give up such a darling piece. The minute hand on the clock above the registration desk trembled and dropped to fifteen. It probably wasn't 10:15 already but could be close.

"Hello?" Drat, she forgot to answer it with *The Painted Lady Inn, how can I help you?* As a full-time innkeeper, she'd need to get that part right.

"Donna?" a masculine voice whispered.

"Yes. Who is this?"

"It's me, Herman." His voice grew a louder.

"It sounds like you now, but I couldn't tell at first. Why are you calling so late?"

"Is it late? I don't have a clock in my room."

Did he not have a window, either? "Yes, it's after ten. I never knew you were such a night owl."

He forced a laugh. "That *is* late. I have a quick question, more of a favor."

"Go on." She wasn't all that sure she had the ability to grant any favors, though she missed her neighbor. He used to pop in at the end of the day for coffee and a snack and always repaid her in gossip. Some gossip was current, but most happened decades ago. His impulsive move to a retirement home in Indiana had worried her. Knee jerk reactions, for whatever reasons, usually didn't turn out well.

"I'd like to come down earlier and meet up with my old friends and all."

Old friends? That was a puzzler. Herman insisted he needed to move because he didn't have any friends or relatives in the area. "Okay, what about your friends who were coming with you?"

"Still are. I'd like to show them Legacy."

"When are you expecting to be here?" She hadn't asked if he expected to stay here, but she assumed it was a foregone conclusion, since she volunteered to put the three up. There was a lengthy silence at the other end of the phone, then Herman cleared his throat.

"I was hoping you could put us up. Right away." A wheedling tone entered his voice.

Since she was already at the registration desk, she opened the calendar. "The weekends are my busy times. Define right away." Maria had penciled in names and put room numbers by the names.

"That's why I called. We should be there by tomorrow."

"The best I could do is put you in the family suite that has two beds and a couch that makes out into a bed."

"Sounds great. Can't wait to get there."

"See you soon."

"Bye."

Donna hung up the phone and pivoted to return to the kitchen. She paused as she realized she needed to write in that the suite would be filled on the calendar. Maria could rebook the same room if she failed to make a note of it. As a busy mother, her sister-in-law wouldn't be as available to help. Just another reason for her to be a full-time innkeeper.

In the kitchen, Mark had a chip bag upended over his face but put it down when she entered.

"Go ahead and finish the bag."

He gave it a final shake, then threw the bag away in the trash can under the sink. "Who called?"

"Herman."

"Why?"

"He wanted to come down early to visit with friends."

"What friends?"

"Exactly. He started off by whispering, too, which I thought was weird."

"He could have a roommate. I imagine in a retirement home, everyone goes to bed early."

"Maybe. It just didn't feel right to me."

Mark picked up the empty soda bottles and carried them to the sink for rinsing before they went into the recycling. "The man misses his old life. Don't go imagining conspiracy scenarios where none exist."

"I suppose. If Herman comes early, we could get married earlier, too."

Mark splayed his hand against his chest. "Are you kidding me? When I suggested getting married on the ship, you pooh-poohed the idea."

"I know I did. After spending an entire day wedding shopping,

I'm overwhelmed with all the hoopla."

"I know." He turned away from the sink and strolled to where she stood just inside the interior door and wrapped his arm around her shoulders, pulling her close. "Today was hard. You might feel different tomorrow."

"Maybe." Insurmountable problems did usually shrink after a good night's sleep.

"You off tomorrow?"

"Just the morning. I still go in at two."

"I'll swing by around ten and pick you up. We'll head to the court house to get the wedding license. You'll need picture identification and your social security card."

"Do you want to get married earlier? I've already had a half dozen people tell me it couldn't be done."

"That's not the reason for getting the license now. Figured we should since the clerk's office is a one-woman operation. If Glenda gets sick or takes time off, you don't get your license. We better do it now as opposed to waiting, and they're good for sixty days."

Donna rested against Mark's sturdy form. He represented mainly all that was right in her world. "We could do that. You're not sneaking me off to be married by a judge, are you?"

"That would involve making an appointment and most of them aren't as free as you might think."

A twist of her neck allowed her to see his chin, dark with five o'clock shadow, but not his eyes to be able to judge his seriousness. "Surely, you must be friends with at least one of the judges."

"I am. Judge Conner, the traffic judge."

The thought of standing before a judge who listened to sob stories about someone accidentally exceeding the speed limit, especially when that someone could be a family member, did not appeal. "No thanks. I'll hold out for Herman. Do you think his Justice of the Peace license will still apply?"

"I don't see why not since he hasn't been gone long enough to lose his residency."

She hadn't thought of that. Now that Mark brought it up, it made her glad they weren't going to wait too long. The only thing she really wanted to do was work out a few issues, but her mother's carefree attitude about driving and traffic rules had worn her out. On top of that, her right foot was sore from stomping her imaginary brake. She had volunteered to drive back so she could relax her foot—as much as you can relax while driving an oversized car on the highway.

For reasons beyond her, the size of the car often made those driving smaller vehicles anxious to pass, despite the unwillingness of their 4-cylinder engines to do so. "I'm beat. Not sure about you."

"Me, too. I could only listen to Daniel speculate so many times on something horrible happening to his wife and daughter. I'd have thought you picked up your paranoia from Daniel, but since you're the older sibling..."

Donna pulled out of his embrace and gave him the stink eye. "Stop right there and go home while I still love you."

Mark chuckled and dusted a kiss across her hair. "Will do. My momma didn't raise any dummies."

Donna saw him out the door and locked it. Beauregard was still out there in his tent. She'd be locking him out. If he needed to use the facilities, he might end up watering her begonias. They already struggled to survive with Jasper being around. Undecided, she stood at the door with her fingers resting on the deadbolt until Tennyson popped out of his room.

"That dude who was sleeping outside is upstairs now. After

today, he figured he deserved air conditioning and an actual mattress."

"Good to know." She turned out the hall light and could hear the skitter of dog nails. Her dog was abandoning Tennyson for the comfort of his dog bed in her room. That was another thing she hadn't discussed with Mark. Would he be okay with Jasper in the bedroom?

Chapter Seventeen

A MORE SUBDUED group of re-enactors made their way down the stairs. Unlike the rest of her family, Sue didn't sport a sunburn or bug bites. Feeling cheerful at her upcoming wedding task, Donna decided to scramble some eggs for her guests since she assumed, they'd need the protein. Instead of oatmeal, she made grits with a bit of cayenne pepper and cheddar cheese. Even fried ham, so she could use the skillet for red eye gravy afterwards.

An old song about going to the chapel and getting married came to mind, and she attempted to whistle it badly. Jasper added his voice to the melody, which had Tennyson walking into the kitchen holding his ears.

"Why can't you just knock instead of making so much noise?"

She hadn't though it was noise. Well, nothing was going to get her down today. Nothing.

An unexpected knock sounded on her front door. A quick glance at Ten had the boy sighing and moving to answer. Donna stopped banging dishes around the kitchen to listen.

Masculine voices exchanged too low for her to hear, and then Tennyson pushed open the kitchen door to tell her, "Elevator man is here. Do you want me to send him in?"

Was this everyone shows up early month? "Go ahead." She might as well see what was up even if her plan was to get her funds from the sale of her house to pay the for the elevator.

A youngish man, probably sitting at thirty, entered the kitchen dressed in work pants and a t-shirt with the name of the elevator company.

"Morning, Mrs. Tollhouse." He put out his hand to shake. "Sorry to bother you."

She grasped it and gave it her best I'm no pushover handshake, then released his hand. "That's okay. What brings you out?"

"Cancellation. I was going to put in elevator in a home, but they decided against it at the last minute. Leaves me free today, if you want your elevator done early."

Once she gave up on everyone appreciating the health benefits of walking up several flights of stairs, the elevator loomed on the horizon like a promised treat. Even Ten had commented how nice it would be to have an elevator when people arrived with heavy luggage. It made her wonder who wouldn't want an elevator. "Why did today's client cancel?"

The man directed his attention to the floor, then looked up. "Death. The elevator was supposed to make it easy for her wheelchair bound mother to get around. She passed."

"Oh." She plated the meal and moved the plates to two round trays. Ten strolled in and picked up one tray, and Donna hefted the other. "I'll be right back."

Zachariah accepted his plate with enthusiasm and no complaint about anything missing. Sue glanced up and mouthed some words that Donna couldn't decipher. Good gravy, she might have to break down and go for an eye exam. When she placed a plate in front of the woman, she stuck her leg out enough to bump Donna's leg, not hard enough to make her stumble, but enough to make her wonder what she was wanted.

"Our innkeeper is getting married," Sue stated. "She told me how much help I was yesterday at helping her get stuff organized."

Donna couldn't remember ever saying that. Sue's honest feedback about the dresses had been helpful, but most of the time Donna had no clue where the woman had disappeared to once they entered a store. Not sure what Sue was after, she went along with the woman who probably wanted another respite from the re-enactment.

"Susannah did help a great deal," she started, earning a dark look from the husband. Her sentence was uttered with about the same amount of finesse as a first grader in a school play.

"Maybe you could use my help today?"

It sounded to her as if Sue should have said, "*Maybe I could hit the beach.*" She couldn't begrudge the woman a day at the beach. "Sure."

Gisele's head jerked up. "I'm good at…" She stalled, probably realizing teenagers would not have any expertise at weddings. "…picking music. It's a very big part of the ceremony."

It could be, not that Donna had even thought about it until that very second.

Thaddeus, her cousin, smirked and pointed to Gisele. "She doesn't want to go back because she was flirting with this guy that turned out to have a girlfriend who was at the battle."

Well, that was unfortunate and probably embarrassing. No wonder she didn't want to go back. Gisele's face flushed as her cousin went into detail about the girlfriend going bonkers.

Zachariah cleared his throat. "I think it would be beneficial for the women to stay clear of the battle field. It will help us men concentrate on what is important. Our great grandfathers couldn't have encouraged their women folk to be at the battle site. Neither should we."

The brother-in-law merely nodded and continued to shovel in

food. Thaddeus's mouth dropped open as he shifted his gaze between his father and uncle. "That means there won't be a cat fight without Gisele there." He gave a hefty sigh and flopped back into his chair.

That sounded like something everyone wanted to avoid, except Thaddeus. Obviously, the boy wasn't the polite teen she originally thought he was. Turns out he was normal.

Tennyson had made it back to the kitchen before she did and had already given elevator guy a cup of coffee. Her little boy was growing up. Not that Ten was very little. He already towered over her when she hired him.

She didn't have time to waste since Mark would be coming by to pick her up.

"I wasn't expecting to pay for an elevator today. I was waiting for my house sale to finalize."

"Will it be final in thirty days?"

"It will."

"Then you can pay me in thirty days. Does that work for you?"

"Well, okay. Are you starting today? I need to run some errands."

"Simple walk-through. We discussed putting the elevator shaft behind the house to keep from changing the exterior appearance."

"I'll do some measurements. Find out what the wall is made of. Figure out where your structural beams are."

"I don't want to take out a bearing wall." He needed to know he wasn't talking to someone who didn't know anything about construction, although she wished Daniel was there to ask the important questions.

"We'll have to dig a foundation for the shaft, too. I'll need to inspect the basement to make sure I don't dig into it." He casually mentioned the possibility and then sipped his coffee.

She rubbed her forehead with her fingers. The mother of all headaches was building underneath her skin. Why did everything have to be so hard. Battered infantry caps passing her kitchen window meant at least the men were gone for the day.

"Tell you what. You can take measurements. Check out the basement. Decide what the walls are made of but do nothing more today."

Mark entered from the side door, which resulted in Jasper greeting him enthusiastically. "Hello." He nodded at the stranger, waiting for Donna to introduce him.

"This is…" Wait, she'd never got his name. "…the man who is going to put in the elevator."

"Todd Stevens." He stood and held out his hand. "It's not going to be just me. It will be my entire crew."

Mark asked him some pertinent questions she wished she had thought of.

The man had a crew, which somehow made him more legitimate. It wasn't as if she hadn't researched the elevator and lift systems. She had. Now that the elevator was almost a reality, she had her doubts if it was the right thing to do. She'd put the ramp in to make the inn compliant and even installed extra hand holds in the bathroom, but technically it wasn't enough. No one ever inspected the inn because for all essential purposes it was so small as not to matter. As Maria had pointed out once, it would only take one angry person to complain that the doorways weren't wide enough. Her original intention had been to use her room as the handicapped room when it was necessary, but with Mark moving in, he probably wouldn't be a fan of moving his stuff every time someone needed the room. Without her home to bounce back to, she'd have no place to go when the inn was full unless it was Mark's house.

Not a fan of the nicotine-stained walls, she avoided going to Mark's house. It represented who he used to be as opposed to who he was now. He may have even entertained other women in his house. Not a thought she was easy with. Getting the house livable was a much bigger project than she wanted to take on, but that left them with very limited solutions. What did the owners of bed and breakfasts do? Donna gave Tennyson his instructions for the next couple of hours and darted back to the bedroom for her purse. She passed the entertainment parlor where mother and daughter battled it out in a video racing game.

Purse located, she reminded Ten that the ladies would like to go to the beach. If he had time between cleaning up the dishes and showing the elevator guy around could he show them the short cut. Even though the beach was a mile away by a car, a pedestrian could make it in a quarter by making the right turns. In the winter, when the leaves were off the trees, you could hear the ocean if you left the windows open, not something she encouraged the guests to do.

Mark smiled at her entry and confided in a stage whisper to the elevator guy that they were heading out to get a marriage license.

As they walked to the car, the irritation that had been pricking her expressed itself. "You didn't have to tell him where we were going."

"Are you ashamed of it?"

"No. Still, some things should be private."

He snorted. "That boat sailed once Heloise got wind of it. I'm sure she borrowed the ship's satellite phone to make a call back to Legacy."

"You're right. I wouldn't put it past her. There's so much happening I might be a bit on the snappy side."

"A bit." He winked, trying to play off the remark.

Donna pushed him. "You like to live dangerously."

Mark moved in front of her to open the passenger door and sang. "If loving you is dangerous than I don't want to be safe."

His attempt to change the words to a familiar song made her heart skip a beat. Just when she had her doubts, he did something charming.

"You have a beautiful voice. You should sing more."

Mark laughed and, after she was in, closed her door and then rounded the back of the car to climb into the driver's side. Inside the car, he spoke with more than a touch of amusement in his voice.

"I don't imagine people would be very pleased if I sang the words, 'You're under arrest.'"

"It's possible. Studies have shown that singing relieves anxiety and brings down the blood pressure. Besides, you don't arrest that many people in Legacy. Mainly, it's warnings or information gathering and the occasional hurt dog you rush to the animal hospital. I'm not sure what's with all the murders in the recent years."

A thought occurred to her. Before she could verbalize it, Mark did in a shared sentiment. "Out of towners."

"Exactly. We depend on them to stay financially afloat. They drive into towns with their SUVs, children, and credit cards. Only a miniscule amount has bad intentions. It is those few who have an impact."

"Cheer up. Most are on their way to cities such as Charleston or Panama Beach taking their crime wave with them. Can you imagine what Legacy would be like if we were a spring break location?"

She held up her hand. "Please. Don't start. I have enough potential scenarios to think about."

"Got it."

"How much manpower do you have on the wedding planner case?"

"You're looking at it."

"What?" She must have heard wrong. In a low crime area, a murder should be a big deal.

"Yep. Yours truly. Why do you think I asked for your help?"

Did she want to point out how often she had helped in the past? How her keen observations brought everything together? "Why just you?"

"Davis is on maternity leave. Marcos headed out on vacation before the murder. Lindsey is on desk duty since breaking his leg in the ATV accident. He can still make phone inquiries. There you have the detective staff of Legacy's finest. I can tap any uniformed personnel for help right now if I need them. The captain believes this is a one-time thing, and if we find the killer, that would be nice, but the residents have nothing to fear. As you probably noticed, nothing has been released to the news service."

"I did notice that, which makes Evelynn's knowledge of Charmaine's murder suspicious."

He threw her a searching look and started the car. "Did you mention it to anyone else?"

"No, not even Tennyson knows. Mother and Maria do, obviously. There's a possibility mother might have mentioned it to Simon since he was there when she took the photo."

He murmured something too low for her to hear.

"What did you say?"

Mark gave her a pained look and said, "Men can be bigger gossips than women."

That's what she thought he said. A smile crossed her face as she settled back into the seat. Instead of biting on that tidbit as he probably expected, she gave him the courtesy of changing the subject.

"This is a lovely car. I love how plush the seats are and how roomy it is."

"Not surprised since you basically picked it out."

"I did not."

"I mentioned to your brother that I might replace my old car when I stopped smoking, since I was tired of being surrounded by the smell of smoke. The next day, you handed me a list of suitable cars with this one at the very top. You highlighted it and put several stars beside this model as if I might miss that was your favorite."

A vague memory of doing that coalesced. "I was only trying to be helpful. You could have bought the car you wanted."

"I did. After checking out several models, I decided your original choice was the best. Figured if I got the car you wanted, you'd be more likely to ride around in it with me. I had to find some way to hang onto you."

"Here I thought it was my cheesecake you wanted to hang onto."

"That figured into it, too."

Donna's phone chirped interrupting the conversation. The mood in the car was lighthearted, and she didn't want to ruin it by some daily triviality. It chirped again causing Mark to urge her to answer it. She did as he started the car.

"Hello." She expected possibly another call from Herman, since he did know her cell number.

"It's Grace. Would your handsome fiancé be with you?"

"Yes, he is. Why?" Her sleuth skills picked up on the panicky tone of her voice and that she called Mark handsome. Donna had already had one groom stolen out from under her before she made it to the altar.

"I received a threatening note stuck into my morning newspaper."

"Did you call the police?"

"A second ago. Then I called you, since we had planned to do some wedding planning together. I can't now because of the note."

Donna put the phone on speaker and asked," What did it say?"

"It will be funeral bells for you if you participate in any more weddings."

Mark reversed out of the driveway and idled for a second. "Give me your address. We'll be right there."

Chapter Eighteen

T HE MODEST RANCH and Cape Cod homes could have perched on most any street in Legacy with their well-groomed yards and pots of blooming flowers dotting their porches. Even though Donna wasn't familiar with the street, it presented an atmosphere of gentility and good manners with its similar mailboxes and lawn furniture on the front porch. Here were people who still sat outside and visited with one another on humid evenings. Donna could vaguely remember doing that as a kid. More correctly, she could remember chasing lightning bugs and her parents doing the visiting.

Mark pulled up to a house with a neat picket fence. Grace was one of the few who did rate a charming cottage with a white picket fence around it. Despite its diminutive size, the front yard was a showcase of blooms. It could have easily served as a cover for a bulb catalog.

A black and white unit sat parked at the front with the officer still inside. The officer immediately left his car once Mark pulled in behind him and approached the driver side of the car while Mark put down the window.

"Glad you're here."

Donna peered around Mark. It was Officer Wells, the young officer who had helped them on a previous case. Not too surprising since Legacy didn't have numerous first responders.

"Catch me up, Cory."

Not a first name she'd expect for the officer. The name suited some character in a movie about teenage geeks more, but she knew enough not to mention it. Besides, it would be better to hear what the man had to say as opposed to speculating on his name.

"The homeowner called the police. Stated she felt threatened but refused to explain or let me enter the premises. She informed me she'd wait for you."

"All right. You can enter with me." He glanced over at Donna. His eyes had a slight twinkle. "I expect you to come, too."

Donna had the door open already, not even giving her fiancé a chance to play the gentleman. She circled the car with long strides, leaving the men behind as she opened the gate. A few hurried footsteps put Mark directly behind her.

"Since I'm the one with the badge, I like to take the lead. You can be the sympathetic friend."

She could do that, although she felt Grace and she were more acquaintances than friends. She did like the mild-mannered mother who made a business out of something she did well. Six daughters in this cute as a button dollhouse had to have been tight. The mother was probably very much in favor of them moving out. It made her wonder how her husband felt about having an empty nest.

Grace greeted them with a handkerchief in hand and a slight sniffle in her voice. "I've been so scared ever since I got that letter."

"Where is it?" Mark peered around the well decorated room as if expecting the object in question would be prominently displayed. Wells came up behind her, forcing Donna to step into the home despite the fact she hadn't been formally invited, which was a major breach of her upbringing.

The front door opened into a living room dining combo in a L-shape. Mark stood in the living room talking to Grace who stood too close for Donna's comfort, but maybe that's the way it was with hysterical women. They moved close to authority figures, hoping to draw some security from their presence.

Anyone who could raise six daughters and plan their weddings along with numerous non-relations' weddings had to have grit, although, the balled-up handkerchief didn't fit with the full makeup. Not a mascara smudge in sight, which caused Donna's bogus antennae to go up. Her reaction might be due to all the utterances coming from the living room.

"I'm so glad you're here. I feel so much safer with you in the room, Detective Taber."

Donna made a gagging gesture, but luckily, she'd drifted to the dining room where no one could see her. It never occurred to her that during his work women threw themselves at him. It didn't help that Grace was still pretty in that well-preserved way that hinted at night creams and facial exercises.

Behind the dining room table stood bookcases filled with trophies. Most of them had some sort of female figure on the top. A few had fake oversized diamonds or crowns. A few even had little girls. Her daughters must have been quite the contest champs.

A closer examination revealed the names on the trophies. Little Miss Pumpkin Pie, Miss Teen Cottonwood, and Miss Congeniality in the Miss Teen North Carolina contest. All had Grace's name on them. Donna worked her way down the book case, narrowing her eyes to bring the words into focus. As much as she hated to admit it, a pair of reader glasses might help.

Every single trophy belonged to Grace. Her husband must be pleased to be married to a beauty queen. It would be hard to think of a man who didn't think of that as something of a personal triumph. It made her wonder how the daughters felt about their mother's various victories. Most would declare that such things were all in the past, but seeing the trophies meant Grace didn't feel the same way.

Donna strolled into the living room as Mark placed the note in a bag using a pair of plastic tweezers. Wells was busy making notations on his tablet that would feed into the police computer system as soon as he pressed Send, making Donna a little envious. The hospital didn't have a system as efficient.

Grace took a step back away from Mark when Donna entered the room. Her mouth pulled to one side indicative of some disgruntlement. The woman probably thought Donna had been inspecting her house. She had, in a way, though not in the usual fashion such as peeking into medicine cabinets to see what drugs she was on.

Not sure of the proper protocol when confronting someone you knew who was involved in an actual case, Donna gave a little finger wave. It wasn't like Grace had done anything wrong. She was the victim.

Mark continued to run down options for her. "You could stay with one of your daughters or friends."

"What about her husband?" Donna knew good and well she'd seen a wedding ring on Grace's finger. A wide plain band, but a wedding ring all the same.

"She's a widow," Mark interjected and returned to listing how Grace should proceed.

The woman gave an emphatic nod as she focused on Mark. If the attention she was doling out to Mark was any indication, she wasn't exactly a grieving widow. That made her curious about the ring. Grace could easily marry again. Why wear a ring if she was interested in a little romance and a possible wedding of her own? If Donna didn't know better, she'd think the woman was gunning for her man. Mark had been in Legacy forever and single about as long.

Every female in the surrounding area already had their chance.

As Wells and Mark turned to leave, Grace hurried up to her and placed a hand on her arm. "With everything that is happening now, I can't help you with your wedding. Both Keith and Evelynn are booked solid, so you might have to postpone your wedding until everything blows over."

The unspoken message was that Donna wasn't competent to plan her own wedding. As far as she knew people had been planning and having weddings for centuries without the help of a wedding planner. No reason she couldn't do the same. After all, it was an intimate affair and not a big shindig.

"Thank you. I'll keep that in mind." What she really wanted to say was she could do anything better than Grace, but part of her knew it wasn't true. She didn't have a bookcase full of trophies. Her confidence took a toe stub as she followed Mark.

Inside the car, she asked. "Can I see the note?"

"I sent it to the station with Wells. They can start an analysis on it right away."

"Don't bother checking it."

"Come again? You're talking nonsense."

"Trust me. I was in the dining room, and the woman had a wall full of trophies she won being in various beauty pageants."

A snort answered her revelation. Not at all what she wanted. Donna continued. "I know pageants were a way of life for most southern girls, especially the older ones. They're not as popular as before, although I think some of the reality television shows have stirred it up again. I'd even say as a youngster Grace may not have had any control over whether she was in a contest, but those trophies even go to contests such as Mrs. America and the Mommy and Baby Pageant. She had to enter those on her own."

"Okay, she's competitive. I happen to know someone who's also competitive, and I love her."

Mark held his hand up to Officer Wells who drove away with the evidence she hadn't a chance to examine. The car engine purred to life, and they were back on their trip to the courthouse. The man thought he was being funny but was blind to what was right in front of him.

"She was flirting with you. The woman wants you."

His full-bodied laughter filled the car. "That's a good one. Don't feel obligated to make remarks such as that to boost my ego. You're all the woman I need. Women don't go out of their way to give a graying, middle-aged police detective the time of day. Maybe you have wedding nerves."

Wedding nerves? Was that the excuse for her cranky moods or second thoughts? How could he have missed what was right there? "I wouldn't be surprised if Grace wrote the note herself."

"I thought you liked Grace?"

"I did, but that's before she set her sights on you, and I discovered all those trophies, many listing her as Miss Congeniality."

"What does Miss Congeniality have to do with anything? It would mean she was friendly, which people tend to like in another contestant."

Why couldn't a smart man understand? Of course, as a man, he missed out how a woman's mind operates. "Women enter pageants for a variety of reasons. Some hope it will be a chance to jump into modeling or acting when an agent spots them. Others are there for the big money or scholarship prizes. Still others hoped to meet the celebrities involved with the contest and make a connection that could lead to a future opportunity. There are even a few who believe strutting their stuff will lead to the most elusive of prizes: a rich, indulgent husband."

He whistled, then made a sharp turn into a parking space. "I had no clue that you were a pageant bunny."

"I wasn't. Janice was. Making friends is not one of the reasons a person enters a beauty contest. Everyone in the contest is your competitor. You can try to eliminate them by being the best talent or the most beautiful, but judges tended to like beautiful, talented, nice girls. The only problem is most of the girls aren't nice. They'd steal each other's acts if they thought they could do it better. Clothes and makeup would go missing. The girls who managed to keep a façade of niceness and gentility were never fingered as the culprit, and they often won the contest or at least the congeniality award."

"I realize Janice is your friend, and you go back fairly far. I don't remember her being overly nice. Why would you believe her anyhow?"

"Janice isn't good at acting. She's never gotten that whole south-ern charm bit down like butter wouldn't melt in her mouth."

She could feel his eyes on her so Donna kept talking. "Okay, I'm not much good at it either. Anyway, Janice had no reason to lie to me. It's been more than thirty or more years ago, but she had been a runner-up in the Miss America contest. She was gorgeous then and could play piano like nobody's business. She didn't win and failed to score a rich husband, but she did get enough scholarship money for nursing school. That's when we met. She used what she made as a nurse to start her restaurant."

A figurative lightbulb glowed above her head. Janice would have been in the Miss North Carolina contest as would Grace. According to Janice, hopefuls often entered the contest as many times as they could, hoping for the big title. What if they were both in a contest at the same time? If they had been, would Janice remember anything about it? She certainly hoped so. It may prove nothing, except that Janice and Grace were equally competitive.

Her door opened as Mark put out a hand to assist her. Donna smiled up at him, thinking she may not have been a pageant bunny, but she did score big. They walked hand in hand up the cement stairs to the courthouse. A large maple tree shaded some teenagers who leaned against the tree as they focused on their cell phones as opposed to each other. Every now and then, one would hold out their phone to the other. If this was flirting, it had changed immensely.

"Look at the kids over there. Do you think they're flirting?"

"Hard to tell. I will say with the introduction of cell phones, I don't do as many disturbing the peace calls. They all are plugged into something, listening to who knows what. It's as if they exist in an alternative world."

"I used to tell my parents they were from outer space."

"And they still kept you around."

Several people greeted Mark, who promptly announced they were getting their marriage license. All wished them well and a few patted Donna on the back. It probably took fifteen minutes to make it to the clerk's office, which had a closed sign on it.

Donna stared at the words as if she couldn't register them. The hour hand on her watch hadn't even reached eleven. The clerk couldn't have left for lunch.

Mark flagged down a passing employee by name. "Jay, what happened to Glenda?"

"Toothache. Dr. Fordyce was willing to see her, so she hightailed it out of here."

"When will she be back?"

The man shrugged. "Doubt she will. She'll be so full of Novocain, she'll be drooling on herself. Not a good look."

Great! If Donna didn't know better, she'd have thought Grace had caused this to happen by having to talk to Mark about her note. Still, logically she knew toothaches happened, and there wasn't a great deal you could do about them, other than see a dentist.

"Thanks." Mark held up his hand to the man, then turned to her. "Tomorrow is another day."

"It's Friday tomorrow." She wondered what other disaster might prevent them from getting a license. "That's the last day we can get a license before the weekend."

"You'd be wrong. Due to the destination weddings and the no waiting policy, out of towners with proper identification show up on Saturday morning and can get married that evening."

"Knowing that, I should put a link to the clerk's office to encourage people to use the inn as a wedding venue."

"Sounds like a plan. Let's head back to the inn and see what chaos has happened in our absence."

The thought horrified her. A gentle elbow to the ribs delivered her feelings about his suggestions. "I have enough actual stuff to worry about. I don't need anything else. Maybe Herman and friends will be there. It would be great to see him."

"I miss him, too. Maybe, he could finish the missing jewel story for me."

Donna laughed as they exited the courthouse. "There is no ending. They were never found. Tennyson even delved into the possibility that I could claim the jewels if they did eventually show up on the property."

"And?"

"If there is no active insurance claim, then yes, due to the fact I bought the house and whatever was inside of it in good faith."

"That would be quite a treat."

"Yeah, but I don't expect to find them. Plenty have tried. Nada. Besides, I like my life just the way it is."

"Glad to hear it. I predict more of the same."

He cupped her elbow and steered her in the direction of the car.

Even though they had missed getting a wedding license, a happy contented feeling settled on her. They had almost an entire month, even though right now, it seemed like forever. All too soon, it would be here. She needed to make plans—now—as did Mark.

"Have you got our honeymoon planned?"

He sighed and gave her a woeful look. "I've been meaning to talk to you about that."

The happy contented feeling ebbed away a bit. "Go on."

"As you know, Legacy doesn't have the biggest police force around. We are thin on detectives with one being on maternity leave and the other one restricted to desk duty."

"I know that." It didn't take a genius to see where this was going.

"The Gen Con is the exact time as our wedding, too."

"The what?" Donna hadn't heard anything about this.

Mark's free hand went up over his face in his usual stalling gesture. In more generous moments, she called it his thinking pose. He dropped his hand and continued to walk. "The guys at the office told me it had something to do with games and people walking around town in costumes, which would be the perfect cover for a robbery or even an assault. Heard every room in the area was booked. It's supposed to be a major coup for Legacy since we stole the convention from another city."

"I can't figure out why I hadn't heard about this." Better yet, if every place was booked in the city, why hadn't the inn received any inquiries? Had she somehow missed out on being on a list, because she hadn't made it to the chamber of commerce meetings? You'd think at least Janice would have told her.

"When did this happen?"

"Apparently, a couple of weeks ago."

"That explains it. Either I was planning for the cruise or was on it." Even though she was a little miffed not to get a part of the convention crowd, she would consider it later when her own life became a little less turbulent. "Let's head back. I might even get home before Herman and friends arrive.

Chapter Nineteen

ERMAN'S BLUE SEDAN, that she'd joked was large enough to hold a baseball team, resided in the far end of the parking lot under a shady tree. Tennyson's truck remained, but the contractor's didn't. A bright yellow trailer, the type commonly used to haul riding lawnmowers, was left in the gravel lot. She pointed to the trailer as Mark pulled in.

"What do you think he needed that for?"

"Excavator, possibly."

"Yeah, he said something about having to put in a foundation. I just wonder if I'm doing the right thing."

Mark put the car into park and shut off the engine. "You need to quit overthinking this. You own an inn that is open to the public, which means it must be handicapped accessible. An elevator was pretty much a given."

"You're right. It's such a big step, though."

He shot her a look of disbelief and swung open his car door. "Is it any bigger than starting a bed and breakfast? Putting your life on the line hunting down murderers? Or even agreeing to marry me?"

"Well, put that way, it isn't a big deal. Best of all, I don't have to do any of the work." Donna waited for Mark to open her door before exiting. If he wanted to be the gentleman, she shouldn't discourage him. There were too few gentlemen in the vicinity, which might be the reason Grace had suddenly focused on Mark. She told him what Grace was up to, and he laughed it off. Even told her she was imagining things. Maybe she was, but a woman could usually tell when another female was after her guy.

They walked into the house discussing when they could take their real honeymoon. A strange silence hung over the interior, if she excluded the sound of the subzero fridge. Even Jasper stood barkless, but he did act suspiciously. Inside the kitchen, nothing appeared out of place. Tennyson had tidied up and placed all the dishes inside the dishwasher. Okay, nothing here. She needed to check out the other rooms.

Without saying a word, she pushed open the swinging door. The smell of dust and diesel exhaust wafted on the breeze. *Strange.* Two elderly men had their backs to her, but she recognized Herman's thick head of silvery hair. The other head was mostly shoe polish black.

"Herman!"

Both men turned slowly and appeared somewhat chastened. The breeze came again ruffling Donna's hair. Mark came up behind her and put one hand on her shoulder.

Her former neighbor tried for a smile but didn't quite make it. "Donna. Mark. Congratulations on your nuptials. Appreciate being picked as the officiate. Hope you'll still let me be the one who joins you two together."

"Why wouldn't I?" A little more of her contented feeling left, only to have an uneasy thought crowd in to take its place.

Both men stepped aside revealing a hole in her inn. There was a ragged rupture at the very end of the corridor. Her hand landed on her chest, if only to push back the heart that appeared determined to leave her chest.

Her feet carried her to the hole without even contemplating her action. A wizened face popped up into the opening, causing her to stumble back. The unknown face spoke.

"It's not such a big hole. An appropriately sized picture should cover it."

Who was this person who'd cover a hole in her inn with a picture? Donna crouched the better to peer into the hole, and addressed the house assailant. "Who are you, and what have you done to my inn?"

The face grinned at her. It was such an infectious expression she found herself smiling back despite her upset.

"I'm Gus, Herman's friend. When we arrived, I saw this man unloading the mini excavator. He drove it to the back of the house. Told us he had to go get something else. After he left, I decided to check it out since he left the keys in it. It was an accident. Sorry."

Someone groaned, but it could have been her. "Where was Tennyson?"

"Who?" Gus Inn Destroyer, asked.

Herman answered. "He took the women to the beach. He asked if we'd be okay. I thought we would be. There was no reason for me to anticipate this."

She felt a full-fledged rant coming on, but Mark's hand on her shoulder delivered a light squeeze as he said, "Looks to me like you got an early start on the elevator."

The hole was about two feet from the floor, but yes, it would be exactly where she'd put an elevator door. "What about my guests?"

"They don't strike me as the type to notice such a thing. We'll tarp it up and move a chair or something in front of it."

She shook her head in disbelief. Did he think moving a chair in front of it would solve it? Donna held out her hand and stared at the tremor. She prided herself on her strength and here she was shaking like a leaf.

Mark's hand covered hers, turned it over, and carried it to his lips, allowing him to place a kiss on her wrist. A sweet gesture that made her sigh. He promised, "In a couple of months, we'll laugh about this."

"You're right."

"I'll take care of this. You can visit with Herman."

"Thanks. I'll do that." She glanced back to the man whose face had filled the hole. He had vanished. With the re-enactors, a wedding to be planned, and a murder to be solved, she didn't need a loose cannon in the mix.

Donna gestured to Herman and friend and led the way to the kitchen where she put on a pot of coffee. Mark rooted through some cabinets gathering scissors and duct tape. "Do you have any tarps?"

"In the shed out back."

Donna located some cookies in the freezer and put them in the toaster oven to warm up. The sound of footsteps over her head froze her in mid-action. There should be no way the man from outside could be on the floor above, but then, there shouldn't be a hole in her inn, either.

"Herman, do you hear footsteps?" She pointed to the ceiling.

Before her neighbor answered, his companion did. "That's probably Eunice. She's checking out the rooms to see which one she wants."

Herman nodded. "Jake's right."

All she remembered about Eunice was the woman masqueraded as a guest a while back. The chatty senior citizen was always trying to scam Donna into letting her have a free room because she helped. The help she offered, at best, was questionable. In the end, her daughter showed up. She'd tracked down her mother, who had covertly left her senior care home. What were the chances Herman and Eunice would be at the same home? "Did you pick her up hitchhiking?"

Her former neighbor shook his head while his companion laughed. The backscreen door slammed, drawing her attention. The man who had been staring in through the hole wandered in and boosted himself on a stool.

"The cop ruined all my fun. Took the keys from the scoop away from me. Told me he'd arrest me if I didn't turn them over."

Donna closed her eyes. Why hadn't she even considered the possibility of this stranger running rampant through her azalea bushes? Maybe he already had. Thank goodness for a fiancé who had experience dealing with joy riders who chose heavy equipment as opposed to cars.

Herman gestured to the short bald man. "This is Gus." He angled his head to the thin man sitting beside him. "Jake. Forgot to introduce you with, ah, everything."

"That's understandable. Hello, Jake." She turned to Gus and placed her hands on her hips. "Gus, this is my inn. My rules. If you ever had any doubt about doing something. Don't."

The culprit's eyes sparkled. "You're right, Herman. She is feisty!"

Feisty? She never thought of herself as such, but couldn't be distracted by it, especially with Eunice snooping in her guest rooms. Memories of the woman pawing through other guests' belongings in the name of investigating came back.

"How did Eunice end up with you?"

Herman directed a meaningful look to the coffee pot. How could she have forgotten her former neighbor seldom provided needed information without enticement? Donna placed cream and sugar on the island counter and then poured three cups of coffee.

"I think she overheard us talking about coming here."

Jake interrupted. "You told her! Even bragged about the good things you'd get to eat."

Herman's face flushed, and he busied himself with his coffee.

Gus joined in. "She's a sly one. If it hadn't had been night when we left, we might have noticed she was sitting in the car with a blanket over her head."

They hadn't noticed the woman sitting in the car with a blanket over her head? "Surely, you had to see her when the car dome light came on?"

Jake and Herman exchanged looks, while Gus volunteered information. "Herman had switched off the light earlier so it wouldn't show when we left afterhours."

It sounded odd to her, rather like some action movie. She'd run it past Mark and get his opinion later.

The object of their discussion strolled into the kitchen. "I thought I smelled coffee."

"Hello, Eunice. What brings you to Legacy?"

The woman grinned as Donna handed her a cup of coffee. "The wedding, of course. I predicted you two would tie the knot."

She hadn't predicted any such thing. "The wedding isn't for a while. Won't they miss you at the center?"

"Oh, no, I took care of that before I left."

The words didn't make Donna feel the least little bit at ease. Having both Eunice along with the impulsive Gus as guests was growing old fast.

"You do understand the wedding isn't immediately."

"I know. I could use a vacation. I'm grateful you planned it in the summer. The North Carolina Coast doesn't exactly welcome you in the winter."

"That's exactly why we planned the wedding the way we did." No way, would she be foolish enough to mention they were working around a trial for murder case and the wedding planner investigation. She wasn't sure how Eunice could dig through a case from far away, but as she so aptly demonstrated, she could get somewhere if she set her mind to it.

"Besides, these three refused to let me into their secret cold case club, and there wasn't much to do."

"What cold case club?"

The three men directed accusing stares at Eunice. Herman wrinkled his nose. "It's not exactly secret, especially if Eunice knows."

The tiny woman straightened her shoulders and glared back at Herman. "I sleuthed it out."

"Eavesdropped would be a better description," Gus shot her a disbelieving look. "I opened the door, and you fell in."

Herman held up his hand. "The six of us meet to go over cold cases that Marcy gets. She's a former detective and fellow resident. She figured working the cases would keep her mind sharp. At first, she did this on her own, but would occasionally ask our opinions. Gus and Jake grew up in the area and could tell her all the old names of places and streets."

The sound of tires on gravel drew her to the front window as she watched Mark's car bump out of the front driveway. What was that about? He couldn't even tell her he was leaving? Personally, she wouldn't mind some help with this crew, and he takes off without a word. The back door slammed making her question if The Painted Lady Inn had turned into Grand Central Station.

Tennyson walked in and held up a hand in greeting. "I got the women to the beach. Super day for swimming."

She suspected the last statement was more of a hint than anything else. "That sounds good. Maybe you'd like to take Herman and friends to the beach."

Eunice slapped her hands together. "Sounds like a deal. It's been a long time since I've been skinny dipping."

"You'll have to wear a suit," Donna interjected, not wanting to deal with one more problem. "How about taking Gus and Jake along since they've never seen the coastline?" She hadn't asked them, but assumed they hadn't, and she wanted to talk to Herman alone. After all she had a wedding ceremony to discuss.

Tennyson's long face worked well to portray suffering. Yeah, she'd have to do something extra special for him. Maria's recent addition to the family meant there'd be little help coming from that quarter, although she'd promised to manage the booking and website from home.

After the cookies and coffee were history, Tennyson volunteered to escort the three seniors off to the beach, although they'd settled on wading as opposed to a swim. Gus mentioned getting an eyeful of girls in bikinis that caused Tennyson to roll his eyes. Whatever she did for Tennyson would have to be extra nice.

A long floppy hat shielded Eunice's face from possible sun, and she carried an umbrella too, which would be no small feat to hold onto with the strong beach winds. Tennyson nodded in Donna's direction.

"Oh, I almost forgot. Mark got an emergency call."

Ok. That explained why he charged out of the place. "Why did you wait to tell me?"

His thin shoulders went up in a shrug. "There's a lot going on today. By the way, is there supposed to be a hole in your hallway?"

"No. Yes, I knew it was there. Gus made it."

The man waved his hand as if everyone had forgotten who he

was. "It was an accident." He giggled, making Donna question the accident part. Most people were apologetic when they had an accident as opposed to being amused.

Once the four of them trooped out, Herman gave a heavy sigh and planted both elbows on the counter. If anyone should be sighing it should be her. After all, she wasted time at Grace's house when she should have been getting a marriage license. The visit was based on what she was sure was a bogus call. It could, possibly, have been a prank by a local kid who'd heard about Evelynn and knew Grace was a wedding planner too. One thing Donna had learned in the amateur sleuth business is that criminals were seldom original. People had been wiping each other out for thousands of years for similar reasons.

"What do *you* have to sigh about?"

Herman gave her a long look before answering. "Eleven hours in the car with those three. My night vision isn't the best. At one point, I allowed Jake to drive. I must have dozed off. When I woke, we were much farther than we were previously."

"That's good."

"In a way. I discovered Jake hadn't driven in a while, and he confused the highway designation for speed limits. We were fine on 64, but when he got to 168..." Herman trailed off.

Donna pressed her hand against her chest, imagining people swerving out of their way. "I can only hope there weren't too many people on the road."

"Less than you would think since it is a toll road."

"Did you stop, then, for the tolls?"

"I think Jake blew through them all."

"Goodness. I'm glad you're still alive! On the way back, your friends might want to fly or you could get Gwen to drive."

"Yeah, I considered that."

"How's the home?" Donna corrected herself. "I meant retirement center."

"Horrible. Boring. The cold case club has saved my sanity." He shivered as if the idea chilled him. "Everyone is so old there, except for Marcy."

It probably wouldn't be a good time to point out that Herman was in his eighties. "I thought you wanted to move there to be with your friends."

"I did. I do. It's hard to go from living alone in a big house to going to a two-room suite and having people in your face twenty-four seven asking what you want to eat, play bingo, or attend ballroom dancing lessons, or whatever else they've dreamed up. I will say they have a great deal to do, but it all seems the same after a while."

"Why is that?"

"Most everyone is stuck in near death mode. Many sit all day in their rooms and watch conspiracy television news. Then, more than a few have senior moments. I'll talk to someone one day and have a decent conversation. When I see them next time it is as if we have never met. I miss seeing you and Tennyson. When I found out Marcy was working on cold cases, it reminded me of when I helped Mark on his cases. I needed to be a part of it. Marcy very kindly let us help."

"I'm sure she benefited from your help." His hangdog expression made her want to cheer him up in some way. "Here's a thought. Mark has a case that maybe you could help with it. You'll have to keep it secret."

"I can do that."

"It's not common news." Although, it might be more common

than she'd originally thought.

"Lay it on me." He shifted on the stool, sitting more erect, and his eyes sparkled.

"My mother attended a wedding where the wedding planner ended up dead in a cake."

"Who?"

"Charmaine Sanders."

"I know her."

"You do?"

"Yeah, in a way. I knew her second husband Buddy, better. She was a sweet girl without a mean bone in her body. Still, Buddy was the soft-hearted one."

"So, why did they divorce?"

"Buddy claims Charmaine was on the hunt for the mythical perfect man. It could have been more of Buddy's allergy to work."

"Does he live around here?"

"Did. After Charmaine left, he decided to show her he *could* hold down a job. Unfortunately, he was hit by a truck crossing the street to a job interview, which proved the man was allergic to work. In the end, it killed him."

Donna forced a small chuckle to appease Herman, although the subject wasn't amusing.

"Anyhow, another one of wedding planners had her car blown up. Another one received a threatening message this morning. It looks like someone is trying to wipe out the Legacy's wedding planners."

"Angry bride? Mad vendor?"

"I wish I knew. Maria, Mom, and I have talked to the other planners and have received three different stories about Charmaine. The only male planner, Keith, refused to talk about her, afraid it might bring him bad luck or something. Before she died, he had plenty to say, referring to her as traditional and inexpensive."

"Yeah. There's an insult." His face folded into a smirk, counteracting his words.

"It translates to boring and low class."

"I'm certainly glad you can do the translations. So, what is your take on all this?"

Donna's index finger tapped her cheek. She had been turning possibilities around in her mind when she hadn't been freaking out about everything else. "There's a fourth wedding planner, Ramona Edwards."

"I know her mother. Nice lady. So, what's up with her?"

"She's mysteriously disappeared." Donna poured herself a cup of coffee and sat down at the island. "Her mother hasn't seen her in quite a while. No phone calls, no emails, nothing."

"Can't remember any bad blood between the two. What's the reason given for her absence?"

"General rumor is she ran off with a carnie."

"Hmmm. Doesn't seem likely. Coming from a staunch church-going family, but sometimes forbidden fruit is the most tempting. What's your theory?"

She couldn't find out anything about Ramona and couldn't get Mark too interested in the missing woman. His question about her car was probably to placate her. She held up two fingers. "Now, I have two theories. Number one, Ramona faked her disappearance and is responsible for killing Charmaine. Number two, is she could be a victim too."

Herman reached for the empty cookie plate and pushed it around demonstrating its empty state. Recognizing the hint, she slipped off the stool. There was a package of shortbread and another one of blondies in the freezer.

As she made the trip to the freezer, Herman spoke. "What's her motivation?"

"That's kind of the issue. I've nabbed around on the Internet to see how many wedding planners an average town can support. A population for sixty-thousand usually has five wedding planners."

"We don't even have close to that number."

"Exactly."

"Still," Herman rubbed the space between his eyebrow with his bent finger. "There has to be a better way to deal with the competition than killing them off."

"I agree. I truly think the wedding planners were trying to do that. Keith prides himself on his hipster weddings while Evelynn promotes her image as the high society wedding diva, and Charmaine was cheap and extravagant."

"Sounds to me like Charmaine got most of the business."

"I think so. She even threw business Grace's way, who was just starting out. I'm not surprised she didn't send any to Keith or Evelynn."

"Do you think either one of them are the guilty party?"

"I want to, since they're both petty and malicious. It feels like a natural fit, but I want to go back to Ramona as the absentee killer." She opened the freezer and pulled out both packages. It had been her experience if she warmed up anything, it would be eaten in a matter of minutes.

Herman cleared his throat. "I'm familiar with this type of situation. It's always a favorite in mystery novels. Killer stages his own death with accomplices, then comes back to murder with no one being the wiser, except for the very smart sleuth." He directed a grin her way.

"I wish that was it, but I can't find anything on Ramona. I've looked. It's possible she changed her name." She blew out a breath. "It probably more possible she's dead."

"Why?"

"Wedding planner." She held up her index finger as she announced what she thought was obvious.

"So, you think another wedding planner or an anti-romance psychopath is taking out wedding planners?"

That is what she thought, but when the words came out of Herman's mouth, they sounded wrong. "I did. What's your take?"

"Something personal."

"Weddings are fairly personal."

"No, something between Charmaine and the killer."

Well, that brought the investigation full circle again. "Both Mark and my mother have been delving into this. Two of the five ex-husbands are dead. The other three re-married. That doesn't appear to be an issue. Evelynn had hinted that Charmaine had accidents at her weddings, but Grace helped at some of those weddings and explained Charmaine was very careful. It seems to me like someone was trying to make Charmaine look bad. It wasn't working even when the incidents happened. She still managed to fix things and the weddings went on. If someone was trying to ruin Charmaine's reputation, they must have been getting frustrated."

"Frustrated enough to kill."

"What if they really hadn't meant to kill, but wanted it to be just another accident to ruin a wedding?"

"I think you might be getting closer to the killer if you knew who was staging the accidents. Are the cookies ready?"

Donna opened the toaster oven and poked the side on the foil wrapped package. "The blondies are almost there. Still, we have the exploding car, the threatening note, the vanishing Ramona? How do these fit into this? Better yet, what was the personal motivation?"

Herman rubbed his hands together. "This is grand. I love delving into a current crime. It could be they're not connected. People assume everything is connected, when it's not. They could be red herrings to lead you away from the killer. Then again, they could be something totally unique to the situation."

Donna circled the island to hug Herman. "I've missed you and your voice of reason."

"Yeah, I missed you, too." He patted her hand resting on his shoulder.

"You're thinking of coming back?"

"At first, I did. However, there's the fact that I sold my house and signed a contract for five years for my little suite."

"A smart lawyer could get you out of it."

"For a price, a big one. Also, there happens to be a lady there I'd like to get to know better."

She raised her eyebrows at the pronouncement. "Oh, now I see."

"Gus and Jake need me to keep them in line."

"That's the truth."

"How close are you to being ready to marry?"

"That's an odd question. I already told you the date." She dropped her arms and moved where she could see Herman's face better.

"Well," He spoke, but then looked away in the direction of the cabinets. "I'm not too sure how long we can stay."

"I told you I had room. Not for Eunice, I may have to have her sleep in the linen closet when my other guests roll in."

"When I signed the contract for the home, it was in very tiny font. Ridiculously small when you consider the age of the residents.

They have some strict rules about coming and going. I was one of the few residents who have a car. Most people there have been placed by relatives and don't have the ability to come and go as they please."

The lack of car interior lights and leaving in the night was starting to make sense. "I assume Jake and Gus weren't supposed to leave, either."

Herman nodded. "Eunice, either."

"That one I figured out on my own from last time."

"We just wanted one last road trip together. I guess I thought it would make me feel young."

Patients escaping from a rest home wasn't a crime, or was it? The better question would be if she'd be charged with aiding and abetting. "You need to call the home. I can explain that you wanted to be at the wedding. That might carry some weight."

"Okay," Herman agreed in a soft voice. "Do you think the two of you could get married sooner?"

Donna closed her eyes. A Vegas wedding would have been so much easier. "Let me make a few phone calls. First, we need to call your retirement center."

Chapter Twenty

BEFORE DONNA COULD even look up the phone number of the retirement center, a sedan came careening into the parking lot followed by a squad car with sirens blaring. What now! She was officially on overload and refused to accept any more spontaneous disasters.

The back door slammed, which brought her head up fast. Were the police letting themselves into the house, now? That's what she got for not locking the door. Mark rushed in looking harried with his hair standing up in spots as if he had shot his fingers through it in frustration. Officer Wells came up behind him and bumped into him at Mark's sudden stop.

Her sweetie glanced back at his colleague. "I told you the sirens weren't necessary."

"It's a kidnapping, which is serious. A senior citizen was carried across state lines."

Donna had no clue what they were talking about, but Herman scrambled from his stool and kept one hand on the counter, looking ready to push off into a fast walking escape.

Nothing made sense. She felt like she had stepped into a play without a clue to what her lines should be. "Who's been kidnapped?"

"Eunice Ledbetter."

Herman groaned and sagged against the counter. "I should have known."

Mark glanced at the elderly man. "You've been named as a person of interest along with your friends, Jake and Gus."

"Seriously?" Herman leaned even more on the counter and was almost to the fainting stage. She scurried around him, placed one arm around his waist, managed to take some of his weight, and hefted him up to a standing position. Without asking permission, she led the man into the front parlor where he could sit in a wing chair. In his condition, a stool wouldn't serve. The two men followed her in.

Officer Wells did his best to look intimidating, which was about the same as a Yorkshire terrier trying to look fierce. It must have worked on Herman, though, because he threw both hands in the air.

"I had nothing to do with any kidnapping. The guys and I planned on having a road trip to Legacy for Mark and Donna's wedding. Eunice was not invited. When she asked, we unanimously told her no. The woman is an extreme wild card. Who'd take her anywhere? She hid under a blanket in my car."

Wells crossed his arms and kept his gruff expression while Mark's eyebrows inched up. "Could you explain this?"

Herman moaned. "No one can explain Eunice Ledbetter. It's best just to keep your distance. At one time, she'd fancied me. Scariest time of my life until now."

Oh, my goodness. When Eunice made her previous appearance, Donna never had any clue what she'd put her former neighbor through when she'd suggested Herman should take the woman out to keep her out of the way. She held up her hand as if in class and waited until Mark nodded his head.

"I think I know what happened. The men, Herman, Jake, and Gus, wanted to take one last road trip for old time's sake. They didn't totally clear it with the staff and snuck out in the night, making sure the interior light of the car wasn't on as they made their getaway. I bet you didn't even turn on your headlights until you were off the property."

She glanced back at Herman who acknowledged her query with a head bob before she continued. "Anyhow, Eunice snuck into the car and hid under a blanket. That should teach you to lock your car."

"Always, from now on." Herman made an air cross over his heart, signifying his oath to lock his vehicle.

"Good. Anyhow, Ten took Eunice to the beach—"

"She's at the beach." Mark's chin worked to one side, then the other. He looked like he wanted to say something else, but he didn't.

"Oh, she's safe. Eunice isn't swimming."

Mark shook his head. "I'm more worried about everyone else."

"Got it. Anyhow, she claimed she'd taken care of—." She broke off in a groan. "Okay, she lied. All she said was she'd taken care of it when I asked if they'd miss her."

Officer Wells dropped his arms and his I mean business expression. "She left a kidnapping note. One of those with letters cut from the newspaper. It said the kidnappers wanted an unlimited movie warehouse gift card, a case of wine, and fifty pounds of Belgian chocolate and to leave it in Eunice's room. That made the staff suspicious along with the disappearance of three other residents and Herman's car. The sedan was spotted running a toll booth, so we had a general direction. It was assumed Herman was driving and heading to his former residence."

The subject of their discussion placed his elbows on his knees, rested his head in his hands, and groaned.

"Look at him!" One balled fist found purchase on her hip. "You've gone and scared him silly. What's wrong with senior citizens going on a lark?"

"Donna." Mark moved closer and touched her arm. "Herman can do what he wants because he's mentally capable. He checked himself into the center. He can also check himself out. With the others, that's not the case."

Herman's head shot up. "Of course, I can take care of myself, as can Gus and Jake. I'm not sure what you mean."

Donna decided to point out the obvious. "Gus did jump on an excavator and put a hole in my house. That's not the action of a mentally competent person."

"He was just looking for the missing jewels."

Wells repeated the last word turning it into a question. "Jewels?"

Instead of answering him, Mark held up a hand for him to wait. "That's beside the point. Let's forget about the jewels and the hole in the inn."

"It's a little hard to do that." Donna commented, considering she'd have to pull off a wedding in twenty-four hours in her damaged inn, and she had no clue what she'd do with her Civil War guests. She guessed she'd have to invite them if they were here at the time.

Something dark scurried past the open parlor door. Too big for Jasper. Besides being the wrong color, she'd never witnessed her dog moving in such a furtive fashion. Jasper's modus operandum depended on people noticing him and giving him his proper canine due. "I think there's something in the house. Wildlife."

"Donna, I realize you're trying to distract me. I'll go easy on Herman, and I think I can straighten everything out without any charges being pressed. I imagine the various children and guardians of your three fellow travelers are heading to Legacy."

Her eyes flickered shut, and she gave a hearty sigh. Should she invite the upset children to the wedding, too? At this point, she had no food and had seriously depleted her frozen food supply. Maybe Maria could run to the Piggly Wiggly and pick up a sheet cake. Better, Daniel, since he wouldn't be loaded down with a baby.

The clatter of dishes breaking had her dashing out of the parlor and into the kitchen just in time to see a striped tail disappear around the corner. "Raccoon!"

She charged after the animal who took a sharp left at the open basement door and headed downstairs. "Ah-ha." She slammed the door in triumph.

She strolled back through the kitchen and met Jasper who chose at that moment to leave his bed and yawn. "Don't tell me you missed out on that home invader."

The interior door swung open, and Mark strolled in just in time to hear her scold her pampered pooch. "Don't be so hard on him. Good chance he was playing possum as a form of self-protection. Raccoons have nasty claws and teeth."

"Right now, rocky raccoon is in my basement. I'm sure it came in through the hole in the wall. It may have led the migration from the outside. The entire family could be moving in. What am I going to do?" Her voice grew ragged as she spoke, wanting to dissolve into a wail, but she kept it steady, always doing her best to be the no-nonsense family member.

Mark wrapped his arms around her. "I'll take care of it."

Her eyes grew glassy as she looked up at him. "You'll go down there and show that varmint who's boss."

He pressed his lips together at the mention of such a plan. "Nope. I'll call Critter Ridders."

The option was a little less heroic than man against nature, but it worked. "Okay. What about Herman?"

"We're working that out. I can call the home and promise to

place the quartet under protective custody. I still imagine we'll have some anxious children showing up. If not, I'll personally drive them back to Indiana."

"That's so sweet." She rested her cheek against his chest. "Did Herman mention that he wanted to marry us immediately?"

"Really wasn't any time to mention it with you screaming bloody murder."

He dusted a kiss on her head that made her simper and go soft inside. Who'd ever believe Donna Tollhouse would go gooey over a man?

"Let's make the call and get things cleared up first."

Herman and Wells entered the kitchen. Mark dropped his arms and informed the two of his plans. Donna made more coffee, because she couldn't think of a time when a cup of joe wouldn't make the difficult easier.

"I'll put this on speaker." The phone rang, sounding tinny in the kitchen.

"Pleasant Valley Retirement and Convalescent Center," a chirpy voice answered.

"This is Detective Mark Taber from Legacy, North Carolina. Could I speak to your director, please?"

There was an intake of breath before the woman added, "Just a minute."

Once the director heard that all the residents were safe and no kidnapping had occurred, she was more willing to consider Mark's suggestions. She readily admitted they were suspicious of the kidnapping note, since it was a well-known fact throughout the Center that Eunice could be a prankster who loved her movies and chocolate. She probably threw in the wine to throw them off.

"As for Herman, he had no clue the others weren't allowed to leave the grounds." He winked in Donna's direction and continued. "The three had served together during the war. It was the veterans' one last hurrah. I also suspect Herman didn't thoroughly read the contract. Few people bother with those legal disclaimers written in such tiny font."

"I agree." The director's voice remained even, not displaying any of the tension she may have felt at misplacing four residents. "What's your plan?"

"Well, they made the road trip for the wedding. I figured the nuptials could be moved up then I can personally drive them back. I may enlist the aid of a uniformed officer since we both know Eunice can be tricky. This is dependent on their families not swooping in and taking them back."

"That sounds wonderful. I'll notify the families immediately to save them a trip, but Eunice's daughter may already be on her way. The woman felt she knew where the group was headed once the car had been spotted in North Carolina. Her mother had a special affection for The Painted Lady Inn and its innkeeper."

Donna whispered, "Yay," hopefully quiet enough for it not to be heard by the person on the other end.

Mark picked up the phone and switched off the speaker. "I'll call before we leave to give you an approximate time of arrival."

Disconnecting, he turned to Donna and Herman. "Okay. What next?"

Herman stood. "I need to talk to the rest of them."

"Sounds like a plan." Mark agreed and caught Wells' eye. "Let's head out to the beach. We might as well take the cars because we might need them."

Did they take the cars thinking the seniors would be too tired to walk back home, or did they assume Eunice would make a break for it? Probably both.

A thump and a resulting tinkle indicated the demon raccoon had found its way into her wine cellar section.

Good gravy! Everybody left, leaving her with a furry inn wreck-er. First, she'd call Critter Ridders. Second, she'd push something big and heavy in front of the hole. Then, she'd have to shift into wedding mode. It was unfortunate she was upset with Grace since she was sure the woman could have pulled a few strings.

Chapter Twenty-One

A FEW PANICKY phone calls netted her a kitchen full of women with note pads and cell phones gathered around the kitchen island. Maria had spread out Cici's blanket on display as if she were the main dish. She certainly was the main attraction as various women cooed at her or dangled everything from keys to hospital lanyards in her face.

Her mother had her tablet open, scrolling through possible caterers. Janice, who had come in at the last minute, peeked over Cecilia's shoulder.

"Forget the caterers. I'll bring the food. I even brought the menu. You can have whatever you want from seafood gumbo, shrimp skewers, pineapple pork, to coconut cream pie. I don't have any wedding cake, though."

"Really?" Donna couldn't believe it. She made a dash for the opinionated redhead and hugged her. "You're so nice. Probably the nicest person I've ever known."

Her mother made a slight reproving sound, which forced Donna to tack on, "Non-related nicest person, I mean."

Shelley, her co-worker, had shown up with a box of wedding toppers. She opened the first box and pulled it out. "Since my cousin does wedding cakes, I stopped by there and grabbed what I thought were the most unique ones. I'll return the ones you don't want. I love this one."

She flourished a bride and groom where the tuxedo groom appeared to be trying to escape while a determined bride hung onto his collar.

"I don't think so." She didn't feel as if she were forcing Mark to do anything. There was no humor in such a display.

"Really? I thought it was hilarious." Shelley pulled out another box and unwrapped an unsmiling older couple.

"Certainly not."

"I just brought that one to see your reaction. Okay, this one you will love. Guarantee it."

Considering the previous ones, she had definite doubts. Her friend displayed a pleasant couple in casual dress with a dog at their feet. It didn't look the least wedding cake topper-ish. She picked up the figurine and stared at it. The woman with her blonde bob similar to her own. The man did look somewhat like Mark if he wore casual clothes, which happened rarely. "They look like us."

"I thought so."

"I love it." And she did.

The front door bell rang, making Donna hold her breath for a second, afraid to guess who else or more likely what else had descended on the inn. Gisele and her mother peeked into the kitchen. "We saw all the cars and wondered what was going on."

Oh, yeah, she did still have actual paying guests. Good gracious, what was her plan to work around the guests? She thought she had one earlier, but now not so much so.

Maria turned to the two with an excited expression. "You're so lucky. You'll get to witness the very first wedding at the inn."

Sue, the mother, clapped her hands together. "What fun! Here I thought this historical re-enactment would be boring, but this has turned into a super getaway."

"Can I be in the wedding?" Gisele asked with an avid expression.

Donna wasn't sure what the girl could do, but Cecilia held up a finger, answering for Donna. "You can oversee the music. Since we don't have time to hire any musicians, we'll have recorded music. It will be your job to turn the music off and on when signaled."

"I can do that."

"I'm glad." Donna forced a smile. "Does anyone have a CD of the wedding march?" It wasn't like it was easy listening music.

"It doesn't have to be that song, it can be anything you like. It's your wedding. Maybe something by Elvis."

"That sounds good." Already her wedding was coming together with Janice's generous offer to cater, Shelley's cake topper, and Gisele being the official CD music operator. She waved her hand in front of her face, suddenly hot. She blew out a long breath as she considered everyone gathered around the table.

"Here I thought I needed a wedding planner to pull this off. I even sort of considered Grace since she was the nicest of them."

Janice made a loud snort. Her friend never shied away from making her opinion known, which was something she liked in the woman.

"What? I know you have something to say."

"I do. Grace Cummings excels at making people think she's nice. I know the real person. I had a flash of it at the Miss North Carolina pageant."

Well, she knew her friend had taken the title, but wasn't able to extend her fifteen minutes of fame into more than a scholarship. "What did she do to you at the pageant that made you distrust her?"

"Not me. Charmaine. Grace's act was a patriotic baton twirling medley. When they went to start her music, it wasn't cued up right. Grace was convinced Charmaine had messed it up since she was next up and waiting in the wings. She stomped off the stage and swore to get even. That was one contest where she didn't win Miss Congeniality."

"What happened to Charmaine?"

"She had an allergic reaction to nuts and had to be rushed to the hospital. She never got to finish the contest. The girl did have some pipes on her. She would have given me a run for my money and would have at least been a finalist. Grace didn't even place with her messed up performance and major hissy fit. I must admit her outburst was unusual. She usually kept her competitive streak buried so deep you never knew it was there. Judges love that. They foolishly think there are people in the contest who only want the best for each other."

Janice stuck out her tongue and made a gagging sound. "I saw her eyes when she came off stage. You've heard the expression if looks could kill. Well, she definitely had the look. That means I didn't really win the title. I got it by default." Janice slammed her fist into her hand.

Cecilia looked up. "It's in the past. Did you have fun as Miss North Carolina?"

"I did."

"That's all that matters. If these competitions are so cutthroat, it isn't the first time something screwy happened."

"True. Okay. Back on track, what about the cake?"

Maria answered. "I ordered a simple layer cake. Well, it's a bit larger than normal. It's one of the bigger ones with plain white icing and white trim. All we have to do is stick the decoration on the top. Daniel agreed to pick it up."

All good. The idea of Charmaine allergy attack replayed in her head. Even with all the hype, those with nut allergies seldom had a reaction from the smell or casual contact. It made her wonder if something else had been involved. "Are you sure Charmaine didn't drink or eat anything in between the pageant segments?"

Janice rolled her eyes. "That's been thirty years ago. Even at the time, I was more concerned about my performance as opposed to what the contestants ate or drank."

There would be no way to know if Grace had somehow caused Charmaine's allergic reaction, but the bookshelves crammed with trophies inside the wedding planner's house alluded to someone who needed to win. Donna initially considered it peculiar there were no trophies for her children. Pageant queens usually expected their daughters to follow in their footsteps, although the kids could have taken theirs with them.

Thinking what she'd missed, she said, "Thanks, Mom."

"What for? I think I have your flower arrangements, red roses and carnations. Will that work?"

"I guess." They sounded rather traditional, but flowers were flowers. "Thanks for not being a backstage mom and pushing me into doing pageants."

"As if I could. You resisted all my efforts to get you to go to charm school and modeling. With your height, you could have pulled off modeling until you opened your mouth and told them how chauvinistic they were being or how they weren't using the best angle. Just as well, it sounds like the whole thing was filled with backbiting females."

"Hey!" Janice objected pointing to herself. "I'm in the room. Besides, I wasn't petty. I prefer the term opportunistic. I could afford the entry fee, which was all I could afford. My goal was the scholarship to any state college."

Her mother shrugged. "You know I didn't mean you. I'm going

to slip off into the next room and order the flowers. They deliver."

With everyone talking and the occasional delighted coo from Cici, it was a little loud, but it hadn't prevented anyone else from calling on their cells. She had half a mind to follow her mother to make sure the woman wasn't making some grand over-the-top gesture like a horse drawn carriage.

"How many people are going to be at your wedding?" Janice asked brandishing her cell. "I'm calling in the order now."

Inviting people was the last thing on her mind. "I need to call Mark's mother and sister."

Maria waved at her. "Did that."

She raised her eyebrows at the statement. "Ah, did you mention anything about the wedding being in a rush as a reason for me not calling."

"Did that. Just as well. Mark's mother is thrilled he's getting married, but Eileen on the other hand is not a fan.

"Of me?" Her voice swung up to upper registers. It wouldn't be the first time someone didn't like her.

Maria smirked a little. "Not you. You're fine. She even thinks you're a suitable match to Mark, but she's not a fan of marriages, wedding, and love. Claims it's a sham by wedding related businesses to make a buttload of money. She even told me that Mark's idea of her helping was ludicrous."

"WELL, THEN," JANICE glanced up from the list she was making, "she'll probably show up in black to protest the entire ceremony."

Maria and Janice both laughed at the possibility, but Donna was far from amused. Didn't she have enough to think about?

"You never told me how many guests."

The mention of her future sister-in-law possibly boycotting her brother's wedding distracted her. "Well, all of you are coming, of course."

They nodded and murmured their agreement. Shelley piped in. "Not sure if you have a time set for the wedding, but could you do it in the morning so all the post-surgery staff can make it?"

"We were having it in the morning so Mark can escort some of our guests back to the retirement center. It's a long drive."

She added the numbers in her head. "I think thirty should be plenty. That's including five extra people Mark might invite."

Janice winked. "I'll make it forty. Some people get confused about what is a serving. That should cover everybody. Who's going to be your maid of honor. Hint. Hint. Nudge. Nudge."

She caught Maria's eye. "Sorry. My apologies to my good friend, and also to my generous sister-in-law. I'd like my mother to be my matron of honor. If she hadn't been pushing men at me, I'm not sure if Mark would have proposed. We'd be like one of those couples you hear about who dated for thirty years."

Janice pouted the tiniest bit and muttered loud enough for everyone to hear. "Never a bridesmaid." She tacked on, "I understand."

Maria laughed. "It is just as well. I wasn't sure how I would have handled Cici during the wedding. At this point in her development, she prefers for me not to be out of sight. As for you dating thirty years, that would never happen. Eventually, you would have told him to stop wasting your time."

"Could be." She doubted she'd ever say that since she never thought he was wasting her time. Just the opposite.

"So," Shelley grinned at her, "You're being cheated out of a wedding night. I'm sure you're expecting a spectacular honeymoon. Maybe an over-the-top new house."

"Honeymoon is delayed to after Gen Con."

Maria's head went up with a jerk. "Oh, I forgot to tell you that you're totally booked for that."

The news had the same effect as a good wallop to the solar plexus. Donna inhaled deeply as she tried to get her head around people costumed as video game avatars bopping around the inn. "Well then, I guess it is good we're getting married tomorrow."

Instead of pointing out that Maria hadn't added it to the calendar, Donna decided to keep her mouth closed for a change. A new baby was more than reason enough for forgetting.

The sound of masculine grumbling heralded the entry of sandy and slightly sunburned Gus and Jake. Gus made an elaborate bow.

"Who knew there would be even more lovely scenery here than on the beach?"

A few of the women chuckled. It was easy to tell who had been the womanizer of the group. Jake looked back to Tennyson emerging from the hall.

"Keep going to the parlor with the big screen television. I'll get the movie started and get your drinks and popcorn." Tennyson waited until the men were through the door. "I got the easy ones."

A shrill complaint split the air. "I did not take that brat's bucket. He wasn't using it. That's not the same as stealing. Haven't you heard of Reduce, Reuse, and Recycle. I was in the second part, the reuse."

An even sandier Eunice appeared, turned halfway to yell over her shoulder. "I will report you for police brutality!"

Mark showed up behind her a little rumpled looking with a large wet blotch on his shirt and pants.

Corralling three seniors shouldn't result in that much disarray. "What happened to you?"

His head jerked in Eunice's direction. "That one has amazing aim for her age."

Wells crowded into the kitchen. His uniform showed wet patches, too. Apparently, the woman had very good aim. It wasn't hard figuring out what she'd done with her purloined bucket. Along with the sea water, sand was dripping all over her floors. She stood and picked up a dish towel. "Let's go outside and rub that sand off."

Eunice giggled. Donna included the woman in her glare. After she got the three of them less sandy, Wells escorted Eunice to the room she'd selected on the third floor. He agreed to stand guard to assure the sly senior stayed put.

"I wouldn't put it past her to make a sheet rope," Mark gestured to a third-floor window with Eunice's white face at the glass.

"Good luck with that! Daniel and I unintentionally painted the windows shut. I haven't a clue when was the last time the third story windows were opened. Is her daughter coming?"

"She is. I didn't mention it to Eunice, of course. She's bringing her husband since I suggested she might need assistance."

"I hope they don't end up locking her up somewhere. Eunice can't help what she is."

Mark flattened his hands on his wet clothing. "You might think differently if she was throwing cold seawater at you. Even got it in my eyes. I think she's enjoying a second childhood. Must have been an ornery child."

Mark's text alert went off, causing him to check his cell. "There's a fire at Grace Cummings's house. I need to check this out."

"Wait!" Donna jogged after him as he headed to his car. "I need to talk to you."

"Not a good time. This could be another deliberate attempt to eliminate another wedding planner."

She opened the passenger side door and jumped in. "That's why

I need to talk to you. Grace might be the killer. I'm almost sure of it."

He gave her a double take and started the car. "She'd set her own house on fire?"

"She would if it would shift any focus off her as the killer. When we get there, we need to examine where all her trophies are. She'd never let those burn up. Either she started a small fire, which is easily extinguished, well away from the trophies or moved the trophies all together. I'm sure the house is insured, and it could be that Grace is looking to relocate."

He reversed fast throwing some gravel and put on his dash lights, but not his siren. "Buckle up. Then tell me how you reached your conclusions."

"Herman and Janice. Something each of them said."

He swerved around cars that appeared not to know what flashing lights meant while he asked through gritted teeth. "Details?"

"Herman mentioned Charmaine's death could have been accidental. Charmaine had been struggling with incidents at her weddings that made her look bad. Grace was kind enough to point out that she was at the wedding of the bride on fire, supposedly helping. I imagine when you delve into it, you'll discover she was at all the weddings with accidents. That gives her opportunity."

"You got that, but what about motive?"

"Janice helped me there. Charmaine, Janice, and Grace were all in the same Miss North Carolina Pageant representing different counties. Janice remembered the music being wrong for Grace's act, and Grace blamed it on Charmaine, since she was the next act up. Grace swore she'd get Charmaine back."

"Janice heard this?"

"Yes, as well as some of the officials, which may be why she didn't get the Miss Congeniality award that time. Charmaine never made it to the next round due to a nut allergy reaction. She ended up being rushed to the hospital."

"Do you think Grace did it?"

"Hard to say. When I found out how cut-throat the pageants could be, I decided it could be anyone. I imagine security is much tighter now. My point is she mentioned she'd get Charmaine."

"It's been thirty years."

"I know that, but maybe the opportunity never presented itself before now. Could be that Grace really wants to be the ruling wedding planner and that set her off. The same extravagant costumes and displays could easily be applied to weddings."

He made a few sharp turns, running over a curb with one. "If she is guilty, it's not like she's going to confess."

"She's smart, so she won't. You could get her for insurance fraud and arson. If you could find any bomb making equipment, you could threaten her with terrorism."

"That alone is a ten-year sentence. Not sure it would stick."

"True, but she wouldn't know that. She'd confess to accidentally causing Charmaine's death since that is a lesser charge. Then, you can pull up the other incidents that occurred when she was in the vicinity and let the jury draw their own conclusions. Make sure any lawyer prosecuting the case makes mention of her pageant bunny status. The women jurors will understand the implications."

They pulled up to the cute cottage they had so recently visited. A thin steam of white smoke came from the back of the house. The fire department members patrolled the perimeters checking for errant sparks. With a knowing nod, Mark exited the car and moved to the fence gate. Grace flew out of the crowd of onlookers and grabbed onto Mark's arm as Donna opened her car door.

"You're here. I knew you would be."

Acting must not have been the skill she won all those trophies with, although Janice had insisted, she was an excellent actress. Maybe her skills were rusty. When she placed her beringed hand on Mark's chest, Donna swung into action.

It only took four long strides to reach Mark's side and gently pry Grace off Mark. "You must be so overcome with shock, but you have to let the authorities do their job."

She kept a firm grip on the woman, having dealt with more than her share of runners and attackers when she'd worked the psych unit. They stood silently with the neighbors as they watched the drama unfold. An SUV arrived with a dog in the back and its uniformed handler.

"What's the dog for?" one of the neighbors behind her asked.

Another answered. "Maybe it was a set fire. It could be an arson dog."

Grace trembled in her grip, which Donna tightened, certain it was the precursor to running. Donna wanted to correct the man behind her. She didn't think there was any such thing as an arson dog, but what if there was? She'd need to check it out.

It could have been the man's wife who scoffed at his suggestion. "Please. Everyone knows that's a drug-sniffing dog. The woman must have been distributing drugs, and one of the sellers she crossed set the house on fire."

Grace shot Donna a pained look, causing her to feign sympathy. "Ignore them. Next thing, they'll be saying is it's a bomb-sniffing dog they brought in to detect explosives."

"I wouldn't be that stupid," she snapped, then cleared her throat. "I meant I wouldn't want anything that dangerous on my property."

Donna gave an absent-minded nod as she filed the disclosure

under things to investigate, places where Grace could have assembled a bomb.

A fireman came out and waved at everyone as if shooing away hungry cats. "Show's over. Go home. Thank you for your concern."

Mark had entered the house, accompanied by the dog and handler. They came out together. The dog had a ball in his mouth, the usual reward for a successful find. Mark carried a plastic evidence bag that had clothes in it.

Grace tried to lunge in Mark's direction and shouted, "It's not what you think it is."

Mark said nothing but walked across the yard to a squad car that had just pulled up on the opposite side of the street. He pointed in the direction of Donna and Grace. Probably realizing the inevitable, Grace landed a hard punch upside Donna's face. A move that should have made her let go, only made her mad.

She kicked at her assailant's knees, then knocked Grace to the ground and straddled her. Grace attempted to wail on her with her free hand. She caught that one, too. With both hands pinned, she was only a few inches from Grace's enraged face, just close enough for her to whisper.

"I'm not one of your pageant rivals you can so easily dispose of."

The shock that replaced the rage for a brief second assured her she'd hit a bullseye. Mark and another officer ran up to assist after what felt like forever.

"Donna. Let us handle this. What happened?"

"She attacked me."

Grace twisted underneath her and shouted, "You can't trust her. She's making up stuff. She's jealous of me. All the women are. They were never good enough to be in the pageants. They were never queen."

Donna waited until the officer had her cuffed before slowly moving off the culprit. When she felt she was at a safe distance, she yelled, "You were never queen! A few trivial contests that your mother paid for you to be in doesn't count. When it came to the important stuff, you choked."

Grace snarled and tried to lunge at Donna who stepped neatly out of range. A second officer arrived to wrestle the out of control woman into the car.

A nearby neighbor made tsking sounds. "Never did trust her. She was always too much of everything."

Interesting way to put it. Donna would keep that in mind if she ever met anyone who was too much of everything.

Chapter Twenty-Two

M ARK HELPED HER off the ground and guided her to a squad car with an arm around her waist. He dropped his arm to issue some order that resulted in the trunk popping open. Inside the trunk, he located a medical kit and instant freeze pack that when twisted released a chemical reaction that caused a cooling sensation.

"Put this on your eye. We'll do the debriefing on the way to get our license. Glenda is coming in just for us even though her jaw is still swollen up."

Donna placed the pack on her face and settled for nodding as opposed to talking. She allowed him to carefully escort her to the car and help her inside. The woman had hit her fairly hard, but it was the fact she had misjudged her from the first that left her speechless. She'd leave the talking to Mark who'd entered the car, shut the door, and started the engine.

"You were right about the fire being small and easily put out. It wasn't close to where the trophies sat yesterday. No trophies today, which made me think she was planning on relocating."

"The clothes?" She managed to mumbled with the pack half covering her mouth as the car nosed its way into the street.

"Residue from bomb making. Didn't actually find the supplies, but we will. Did Grace say anything significant?"

"The dog showing up rattled her. Neighbors said something about having drugs or bomb making paraphernalia on her property, and she replied that she wasn't that stupid. I pretended not to notice. She took a swing at me because I was holding onto her."

"You naturally fought back." His tone carried a mixture of pride and concern.

"Wouldn't you?"

"Can't fight back. It's part of the job protocol. Feel up to getting a license? We have to if we want Herman to marry us tomorrow. Glenda is coming in special for us, too."

"That she is."

Her fiancé had competently steered his way through the streets of Legacy while they spoke and they were at the courthouse. "Here we are."

The actual process took less than ten minutes, which consisted of Glenda pointing to places where they needed signed. She copied the paperwork and handed the original form to Mark. Glenda finally spoke when they were about to leave.

"You'll need to file the paperwork after the wedding to make it official."

That was news to her. She'd never really thought what happened to wedding certificates. Before, it had never mattered.

Donna pulled the sunglasses from her face long enough to answer. "I'll see that he does."

The clerk spotting her reddened eye, gasped and cut her eyes to Mark. "I thought you had a toothache like me. I never thought…"

"Don't go getting the wrong idea, Glenda." Mark rushed his words together as he tried to explain.

Feeling calmer, Donna gestured to her face, which she judged by Glenda's reaction was coloring up. "Got knocked around by a murder suspect, but I still managed to hold onto her until the police arrived."

"How thrilling." Glenda pressed her hands together. "You live such an exciting life."

Mark raised his eyebrows but chose not to comment. Donna didn't share his reservations. "It has become much more adventurous since I bumped into Mark."

Out on the courthouse stairs, her sweetie decided to address her comment, showing much more patience than she would have.

"I assume adventurous is good?"

She had to lower the cold pack long enough for a mysterious smile. "I'm marrying you. That should be answer enough."

HER WEDDING MORNING came much sooner than it should have. Donna closed her eyes, certain she wasn't ready. Birds twittered outside her window. A cardinal, possibly a chickadee, she wasn't sure if either had any significance.

Shelley insisted she put raw meat on her wounded face while her mother insisted on ice. She switched the two out, hoping to appease both and maximize the healing aspect. Despite the steak and the ice pack, a suspicion lingered that a magnificent bruise would greet her in the morning. At least the hospital had allowed her to switch around her days off for the wedding. Their attitude might have been different if she'd mentioned she planned on quitting. Hadn't gotten around to that. Hadn't done several things such as cleaning out her house or asking Mark where he intended to live. Donna meant to do that last one before marrying the man. Somehow, it got lost in runaway seniors and wrestling a former beauty queen to the ground.

The sunlight penetrated her curtains, letting her know it wasn't raining. An old wives' tale associated rain with how many tears a bride would cry during her marriage. The thing about the old wives' tales is they always ran to the gloomy.

She needed to get up. After all, she still had guests to feed. She still needed to check her dress and the wedding was at eleven. Wait. She sat upright in bed and blinked. Where was her dress? She remembered buying it and putting it in her mother's car trunk.

"Good gravy." She swung her feet out of bed, causing Jasper to yawn and regard her with a quizzical expression.

"Yes, you have to get up, too." She slid her feet into her slippers and had belted on her robe when a knock sounded.

"It's your mother with your dress!"

She swung open the door to be met by the sight of her dress on a hanger, totally wrinkle-free. "You're a life saver. I still need to get dressed and get our guests breakfast."

"I gave the men toast along with grits with the explanation that true sons of the Southern Confederacy would have been glad to get either and sent them on their way. Maria drove the ladies down to the waffle house."

Donna plopped down on her bed. A single tear slid down her face. "You're wonderful. I'm so blessed to have such a caring family. I was up past midnight waiting for the arrival of Eunice's family. I'd rather have anyone but Eunice at my wedding."

Her mother sat beside her and grabbed her hand. "Glad you feel that way because Heloise is coming."

Donna dropped flat to her bed, taking her mother with her since they were still holding hands. "Why?"

"I didn't invite her, but she was convinced you'd be so disappointed if she wasn't here. Currently, she is taking credit for putting you two together."

"That would only be possible if she had left a dead stranger in my inn for me to find, not that I wouldn't put it past her."

Her mother, still prone on the bed, tried to reassure her. "I told her the wedding was at one, but being the gossip that she is, she might sniff out the real time."

She groaned but dropped her mother's hand and pushed up. "All in all, Heloise isn't the worst of my troubles. I need to check to see if Critter Ridders returned my phone call. Raccoon in the basement is probably right up there with Heloise. Remind everyone not to open the basement door."

"I think you already have, but I'll do it again. Maria has brought some supplies to decorate the dining room. Gisele and Sue volunteered to help. B-T-W, Gisele is on the music."

Did her mother just say B-T-W? "B-T-W?"

"It means by the way."

"I know what it means. I just didn't expect to hear you say it."

"I'm hip." Her mother pushed off the bed and struck a pose with one hand on her hip and her chin angled to one side.

Donna closed her eyes. "Stop it. It's too early."

Her mother's tinkling laughter made her happy. "It's time for your pampering. I can bring you breakfast in bed. Something light. A croissant? Coffee?"

"Definitely coffee. When Maria gets back, ask her if she'll help with my makeup with the bruise and all."

"Actually, it looks okay due to my ice pack. You still need makeup, though." She pointed to the area under her eyes. After her mother brought her coffee, she shuffled to the bathroom and started the water for a bath. She slid into the tub, listening to the sounds emanating from the inn. She could hear the clang of metal pans and guessed Janice and staff had arrived. Jasper erupted in a frenzy of barking that forced her to climb out of the tub and peer out her bathroom window, which faced the parking lot. A hearse was parked beside The Croaking Frog catering truck. What was a hearse doing in her parking lot? She'd bet there was an old wives' tale about that. Had one of the guests died in the night and no one told her?

She closed her eyes for a second, breathed a prayer that it wasn't Herman and felt guilty. Outside the window, a man in a t-shirt and jeans emerged from the hearse, opened the rear double doors and pulled out two flower arrangements. Her mother got her some dead person's flowers. She didn't want dead person's flowers. That had to be major bad luck.

Garbed in her terry cloth robe and her hair wrapped in a towel, she sprinted out of her room only to encounter her mother who was directing the arrangement of the flowers. She moved closer to her mother and hissed, "I don't want dead people's flowers."

The man who held the flowers grinned. "Don't worry. These are totally live people flowers. My father is a florist, too. Not everyone knows that. We even grow most of our flowers. We have three greenhouses."

"Okay." She felt rather silly for her behavior. Still if he didn't want people to think the worst. "Um, your vehicle?"

"Yeah, I know, totally not fuel efficient, but the delivery van had a flat, and I discovered the spare was flat, too. Figuring you wanted your flowers on time, I took the only vehicle left big enough to handle them."

Donna stepped back and regarded the arrangements which were massive. "I see what you mean. Carry on."

Feeling rather awkward, she hurried back to her room to get ready. Carry on? Who said that?

Maria was already in the bedroom laying out cosmetics and hair supplies. "Good, you're here. I'll dry your hair first."

She allowed her sister-in-law to fuss with her hair as she worried about everything that could go wrong with the wedding. "How are things out there?"

"No issues. How about you?"

"I'm a mess. There's so much Mark and I haven't discussed."

"Do you love him?"

"You know I do."

"He's a good man. He had to pull a few strings to get a tuxedo and paid big bucks to have it delivered. It would have taken too long for him to drive to the next county to pick it up, but luckily there was an employee up for a bit of extra money."

"He's wearing something he's never seen or even tried on."

Maria made a face at her in the mirror. "You know how it is with guy clothes. All the sizes remain the same. They very seldom try on clothes. They just buy it, and it fits. He made sure to mention that he ordered a green cummerbund to coordinate with your dress."

"That's sweet."

Maria's reflection arched her eyebrows. "He's a winner. If I didn't have Daniel, I might give you a run for your money with Mark."

"I wouldn't stand a chance."

"Please, the man is crazy about you. Just like Daniel is about me. Speaking of your dear brother, he went to retrieve the cake."

Donna's reflection pruned up as if she'd bitten into an unripe persimmon.

"What was that about?" Maria asked.

"Daniel is more of a big picture guy. A wedding cake is a detail."

"I ordered it. The order will have Tollhouse on it. How much more detail is there?"

"You're right. I'm worried about nothing. Eunice is gone, and Heloise has been told the wrong time. What else could happen?"

"A strange thing happened while we were decorating the dining room."

Did she just think what else could happen? "Strange funny, I hope."

"Oh, yeah. Your measuring tape neighbor showed up and asked if Herman was here. I told her he came for the wedding and asked if she wanted me to get him. She said no but went away with a smile on her face."

The other boot just dropped. "Can you make sure no one even parks close to her house? Most of the neighbors will overlook an hour parking in front of their house, but not her."

"Got it. Let's get your dress on, then I'll do the final hair. I have some tiny rose buds, I'd like to work into your do."

Donna watched her transformation as she mentally ticked off items in her head. Officiate. Check. Catering. Check. The mingled voices of Mark and Daniel had her checking off Cake and Groom. "Oh, no! I don't have a ring for Mark."

"Not surprising how fast you put this together, but your mother thought of that."

Maria reached into her pocket and pulled out a ring that Donna had always seen on her father's hand. Her mother must have slipped it off when they closed the coffin lid. Her hands closed around it, feeling as if her father was with her.

Her sister-in-law held up a string of pearls, then placed them around Donna's neck. "Your mother should have given you the ring, but she was afraid she'd end up bawling and ruin her makeup. She's riding herd on everyone. That woman is an organizer."

"Don't I know it."

The door opened, and her mother stuck in her head. "The photographer is here, and he'd like to get some shots of you getting ready."

"We have a photographer?"

"It's Mark's nephew."

A young, slender man with an oversized camera stepped into the room. "Surely, you remember me. I'm the one my uncle is constantly threatening to disinherit if I write one bad word about you or your inn."

"Oh, right. It's all coming back. Thank you."

He snapped a few shots with the bright flash bouncing off the mirror.

"Act natural."

Why did photographers say that when the act of getting your picture taken wasn't natural? Unless she was a millennial photographing her life for social media. Music from The Wizard of Oz floated down the hall.

"That's our cue. Let's go. Your flowers are in the foyer. I'll get them for you. Daniel is standing by if you want him to give you away."

"No one gives me away. I'm not a worn-out scooter."

"I told Daniel you'd say that. Well, not the scooter part."

Daniel stood in the hallway with Baby Cici on one shoulder while her mother smiled brightly at her. Her smile was a trifle too wide, indicating she was two seconds away from crying.

"Don't cry, Mom. It's a happy occasion."

She accepted the bouquet from her mother and entered through the second parlor. Her co-workers gave finger waves while Shelley gave her two thumbs up. A couple of Mark's colleagues were there in uniform next to a couple of elderly ladies. Heloise, she recognized, but the other she would have sworn was tape measure lady. The dog-walking guys were in front of her. My goodness, some of her neighbors showed.

Ivy decorated the arch her mother must have pulled from the closet. Beneath it, Herman stood stiffly in a black suit, clutching a book while beside him stood an oversized leprechaun. Mark? Whoever it was wore Mark's face, but she never suspected her fiancé would don vivid green tails. Until now, she would've bet they didn't exist.

A flash caught her unaware, and she stumbled. Lucky for her there were no candelabras and cathedral veils. When she reached her intended, she passed the flowers to her mother. Behind Mark stood Tennyson, looking sophisticated for a change in a suit and tie.

Mark took her hands and drew her close. "There was a misunderstanding on the tuxedo."

"It fits well. People will assume we're having a Wizard of Oz theme wedding."

"That's what I love about you, your ability to roll with the punches."

"Said no man ever, until now."

Herman cleared his throat. "I get to do the talking at this event." He smiled out at the crowd and began, "Dearly beloved…"

They came to the part to exchange rings, and she pushed her father's battered gold band on Mark's finger. It fit. It felt like her father saying this one I trust. She'd replace the ring as soon as she could, but for now she liked the way the ring looked on his hand. Taken.

After mutual I Do, the processional had them walking down the aisle past smiling guests. Many waved and a few snapped photos. One woman dressed in black sat with her arms folded. Eileen, Mark's sister. They'd met once. At the time, she'd been more colorful.

Her new husband tilted his head to whisper. "Ignore her. Eileen has been working hard to get in touch with her feelings, and her present attitude toward the entire married state is hatred."

Yeah, she kinda got that vibe. Mark's mother beamed at her and crossed her hands over her heart signaling her feelings.

If she won one out of two family members over, she was doing good. Fortunately, the only member she truly cared about just promised to love and honor her. That's what mattered. They turned right into the dining room where white shirted catering staff stood at attention. Everything was going well. Due to the lack of room, they decided to wait to bring out the cake and champagne for the toast.

Mark drew her into the hall, causing the guests to whisper and roll their eyes.

"I know everything has been so fast. This probably is not the wedding you wanted. I figure we can do it again. Wherever you want, however you want."

"We could, but I'm not sure why I would. Green happens to be one of my favorite colors."

"I'm glad. I have a little surprise for you."

"You do?"

"Yes, it's nothing you can unwrap." He waited to make sure he had her attention. "I decided to sell my house. Haven't even put it on the market, but Cory, Officer Wells, asked if he could buy it."

"Where will you live?" It sounded rather stupid when she heard the words come out of her mouth.

"With you. Right here. Isn't that what you wanted?"

"I did, but now I don't."

Mark rubbed his neck with his free hand. "I'm confused. I thought you'd be happy I was going to sell my house."

"Yeah, I know. Dames. What can you do with them? You have a

good point about not having privacy. Instead of living in a bedroom, I thought we could put an extra unit on the house or something at the edge of the property."

"That could work." He gave her a gentle kiss on the lips. "I love the way you overanalyze everything."

Some heated discussion came from the kitchen. Donna heard Tollhouse hissed as more of a curse than a name as Maria and Daniel entered carrying cake boxes with tight smiles. Maria removed a jumbo chocolate chip cookie while Daniel carried a large sheet cake with a rainbow and the topper that looked so much like the three of them. It was obvious it wasn't the cake they had ordered, but that was okay. People commented on how the rainbow continued the theme and how original to have a topper created to look like the actual couple.

Someone called for champagne. Tennyson announced he'd get it from the basement.

"No!" Donna yelled as she lunged after her fast-moving employee. Mark joined her in shouting out instruction, but the party noise muffled their combined plea. Ten opened the kitchen door and a panicked raccoon sped past her and up the main stairs.

"What in the world was that?" a guest asked in alarm.

Not wanting to ruin the inn's reputation, she improvised. "A ghost. It's not terribly social."

It seemed to satisfy the curious. A few even asked the story behind the ghost. Her mother's guest and full-time beau elaborated with a tale. It might be something she'd need to remember. No telling who'd book the inn for a close encounter of the spirit kind.

Tennyson returned with a chagrinned expression that asked for forgiveness as he delivered the bottle of bubbly. How could she be mad at anyone when everyone worked so hard to pull the wedding off in less than twenty-four hours.

The incarcerated wedding planner hadn't thought it could be done.

Daniel carried a tray around passing out the flutes of champagne, reserving two for the guests of honor. When the room had quietened, Daniel raised his glass. "Here's to my sister and the man I'm happy to call my brother. They met due to a crime, but it would have been a crime if they both hadn't wised up and admitted the obvious: that they're perfect for each other."

The crowd laughed, then sipped their champagne. Donna clinked her glass against Mark's. "Every now and then, my brother gets it right."

THE END

Coastal Seafood Gumbo

Prep Time: 30 minutes

Cook Time: 4 hours

Serving Size: 6 to 8 hearty servings

Ingredients

- 2 tablespoons unsalted butter
- 3 tablespoons all-purpose flour
- 1 onion, chopped
- 1 green bell pepper, cored, seeded and chopped
- 4 cups water
- 2 6-ounce cans tomato paste
- 1 pound of frozen chopped okra
- 1 12. oz. can of kernel corn (drained)
- 2 pounds large shrimp (21/25 count), peeled and deveined
- 1-pound jumbo lump or lump crabmeat, picked over for cartilage
- hot sauce, for seasoning

Directions

1. In a heavy-bottomed pot or Dutch oven, melt the butter over medium heat. Add the flour, stirring slowly and constantly, and cook to a medium-brown roux.
2. Add the onion and bell pepper and stir to combine. Cook until the vegetables have wilted about 5 minutes. Add the water and tomato paste and stir to combine. Season with salt and pepper. Bring to a boil over high heat. Add frozen okra and corn. Decrease the heat to low and cover. Simmer, stirring occasionally, until flavorful and thickened, 1 ½ to 2 hours.
3. Add the shrimp and crabmeat and stir to combine. Continue cooking over very low heat until the shrimp are cooked through, an additional 10 minutes. Season with hot sauce. Taste and adjust for seasoning with salt and pepper. Serve with rice pilaf.

Grilled Shrimp Skewers

Prep Time: 40 minutes
Cook Time: 4-6 minutes
Serves: 12

Ingredients

- ½ cup (8 Tbsp.) unsalted butter
- 4 cloves of garlic, pressed or minced
- 1 Tbsp. Cajun spice (provides light heat; it's not too spicy)
- ½ tsp salt (omit if using salted butter)
- 1 Tbsp. lemon juice (from ½ medium lemon)
- 2 lbs. uncooked large shrimp (21-25 count), peeled and deveined
- 12 medium wooden skewers
* *Note: To save time, you can buy tail-on shrimp that are already peeled and deveined*

Preparation

1. Soak wooden skewers in water 30 min (reduces burning of the sticks). Preheat Grill to med/high (400°F).
2. Combine all marinade ingredients in a small sauce pan. Bring to a simmer then remove from heat. Pour half of the mixture into a custard dish or other small dish and leave remaining marinade in pan (You'll brush on half now and brush on remaining marinade after shrimp are grilled).
3. Skewer 4 shrimp on each damp skewer without leaving spaces. Lay skewers flat on a lipped cookie sheet. Brush one side of the skewered shrimp with sauce and refrigerate for 2 min until butter firms up. Flip shrimp over, brush second side and refrigerate 2 min until butter firms up.
4. Place skewers on the grill and cook shrimp with the lid on about 2 minutes per side or just until cooked through and no longer transparent. Remove shrimp from grill. Don't overcook or they will be rubbery. Brush on reserved sauce and serve immediately.

Serves twelve.

East Meets West Pineapple Pork

Prep time: 15 minutes

Serves: 4

Ingredients

- 2 tsp of vegetable oil
- 16 oz. can of pineapple rings (reserve juice)
- 4 pork steaks (trimmed of excess fat)
- 1 tbsp. of brown sugar
- 1 tsp tomato puree
- ½ tsp chili powder
- 1 tsp Chinese five-spice powder
- 1 tbsp. Dark soy sauce

Preparation

1. Add the oil to a large non-stick pan, season the steaks well, then fry for 5 mins on each side until golden and almost cooked through. Mix the sugar, soy, tomato purée and most of the pineapple juice in a bowl

2. Add the pineapple rings to the pan and let them caramelize a little alongside the pork. Add the chili and five-spice to the pan, then fry for 1 min until aromatic. Tip in the soy mix and let it bubble around the pork and pineapple for a few mins until slightly reduced and sticky. Remove and serve pork steaks with pineapple.

Janice's Unforgettable Coconut Cream Pie

Prep: 2 Hours

Servings: 12

Ingredients

FOR THE CRUST (PREMADE CRUSTS CAN BE USED INSTEAD)
- 1¼ cups sifted all-purpose flour
- ½ teaspoon salt
- ½ teaspoon sugar
- ¼ cup shortening, chilled, cut into pieces
- ⅓ cup chilled unsalted butter, cut into pieces
- 2 to 5 tablespoons ice water

FOR THE FILLING
- 1 cup evaporated milk
- 1 cup heavy cream
- ½ cup sugar
- 6 egg yolks
- 1 tablespoon cornstarch
- 1 tablespoon softened unsalted butter
- ¼ teaspoon vanilla extract
- ¼ teaspoon coconut extract
- 3 tablespoons cream of coconut

FOR THE TOPPING
- 1 cup sweetened, shredded coconut or unsweetened coconut flakes
- 2 cups heavy cream
- 4 tablespoons sugar
- 1 teaspoon vanilla extract

PREPARATION

1. Preheat the oven to 350 degrees.

2. Make the crust: Sift flour, sugar and salt together. Using a food processor or pastry cutter, blend butter and shortening into the flour mixture until pea-sized pieces form. Slowly add the water until the dough just comes together. Wrap the dough in plastic wrap, flatten into a disk, and refrigerate for at least one hour. Roll out chilled dough on a floured surface until it is large enough to create a 1-inch overhang on a 9-inch pie pan. Using a fork, poke several holes along the base of the crust. Finish the rim of the crust to your liking and chill until firm, 30 minutes. Line with parchment paper and a custard dish to hold the paper in place. Bake until the edges are pale golden and the crust will hold its shape, 25-30 minutes. Carefully remove the parchment and dish and bake until the crust is dry and pale golden, 5-10 more minutes. Remove from oven and cool.

3. Make the filling: Decrease oven temperature to 325 degrees. Pour evaporated milk, cream and sugar into a saucepan. Over medium heat, bring to a boil, then immediately remove from heat. Using a whisk attachment on an electric mixer, beat egg yolks until they appear pale and fluffy. Add cornstarch and butter; continue beating until they are fully incorporated. Add vanilla, coconut extract and cream of coconut. Set the mixer on a low speed and slowly add the warm cream mixture to the egg mixture. Pour the filling back into the saucepan and cook over low heat for 10 minutes, stirring constantly, until the custard has thickened to the consistency of runny yogurt. Pour coconut filling into the baked pie shell and bake until the edges are barely puffed and the center wobbles like gelatin when you give the pan a shuffle, about 20 minutes. Remove from oven and allow the pie to cool completely, 2-3 hours

4. Make the topping: Place coconut on baking sheet and toast until light brown, about 7 minutes. Whip cream, sugar and vanilla to stiff peaks.

5. To finish: Place a large mountain of whipped cream in the center of the pie and, using a small offset spatula, create a dome shape. Sprinkle the entire dome with toasted coconut. Refrigerate until ready to serve.

A Bark in the Night

The Talking Dog Detective Agency

Book One

Chapter One

A GROAN ESCAPED the silent watcher as the girl pulled out a bunch of keys to unlock the front door. The dog that had been sitting now silently stood, his ears alert, his head slowly swinging side to side as he emitted a low growl.

"Damn it." He hadn't counted on a dog. Who takes a dog with them to an office building anyhow? He could have knocked down the girl and grabbed the keys, and finally made it into the building. He'd spent the last six months trying to enter the place.

The few remaining offices weren't open to the public. He'd even donned delivery outfits and tried to get buzzed in. All he managed to discover was no one in the building had water delivered or even a pizza. Usually, he received no reply when he buzzed. It could be that the buzzer didn't work. The building itself was circa 1930s and only the bottom floor was stores, while the rest were apartments or offices.

That would have worked fine if there was an actual store on the first floor instead of empty rooms. He'd considered breaking in, but he'd most likely get caught and end up back in the slammer. Something he'd prefer to avoid since he had more enemies inside than he did out. Now, he'd have to rethink the situation. Once the girl and her dog entered the building, he tucked his hands into his jacket pocket to feel the short length of pipe he'd hidden there. A man had to protect himself, but as a felon, a gun would automatically earn a huge fine and possibly incarceration. Things he wanted to avoid.

Hands still in pockets, he strolled in the direction of Monument Circle. Sweat dotted his face due to the early heat wave. He could have pulled off his sweatshirt, but the hoodie provided conformity that made him almost invisible.

In the center of the city stood a huge war monument reaching toward the heavens as if trying to touch the departed or at least send a message they hadn't been forgotten. He couldn't remember when it had been built—sometime after the Civil War. As a kid, his grandfather had taken him there. With each war, more statues and flat memorials engraved with names appeared. He remembered fingering the names thinking the people only became important by dying. That wasn't going to be him. Nope, he'd had enough of being Toby Nobody. Once he got into the building, he'd find what was his by right and buy that sailboat he fantasized about while doing time. Might even sail around the world.

Foot and vehicle traffic picked up as he made his way to the circle. A horse-driven carriage, complete with picture-snapping tourists, passed him on one side. The harness bells jingled with the horse's movements. He was not sure why a person would even bell a horse. The animal was too large to miss. Then again, maybe the owner thought it made the experience more festive. Toby stopped and watched the slow-moving carriage. He'd never taken a carriage ride, never took a gondola ride down the canal, either. Nope, those things were for tourists or people with a lot of throwaway money. Soon, that would be him, as soon as he got rid of the obstacles.

NALA PLACED ONE hand on her hip and kept a tight grip on the leash clipped to a handsome black German shepherd mix as she surveyed the building. The stone façade building rose a good five stories, nothing compared to the other buildings looming behind it on a more visited street in Indianapolis. The morning sun revealed chipped parts of the façade and the crumbling entrance steps, exposing the underlying concrete block structure.

"The building has character." She glanced up and down the street, noticing the lack of foot traffic during the early day. The ground floor windows revealed empty rooms inside where light spots on the industrial gray carpet revealed where furniture once sat. "I was never shown a ground floor office or even one with wrapa-round windows." Her shoulders went up in a shrug. "It is just as well. Anyone visiting a private eye doesn't want to be on display. I probably couldn't afford it anyhow. Let's go see *our* office."

The dog gave a bark as if he understood. Nala's straight hair swung into her face as she bent to pat the animal. "That's right, Max. It's a new start for both of us."

Max and Nala climbed the first flight of stairs in silence. By the time they reached the second flight, a young man with a dark hipster beard and arms full of labeled boxes met them.

"Hey, a dog, cool!"

A bark greeted his assessment while Nala offered her hand, then pulled it back as she realized he couldn't shake. "Hello. Do you need any help with your boxes?"

"No, I'm good. I'm sure you're not coming to see me. I'd re-member if I had a beautiful woman and her equally handsome dog coming to see me."

A nervous laugh greeted his remark. Blatant flirting rattled Nala since it was difficult to pinpoint if it was sincere. Extroverts could reply with clever comebacks in a second, while people like herself struggled for an appropriate reply long after the person had left. "Yeah, right."

Instead of insisting he meant it, the man grinned. "I'm Harry Chafant. I run a mail-order business on the second floor. Didn't know there were any other businesses in the building. There are some apartments in use, though. Maybe you're here to see one of the residents."

Nala shoved her hands in her jeans pockets since she didn't know what to do with them. "Ah, I'm Nala, Nala Bonne." *Oops*, she had lost a chance to try out her new name. "I'll be opening my business on the third floor. Max," she gestured to her dog, "and I are going up to check out the office."

"Really?" Harry drew out the word, and his smile grew bigger. "Today must be my lucky day. I'm headed to the post office, but when I get back, I'd love to show you around."

"Thanks, but I've already seen the building." Regret stabbed her as she watched the man's smile slip. No good would come out of being too friendly to her neighbors. Even if they did hit it off, eventually they'd break up and she'd peer out her door every time a woman got buzzed in, wondering if it was her replacement. Still, she didn't want to sound unfriendly. She held up one hand. "See ya around."

"Yeah," Harry agreed and continued to descend the stairs.

If her best friend, Karly, had witnessed the scene, she'd take Nala to task, telling her she shot down another perfectly good prospect. Maybe she had, but she also avoided a messy emotional entanglement and the possibility of placing another crack in her heart. Some women threw themselves into the dating game with all the intensity of a bullfighter. A failed romance never seemed to get them down. They would just move on to the next guy. The most amazing thing about it was that there was always a next guy. In her experience, most men never passed her father's background investigation test. Oh, the joys of having a father in law enforcement.

On the third-floor landing, Nala withdrew her key to the office and opened the door. The entry office remained dusty and empty. The furniture fairies hadn't appeared overnight, not that she'd expected them to. A few words to her mother would have her scouring the design warehouse for office furniture, but she wouldn't mention it. This was something Nala wanted to accomplish on her own. With helpful, somewhat overprotective parents she seldom felt like she did much on her own. Even with school projects, she had felt they were more a group project.

Her father had built a circuit board that allowed an electrical circuit to run several items at once for the science fair. She, however, had wanted to grow plants and play music to them. When she didn't ace the science fair, her father demanded to know if the fair was fixed. It was obvious the circuit board was the superior project. Her petite teacher went toe to toe with her father and pointed out the circuit board was beyond the ability of a seven-year-old. A third-grader won with an experiment that showed tomato plants grew taller with regular shots of diet cola.

"Let's hit it." Nala dropped the leash and allowed Max to wander at will while she withdrew window cleaner, a rag, and some press-on letters. Her first project would be the exterior door.

"I'm not sure about the clear glass. If a person wants privacy, they don't want everyone and their cousin peering in at them as they come to me to consult about a philandering husband or wife."

"Do people even do that anymore? I just thought they divorced, divvied up the stuff, and sometimes offloaded the family pet to a friend, relative, or took him for a ride in the country."

Nala blinked, knowing good and well no one else was in the office. She dropped her gaze to Max, who had his head cocked as if waiting for her answer. *No, it couldn't be.* Dogs didn't talk, at least not in a raspy baritone. She pinched herself just to be certain she wasn't dreaming. It hurt. *Maybe she just thought he said something. The best thing would be to test out her theory.* "Did your last owners divorce?"

Something must have happened to Max since she had picked him up at an animal shelter the day before he would have been put down. Grown dogs were only kept for a few days at the most. Then again, it could be she wanted Max to talk so she'd have someone to converse with. A fellow traveler in this new life she'd plotted out for herself.

"Nope." He grimaced, showing his teeth. "I made the mistake of talking again. Not the first time I've been ousted from a comfortable home. This last time I was driven from the house by my former owner holding a crucifix and calling me *devil dog*."

"Weird." She shook her head hard still not convinced she wasn't dreaming. I would have thought someone would have put you on the David Letterman show. Whoops, I keep forgetting he retired." *Was she really having a conversation with her dog?*

"You'd think that." He barked a couple of times before continuing. "You gotta remember English is my third language and some things don't translate."

"You speak three languages?"

He lifted his nose with pride. "I do. Dog, of course, the silent language of scent, and I'm reasonably conversant in English. One potential owner tried to speak to me in German. Despite my muddied bloodlines, I couldn't understand a word he said. I wanted to tell him I was born in America. I didn't, since I wasn't totally sure."

"Ah, of course." She nodded her head as if she understood. *Was there anything understandable about a talking dog?* "So, when did you start talking? Are there a lot of talking dogs out there?"

His nose dropped as he stretched out and laid his head on his paws. "All dogs talk in the accepted canine dialect, except for basenjis who do this strange yodeling thing. I haven't met one who speaks English, although most do understand it very well. They might pretend not to know phrases such as stay off the couch, not for you, or not now. They do. Even though they understand English, they freak out when I say something. Something about it being us against them, meaning your kind."

"Ah." Nala searched her mind for how she had treated Max in the few days she owned him. Had she offended him somehow by treating him like a dog? "You never answered how you came to talk."

"Oh, that." He managed a few sharp yips that resembled a laugh. "Funny story. My first owner was a close-mouthed male. Not one to share his feelings or general observations about life. While this didn't bother me all that much, it was an entirely different story for his girlfriend, who happened to be a witch. She always fixed extra scrambled eggs and bacon for me when she visited, so I liked her. Anyhow, one day, she says to the man, 'If you don't talk to me, then your dog will.'"

"Just like that?"

"Took me a while to become a good conversationalist. At the time, I was so excited I voiced every thought." He lifted his head enough to display a doggy grin. "Imagine a constant litany of me listing everything I saw. Tree, grass, dog poop from the poodle two houses down, smells like she likes me. After all, she left it in front of my house. Well, you get the idea."

"Irritating."

"Yep, I discovered immediately that while people yack non-stop, they don't appreciate a talkative dog, especially my first owner who didn't even make the effort to talk to his girlfriend. One day, she was gone. Not sure if they agreed to separate. I just noticed the house smelled less like the sandalwood incense she always burned. After that, I got relocated, too."

"Where?"

"A family with kids. They had a little boy I adored. He wasn't that good at walking so he often hung onto me when he was unstable. It was only natural that I tried to encourage him. His parents were worried about his developing psyche and the dangers of believing a dog could talk. They thought I was a bad influence." Max stood, paced to the hallway and returned to his original place before circling and flopping back down on the floor.

"That's too bad about the kid. I'm not sure what I'll do with a talking dog."

A foul smell permeated the air. "Sorry." Max offered her an apologetic expression. "The Chinese food you gave me yesterday doesn't agree with me. I love it, though. Besides, stress has that effect, too."

Her intention had been to get a dog for companionship. Karly, who worked at the shelter, had emailed her pictures of dogs that would be put down. *Talk about guilt.* Even worse, when they met for lunch, she'd talk about the abandoned dogs, giving them names and listing their idiosyncrasies. Nala pointed out more than once that if Karly wanted someone to adopt a dog it was better not to mention things such as its tendency to rip up anything vaguely chewable or its midnight howling. Karly insisted people had to enter relationships with open eyes.

As if that would ever work. There was a reason behind women shoving themselves into shapewear, piling on the makeup, and clipping on hair extensions. Men didn't want reality, and she was sure women didn't either. On occasion, when they needed a reality check, they'd hire an investigator. She'd specialize in date research. No woman wanted to go on a date with an online prospect or even the cousin of a co-worker and end up battered, broke or, worse, dead.

"We'll have to limit your intake to the weekends. Can't have you scaring off the clients with your toxic farts."

A hopeful gleam appeared in Max's eyes as his ears pitched forward. "Do you mean you're going to keep me?"

"Why not?"

"The talking usually scares people off, but Karly assured me you'd be okay with it. Since you're into magic, psychic skills, and all that." His long tail wagged, hitting the floor. The empty room magnified the sound.

"Karly knew? The woman who never believes in too much information withheld the fact from me that you could speak?"

"She never told you she didn't like Jeff, either."

Nala looked up from pecking at her cell with her index finger. "You mean you and Karly talked about my ex-boyfriend?"

Max swallowed hard. "You know, I could be an immense help around the detective agency."

"How so?"

"Scent. I can tell if people are lying or not by their scent."

She shook her head, imagining how well a large German shepherd mix sniffing them would go over. "I'm pretty sure my future clients and suspects wouldn't go for you sticking your nose in their crotch."

"Please." He managed a huff. "I have excellent scent ability. The nose in the crotch thing is something dogs do just for fun. It's a game we like to play with humans. If you didn't react so strongly, then it wouldn't be as hilarious."

Author Notes

If you enjoyed this book, try checking out the entire series. Available at all online retailers.

The first three books are available in Large Print and Audio.

Murder Mansion

Drop Dead Handsome

Killer Review

Christmas Calamity

Death Pledges a Sorority

Caribbean Catastrophe

- The best way to encourage an author is to write a review
- Do you have an idea for a story, recipe or a character name? Love to hear it. I can be reached through my website www.morgankwyatt.com
- Want to get free books, read excerpts before everyone else, receive special members only swag and giveaways? You need to be on the mailing list. Go over to my website and sign up.
- Do you like humor with your suspense? Check out the new cozy mystery series, *The Talking Dog Detective Agency* coming out in July 2017.
- Love to meet you, check out my personal appearances on the website too.
- Can you do one more thing? Read. It's good for you!

M. K. Scott

www.ingramcontent.com/pod-product-compliance
Lightning Source LLC
Chambersburg PA
CBHW060415180626
46817CB00007B/2589